Bridal Path

Bridal Path

NIGEL TRANTER

EDINBURGH
B&W PUBLISHING
1996

British Library Cataloguing in Publication Data:
A catalogue record for this book is available from
the British Library

Cover illustration:
The Dunara Castle at Iona
by Francis Campbell Boileau Cadell (1883-1937)
Photograph by kind permission of
The Flemings Collection

Printed by Werner Söderström

I

EWAN MacEWAN sighed heavily, even more heavily than usual, flung a monosyllabic but apparently comprehensive command to his yellow-eyed black-and-white collie, and picked Ewan Beg out of the sheep-dip. Holding him at arm's length, he shook him bodily over the trough, from dehydration and drainage as much as from disciplinary motives, whilst taking the opportunity to utter some fatherly if obvious advice to his offspring, mixed rather unsuitably with appeals to his Maker. If neither was audible above the frantic baa-ing of two hundred so-called lambs, all of which were big enough to know better, at least so was the shameless Ewan Beg whose wide-open mouth seemed to indicate vociferous bawling. Things were fast reaching the stage where the minutest of mercies might be worth cherishing.

Carrying the infant by that portion of its small trousering just above where the seat should have been, the man deposited it within one of the lesser and temporarily unoccupied compartments of that seething fank, and frowning horribly, wagged a threatening finger. Whether Ewanie was adequately impressed was doubtful, for before his father was able to give further emphasis to his point of view, hoarse and bellowing laughter penetrated the uproar, overbore and vanquished the uproar. Reluctantly, almost fearfully, Ewan MacEwan turned. Bally's sense of humour did not always synchronise with his own.

Bally was standing at the farther side of the fank, a vast and shapeless figure, a sheep negligently clutched in either enormous hand, and his cavern of a mouth wide. But he was looking in the opposite direction altogether, across the lifting greensward towards the whitewashed house under the birch-wood, in the open doorway of which stood what appeared to be a small girl, three parts naked as to costume and entirely Indo-American as to complexion. Or almost entirely; one portion of her plump little posterior still untinted, she was in process of toning in assiduously, with a lump of the vivid keel, or brick-red dye with which each newly-dipped sheep was presently to be marked for identification purposes. With a strangled cry the young man abandoned his son, leapt a succession of the rough hurdles that enclosed the pens, and ran to the house. Grasping this second child more than firmly, he snatched the keel from her, thrust it into his pocket, and stared.

"Och, my goodness me, my God!" he ejaculated. "Just look at that, whatever!"

Whether or not this request was complied with, little serious consideration developed more locally. The lambs chorused exactly as before, Bally's Homeric laughter diminished nothing—it could be relied upon now to continue thus almost indefinitely—and young Kirsty's smile intensified beneath its ruddy rendering, from the angelic to the seraphic.

Hurriedly looking about him, the man sought and found not. "My suffering Sam!" he declared, in a deplorable reversion to Sassunach contamination from Army days, "was ever a man so caught in the crutch of sorrow, at all!" And bundling his daughter under his ochreous dip-soaked arm, he strode back to the clamorous fank, to deposit her in the pen with her brother.

But Ewan Beg was gone already, vanished quite. At three and a half years, his escalatory faculties were as well-developed as was his lung-power. He might be anywhere amongst ten score tightly-milling sheep—or, for that matter, anywhere else at all. Even now he might be passing through

2

the dipping process. Dropping his emblazoned offspring, Ewan peered urgently around that heaving woolly sea—but the only more or less human being that he could see was Bally, still shaking with his witless mirth.

"Shut you your great drain-pipe of a mouth!" the sorely-tried parent burst out, "or I'll be tearing the flapping tongue out of it to thrash you with!"

This threat was entirely allegorical, of course, for Bally, at six feet seven and a bit, was fully six inches taller than his thus painfully lapsing employer.

But probably this unfortunate breakdown in Highland courtesy went unheard. Bally, at any rate, still hooted. And more than that. He dropped one of his sheep, to point, and backwards, towards the house again. Involuntarily glancing along the line indicated, Ewan yelped. Clouds of white steam and black smoke mixed were billowing out from the open cottage doorway that he had so lately left. The man went leaping, to disappear within the impressively erupting portals.

Quite shortly after, half a dozen squawking hens and a single waddling duck came out, in some haste, followed at more leisure by a shaggy black bullock, and curiously, a bearded nanny-goat still masticating what appeared to be an article of household linen. Certain objects, inanimate, domestic, but swiftly propelled nevertheless, completed the exodus—save for the smoke and steam, of course, which continued to escape for some little time yet. When, at length, the reek thinning somewhat, Ewan MacEwan himself stumbled out into the open air, eyes streaming, it was to blinkingly perceive an elderly man lean precariously on the lichened and venerable fencing of the rough-hewn front garden, combing a handsome silver beard with fond fingers.

"Och, Ewan man—what you are needing is a wife, see you," he mentioned conversationally. "A wife, just, aye." And he nodded, with entire authority.

3

"Hell's bells and damnation!" Ewan said, with the careful articulation of one who keeps himself deliberately from saying much more, and by an effort. "The Devil boil and blister you!" That would have sounded much better, and more natural, in the Gaelic, undoubtedly.

For all that, it was no way to talk to Finlay Sim MacEwan, first man of the island, an elder of the Kirk, and own uncle to Ewan himself, into the bargain.

"God forgive you the ill words," he said, with unfailing dignity.

Ewan MacEwan swallowed, opened his mouth but found no apt and suitable words, and lurched back to his flock, unfortunately more in anger than in sorrow.

It must not be assumed from all this, however, that Ewan was a captious, ill-natured, and unmannerly churl. Far from it. But the best of us are susceptible, at times, to minor irritations—and the distinct minority of Ewan's irritations was no small part of the trouble. Furthermore, there was this to be said for the man; he tended very quickly to simmer down after one of these unfortunate outbursts, and thereafter became his normal quiet and mild-seeming self with commendable absence of fuss. As witness that same evening. With the lambs eventually all dipped, marked, and permitted, leaping ridiculously, to rejoin their long-suffering mothers, two infants salvaged from amongst them, cleansed after a fashion, fed, and barricaded into their sleeping-quarters above, and the humorous Bally dismissed, without at least physical violence, to whatever unmentionable den he laired in—with all this achieved, then, and Ewan feeling in his pocket for his pipe and drifting at last to the wooden seat at the front door to watch the night coming down on land and sea, he nevertheless nodded courteously to the old man with the beard who suddenly reappeared at the garden gate, and gave him good evening.

4

He even offered him a fill of tobacco from his tattered pouch.

His visitor had a longer memory than that. "Aye, then— and is that yourself with a civil tongue in your head, again?" Finlay Sim demanded starchily. But his fingers were busy in the tobacco-pouch.

"Och, then—just that." Ewan acceded, but non-committally. "Bad the midges are, tonight. A bit smoke will maybe be lifting them." And he regained his pouch, gently but firmly.

"Aye." The older man sighed, with profound conviction. "Aye." He seated himself on the wooden bench that faced into the glowing west. "A light you'll have on you . . . ?"

They sat unspeaking, till their pipes were drawing strongly, and longer still, watching the day at its dying. The island of Eorsa lay like a scallop-shell on the fringe of the western sea, its concave face opening to the wide ocean, the sunset, and the strung jet beading that was the line of the Outer Hebrides. The sun was now dipped beyond the far rim of the sea, but the afterglow remained, a warm refulgence that spread its genial benison over rugged land and level water. That seaboard was namely for infinitely more spectacular sunsets than this, but the men who watched made no complaint; any indication of calm weather was apt to be more appreciatively received than was the most brilliant colorific display.

Finlay Sim spoke, at length. "The dipping is by with, anyway," he observed.

"Yes," his nephew agreed.

"A dirty job, whatever."

"Yes."

"Aye." The old man watched the blue pillar of his pipe-smoke climb to join the busy columns of the midges. "Mary will not be up, tonight, no."

"Ah." Ewan had been wondering to what circumstances he owed this second visit of his uncle.

5

"I'ph'mmm. She is away over to her sister's. Jean has her pains upon her, again. Early they are, this time."

The younger man sighed. "A pity." He sounded as though he meant it, too.

"Och, it is just the way with the women—the way that the good God made them," the other pointed out dispassionately. "The sown seed must feel the scythe. What enters in must issue out."

"Ummmm." Ewan, to tell the truth, had not been referring to either profound physiology or to sympathy for the suffering Jean. His regret was the selfish one that Mary his cousin was not going to pay her bi-nightly visit, to perform her recurrent miracle of cleaning and tidying his deplorable house, of soothing and exorcising the two devil-possessed cherubic minorities upstairs, and of washing, darning, and restoring some proportion of his household's unedifying apparel to recognisable and usable condition. "The Lord's will be done," he allowed, if doubtfully.

His uncle considered the single wreath of evening mist, rose-tinted, that tipped the bald brow of Beinn Helival, the nearest thing that they had to a mountain on Eorsa. "Aye, that is so. The Almighty's ways are wonderful, indeed. A shallow vessel He made of the women. It is light pleasure and skirling laughter yesterday, the tears and groaning to-day, and the laughing again tomorrow. But they have their uses, man—they have their uses." And he glanced out of the corner of a rheumy eye to see how the other was taking it.

"They have so." Ewan agreed with some feeling.

"Yes, then." He shook his grey head. "And now here's Mary talking about being away to the Oban or Glasgow or some such haunt of wickedness. Hech-aye, they're all the same, I tell you . . ."

"Mary! Going away . . . ?" Startled now, Ewan sat up. "My goodness—she can't do that! What for would she do a thing like that? Mary's not . . ." He paused. "But, och, it'll be

6

just for a holiday, likely, that she's for going?" he suggested hopefully.

"Nothing of the sort, no. For good, it is—or for ill, more like! It is the little good she'll see in yon Glasgow. A sink of iniquity, it is, no less, and it's myself that knows it. The sights I have seen, yonder . . ."

Finlay Sim ought to have known, certainly. He had spent six years, off and on, in that city of ill-fame, during which he could hardly have wasted his opportunities, for he had managed to put in two years' study on the theological course, two on medicine, and two on teaching at the University there, before returning happily enough to his father's croft without any sort of degree, but with a reputation and fund of diverse knowledge that had stood him in excellent stead ever since. That was a long time ago, of course—but since as everyone knows, times have grievously worsened since then, it is improbable that Glasgow has in any way improved. As his gaze rested, now, on the jagged and terrifying skyline of Erismore, the neighbouring island to the north, a reminiscent gleam came into his eyes. "I mind well the way it was," he declared. "The Devil ravening and roaring . . ."

But Ewan was not listening. He displayed a lamentable tendency to apply ill tidings to his own personal circumstances, instead of either sympathising with his uncle or decently envisaging the perils to which his youthful cousin was thus wantonly proposing to expose herself. He could only visualise his own loss. And with a certain amount of excuse, perhaps. For the two and a half years of his widowerhood, Mary had been taking pity upon him, with a cheerful and unfailing constancy, keeping an eye on his womanless establishment, helping and advising him with his motherless progeny, aiding and encouraging him with her capable brown hands, with her laughing brown eyes, with her soft but nimble tongue. And now . . . ! A sense of loss and a sense of indignation competed within

7

him—and being a man, it was the indignation that he voiced.

"She can't do that! She can't just be leaving me . . . er, leaving *you*, that way. All wrong, it is. What is she going to do, at all, anyway? What is the likes of herself to be doing in such a place! She'll not just find . . ."

"The nursing, it is. She's for taking up the nursing, maybe," Finlay Sim explained. "They do be saying that they're always needing the nurses . . ."

"Nursing! In the name of Heaven—must she go outside of Eorsa if it's the nursing she wants? Isn't it half the island that's in need of nursing!" This was, of course, something of an exaggeration. "Isn't the place awash just with drooling dotards and slobbering babies!"

His uncle frowned, understandably—and perhaps over more than the doubtful biology of the statement. "That is no way to be speaking, Ewan MacEwan," he reproved, tut-tutting into his beard. "Some elderly folk there are, yes, and some not so elderly at all. And why not, indeed? When it's yourself that has a little more sense and experience to you, you'll not be so quick to mock at a grey hair or two. Goodness me, no. There's few that the Lord is less partial to than mockers of their elders." He did not say anything about the babies, for that was something of another story. There *were* rather a lot of babies on Eorsa, considering all the circumstances.

Ewan drew on his pipe in a series of vigorous puffs. "Aye," he said heavily. "Nursing!" The suggestion seemed to rankle.

"Och, she could do worse," Mary's father contended. "She'll make not that bad a nurse, as nurses go. And there's not that much for her here, on Eorsa."

"There's as much as ever there has been, isn't there?"

"Aye—but she's getting on, see you. Twenty-five past, she is . . . and never a man on the island for her to light her eye

8

on." And he gestured down towards the wide sweep of the surf-fringed bay, and the scattered croft-houses of the township that lined it.

"You mean . . . ?"

"I mean that women are the shallow vessels, like I said. Maybe Mary is after thinking that it is time that she was getting married—and not a man on Eorsa that she could wed. Maybe that is what is at the back of her mind in this business, whatever."

For a little there was silence, as, brows furrowed, Ewan considered that. A curlew, calling wearily from the lifting moor behind the house, came into its own. When the young man spoke, at length, the sense of loss had quite won its battle with his fine indignation. "And what am I to do now, then?" he wondered plaintively.

Finlay Sim had him now approximately where he wanted him. "Was I not telling you?" he mentioned, his gaze upturned to the appalling emptiness of the heaven. "It is time that you took yourself another wife!"

This time Ewan did not boil and blister him. He only sighed a long sigh.

There was more than that to be said about the matter, of course. Any number of problems presented themselves, objections abounded. A little wearily, taking his note from the yittering curlew, Ewan selected the most obvious.

"And where am I going to be finding one?" he asked.

That was not merely a rhetorical question. It was entirely pertinent, apposite. There were exactly fifty-seven people on Eorsa, no great proportion of them marriageable females. And of the six or seven—or, at an extremely charitable stretch, eight or nine—that might aspire to such a classification, not one but was related to Ewan in compound first or second degree of cousinship. That was the island's incubus, its burden, its bogey. Everybody on Eorsa was a blood relation of everybody else—with all the social and physical complications that that entailed.

Finlay Sim stroked his beard. "Och, we'll be finding you a wife, surely. We'll not be beat, if we put our minds to it. Let me see, now. There's yon Peig, the Braes."

"My own mother's sister's daughter, by Angus a' Claidh your own father's brother's grandson—him she forgot to marry!"

"Och, tut-tut, yes indeed," the other said, as though he had quite overlooked the circumstance. "My, oh my—that would never do, at all. No, no. Then, there is . . . there's The Partan's Sheena?"

"She was Big Martha's Sheena, as well, mind—and Big Martha was your cousin, too, and so my own father's."

"So she was, mercy me. Fancy myself forgetting the like of that. Well, now." The old man went through the motions of patting his pockets. "A match you will have on you, likely, Ewan? Aye, then. There's Jessie Skelloch, of course, but . . ."

"My goodness—Jessie Skelloch's half-witted! As well, there's scarce a man on the island that's, that's not . . ."

"Wheesht, you—wheesht, man! The ill uncharitable tongue you have in your head, this day. Jessie's a wee thing simple, maybe, but och, she's a decent enough creature, at the heart."

"At the heart, may be—but it's her head, and her, her—och, well, I'd be in a queer state right enough to make a wife of *her*!"

"Aye, i'ph'mmm—maybe you're right. You it is would have to live with her. Man, I doubt it will have to be the mainland for you—for we cannot have you marrying with any that's your cousin, at all. My God, no!" With something of a rush that came, as though he was thankful that it was out. It might have been what he was working up to, all along.

And it was a tall order, a drastic proposition—that Ewan should go to the mainland for a wife, not that he should not marry a cousin. This latter was an accepted dogma on the

10

island—cousins should not marry, especially multiple ones; and as has been indicated, most cousinship on Eorsa was multiple. Unfortunately, perhaps, this excellent doctrine had tended to be accepted more on its non-observance than anything else, more particularly amongst the unthinking and socially irresponsible, for eminently practical reasons. Eorsa lay some six hours' sail into the Atlantic from the nearest mainland port of Oban, and the steamer called only once in the week, weather permitting—and called nearly a mile off-shore at that, a small open boat with a notoriously uncertain outboard engine being the connecting link. In the circumstances, Eorsans, having a wise and truly Highland disinclination towards unnecessary labour and exertion, were apt to be fairly self-contained about their recreation, romantic or otherwise—as indeed they were about most things. For, of course, it was out of the question that there should be any liaisons with the unseemly and degenerate folk of Erismore, the neighbouring island, and as for Mull, twelve miles to the south-east, everybody knew that most of the people there were black Macleans and not to be considered— the Eorsa MacEwans being of honest Clan Donald stock. In the past, naturally, it had been considered better to in-breed with one's own at least decent and namely stock than to open one's bed to such as the Mull Macleans or the disreputables from Erismore, whose ancestry was lost in the fouler mists of antiquity.

This basic principle was maintained, of course, but the non-marriage of cousins dictum had come in to rather complicate the issue. It had been imposed on the island about fifteen years before, when Finlay Sim, happening to be confined to his sick bed for an entire month, got so bored that, through lack of alternative activity, he had read beyond the fourth chapter of his student days' *First Steps in Preventative Medicine*, by Theodore Crick, M.D., and at Chapter Seven discovered that the learned author considered the marriage

11

of cousins to be harmful, deleterious, and eventually conducive to mental deficiency and physical abnormality. Since, unfortunately, there was no blinking the fact that an ever-growing proportion of Eorsa's population, to a greater or lesser degree, showed distinct signs of unusual mental alignment, this barb struck deep. Finlay Sim, who had the greatest admiration for the late Theodore Crick, M.D., arose from his couch determined that henceforward this new canon should be observed on the island, at least in theory. As all that Eorsa had in the way of either schoolmaster, minister, or physician, he was in a singularly strong position to advocate and impose this reform. It should be mentioned that hitherto the island had been ruled with the help of three books; the Bible, *A Groundwork in Primary Teaching, Part One*, and the first four chapters of Dr. Crick's *First Steps*. To these had thereupon been added Chapter Seven of the latter.

But to consider the mainland, in the matrimonial connection, was a major departure. Ewan's late wife, of course, had not been an islander—but that was different. The whole business had been anomalous, the circumstances unique—and certainly not to be repeated. A prisoner-of-war in Germany, captured with the rest of the Seaforths at St. Valery of ill-fame, after four long years' incarceration, Sergeant Ewan when released eventually, had been in a state to marry almost the first woman who smiled at him. He had brought Clayre back from London to a wondering Eorsa— and had not been long in recognising his mistake. Clayre and Eorsa had not mixed, and though both sides tried hard, Clayre was soon back at Stepney—in time to have her first baby. She had never come back. Ewan, with a croft on his hands, had found liaison difficult. Two further visits he made to the south, the second unhappily in response to an urgent telegram that took three days to reach him. He arrived a day late for Clayre's funeral, and made a sad and harassed return presently, with two-year-old Ewanie and the new-born and not yet christened Kirsty. That had been just over two years ago—two extremely full years.

"The mainland, did you say!" Ewan exclaimed. "And how am I to be getting a wife from the mainland, my goodness?"

"You have to go and fetch one, just. What else?"

The young man stared. "But, be damned—they don't just grow on trees, man. . . ."

"Och, you'd find one, easy. There's any amount of women on the mainland. Too many, I hear. They're a sort of pest, like rabbits, or yon Colorado Beetle. Last time I was at the Oban, there was droves of them about the place, just droves. A wicked sight, it was. And that was three years back, so I daresay it will be worse now, whatever."

"Yes, but . . . see you, how am I to get one of them to marry me, off-hand, just . . . ?"

"Ask her, man—ask her! A decent-sized well set up young fellow like your own self will have no trouble at all. They'll just be jumping at you." Waxing enthusiastic, Finlay Sim gesticulated eloquently, and his pipe flew out of his hand to clatter on the ground, spilling its scant contents. "Och, mercy me—look at that!" he cried. "Lamentable, just lamentable. But you'll have another bit fill in yon pouchie, Ewan? Och, surely. Aye, aye—the women will be just jumping at you. You're not cross-eyed or anything. You've got the best croft on Eorsa, God forgive you. And you're a MacEwan."

His nephew rubbed a hand over his jutting chin more than doubtfully. It rasped noticeably—which only added to his dubiety. He was a fairly modest young man, as such go, and could not assess his long dark knobbly features as in any way handsome or attractive to women. Certainly his grey-blue eyes, though apt to be hooded, were not crossed, and his lengthy loose-limbed person, though gangling, was in no way deformed. "M'mmm. There's the children," he remarked.

"Tchach—you wouldn't be taking them with you, good

13

gracious!" The old man thrust out his empty pipe in a gesture, accidentally under his companion's nose.

But Ewan's mind, seemingly, was above tobacco. "*With me!*" he said. "And how could I be going, my own self? Tell me that. It is a croft I have, not a bit shop to be locking up and walking out of. How can I be away to the mainland, seeking a wife?"

"Fine, you can. Isn't this just the grand chance you've got? The hay was early, and here's you with the dipping past. The ewes are clipped, and no hurry to be at the turnip singling. And it'll be near a month before the corn's ready to cut. Man Ewan, it's made for you, just."

"Betsy will be calving in about three weeks. . . ."

"Och, never heed Betsy. There's more than yourself can deal with the likes of Betsy. Besides, you'll be back by then, with a wife, easy. Two weeks will be plenty. Or, maybe, not just with a *wife*, for you'll need three weeks' crying of the banns—but you'll have what you might be calling the raw material of a wife. . . ."

"Two weeks . . . ! Damned, it doesn't give me much time!" the other protested. "It's not a thing that you can be hurrying, too much. Women are like trouts, mind—you've got to give them a cast or two of the fly before they'll bite. . . ."

"Not with the right fly, at the right time, in the right place, whatever! Man—do not sing so desperate small. Remember you are Ewan MacEwan, Corriemore, of Eorsa! You it is that's the catch, I tell you—not the woman!"

Lacking apparent conviction, the younger man shook his head. "And what about Ewanie and Kirsty then, and me away two weeks . . . ?"

"Mary'll look after them . . . before she goes. She can bring them downbye. She says . . ." Finlay Sim coughed, and went on, quickly, "Och, yes—it is just the thing for Mary, before she's for off. A chance, it is—now or never."

14

"You're sure that she would do it? It would be putting a right tie on her. . . ."

"Mary will be doing what I tell her!" her father declared, severely. He frowned at the hills, grey now, with the last of the sunset glow faded quite, and at the endless slate-blue plain of the sea, its warm gold and bronze exchanged for chill pewter, and he shivered and got to his feet. His blood was getting thin—also, there was evidently no hope of further tobacco from Ewan's pouch. "Aye," he said heavily.

The other sat still, his brows furrowed. The curlew was still wheepling, in the heather, but the garret floor of the cottage behind no longer resounded to juvenile shouts and bangs. The night's peace was settling on Eorsa.

"Come you downbye tomorrow's night and we will settle this thing decently and in order," his uncle threw back as he moved off, stiff-legged. "God forgive you the day, and keep you this night, Ewan 'ic Ewan. *Oiche mhath duibh*."

He was passing through the garden gateway before Ewan's rather preoccupied goodnight reached him.

II

E WAN was beginning to reach the stage when he could not keep the feeling of guilt more or less subconscious any longer, and when its persistent surfacing was bound to send him presently in search of his offspring who had been so gloriously if ominously out of evidence for half the afternoon, when, hearing their uninhibited voices upraised suddenly, he glanced up, and frowned and sighed his relief in one. They had appeared around the lowermost corner of the birchwood, on the white track through the heather, and each appeared, at first glance at any rate, to be in one piece and at least able to walk as well as shout. Each had a small fist in the hands of a young woman, who walked between them. It was the latter who was responsible for their father's ungrateful frown.

Nevertheless, he dropped the old iron bedstead and the string, with which he had been repairing the in-field fence, and moved a little way to meet her. Bally, who had been holding nails for his employer in his enormous palm, dropped them likewise, naturally, and followed on, his welcoming grin practically closing his eyes as well as all but engulfing such other features as he possessed.

At the gate which she would have to climb over, Ewan waited, a-lean. Bally elbowed a couple of cattle-beasts aside, and leaned too, concurrently rubbing the back of his shoulder against the gate-post with enhanced signs of reflective satisfaction.

"You found them, then, did you—the borachs?" Ewan greeted, a shade defensively. "I was just coming for them

16

myself—not that they'd been away any sort of time at all, mind you!"

The girl was frowning now, too—though she hadn't really her father's facility for looking severe; an open-faced, laughing-eyed fawn-like creature she was, all golden freckles and tumbling auburn hair. "I found them down in the burn, there, Ewan MacEwan—in the pool that's under the bridge. They might have been drowned on you, the darlings," she announced, as she came up.

Bally roared with mirth.

"Darlings . . . !" Ewan swallowed. "My goodness, you couldn't drown *them*. Eels, they are, just—wicked small wriggling eels."

"Eels . . . !" the girl cried. "Ashamed of yourself you should be, Ewan, to be calling your own flesh and blood such a thing. Horrid brute." She glanced downwards to pick up one of the youngsters, and straightway her hot indignation dissolved into bubbling laughter. "Och, dear me—never did I see such a plump pair of eels, at all! Just look at the wrists of them." She handed Ewanie over the gate to his parent, and reached down for the round-eyed Kirsty. "Mercy— you're wet enough, my lambie, to have half the burn with you yet!"

"There you are!" Ewan complained, taking the second infant. "Objecting to myself calling her the one kind of animal, and calling her another your own self. How is a young sheep better than an eel, at all?"

"Hush, you," the young woman adjured, and lightfooted, part-climbed, part-vaulted, the gate, with a minimum of fuss or unseemly display. She was obviously used to negotiating intricately tied-up gates.

Ewan watched with a preoccupied brow, but a sort of involuntary admiration, whilst Bally, starting to hoot, broke wind instead by mistake, and looked startled but appreciative.

17

Mary MacEwan ignored them both, and proceeded to shoo her small escort up the track towards the house, with soft clucking noises as though they were favourite domestic poultry.

Ewan came along after her. So did Bally. "You weren't up last night," the former said, with a hint of reproach.

"No," the girl agreed, without turning her head.

"Aye. Aye." The man sighed gustily. "You would be busy. . . ."

"Yes."

"U'mmm. Jean—how is she, then?"

"She is well enough."

"Uh-huh. So-oo. And the baby?"

"He is well enough, too."

"A boy, then?"

"A boy, yes."

Furrowing his forehead, Ewan considered her rather straightly-held back. This was not Mary's usual style at all. What had happened to the creature's smiles and lightsome chatter? Strange, it was . . . though it might make it easier to be saying what called to be said. He coughed. "I . . . you . . . I am hearing that . . ."

Half a pace behind him, Bally abruptly slapped his thigh, and chuckled at some conception of his own, with all the fervour of a waterfall in full spate.

"Quiet, you!" the other man flung at him, with a manifest lack of understanding. "What is so funny, at all!"

But it was the young woman who answered. "Maybe Bally has the rights of it," she said. "I am hearing that you're for getting married again, Ewan?"

"Eh . . . ? I . . . och, my goodness—that is a bit quick! It is so." Quite put out, he blinked protestingly at the tossed curls at the back of her auburn head. It was intolerable, unfair, that she should take the very words out of his mouth—though just like a woman, of course. To accuse *him* thus . . .

18

and in her position! Indignantly, he pointed a jabbing finger. "You, it was, I heard was taking that road."

"Me?" She turned her head to look at her cousin, this time, eyes wide. "What nonsense is this you're at?"

Pleased that he appeared to have shaken her, Ewan nodded a knowledgeable head. "Isn't it you that's for Glasgow, or some place, on a road with a man at the end of it?"

"Ewan MacEwan! How dare you talk that way to me! What a thing to be saying. Good gracious—is it daft you are?"

"Do you deny that you're for leaving the island, then?" They had stopped in the track, facing each other. "Are you not for Glasgow, after all?"

She bit her red lip, and made it redder. "I am thinking of it—yes," she admitted. "But it is not for, for . . . it is not for anything like you say, my goodness. I'm just thinking of taking up the nursing."

"H'aye—the nursing!" the man said heavily. "Uh-huh. Just that. Och, yes—the nursing."

"What do you mean? What's wrong with the nursing, then?" the other demanded. "What's come over you, Ewan MacEwan?"

"Och, nothing at all, nothing at all. A grand profession, the nursing, so I'm told. Just the job. Smoothing the pillows of the sick, and making their last hours a real pleasure. And being the right hand of the young doctors—aye, and maybe the left hand, too . . ."

Bally burst into two or three bars of entirely tuneless but hearty song.

Mary, when she could make herself heard, spoke with a quiver in her softly-lilting voice, and an unwonted gleam shone in those brown eyes. "And why not, then?" she wondered. "Why shouldn't I be a nurse—and a good nurse, too? Why shouldn't I leave Eorsa? What is there *here* to keep me, at all? Tell me that, Ewan."

19

Her cousin shrugged. "Not that much, maybe. Just . . . och well, little enough I daresay. Go you, yes. Your dad will manage, likely. . . ."

"My father will manage, yes—he has my mother, hasn't he? And Jean. And Hector. He has the whole island to manage with—and to manage, itself! I have no fears for my father, whatever!" That was a little tartly said.

Ewan inclined his head with a simple dignity. "Myself, no doubt I will manage, too," he acceded.

"*You* . . . ! Yes—you seem to be going to manage very well. A new wife, it is to be, I hear—and from the mainland. Dear me, it's you that's going to be fine and cosy. Have you anyone in mind, in particular, or is it just open to competition? A sort of short leet you'll have, maybe . . . ?"

Ewan found it necessary to concentrate on the shimmering expanse of the Hebridean sea. "No, no. Och, nothing like that," he asserted. "You've got it all wrong. It is just a sort of notion, an idea that we had. . . . I'm needing somebody to look after the house and the children, see you. You know that. . . ."

"What you want," the young woman interrupted, "is an advertisement in the *Oban Times*—Wife required. Apply Ewan MacEwan, Corriemore, Eorsa, any evening after milking-time. Och, you'd have them in shoals, just. They'd be having to hire the *Maid of Lorne* specially—running day trips!"

The man glanced at her warily, out of the corner of his eye. "You have not got this thing right at all, Mary," he protested. "It is . . . quiet you, Bally—will you hold your tongue, man! It is not that way, no. . . ."

"What way is it, then? If it's . . ."

But she was interrupted, her arm grabbed and shaken by Bally's ham-like hand. With the other he was gesturing urgently upwards, towards the house and the small steading —more particularly, towards the bath. It was the only bath on Eorsa, and how it had got there is a mystery. But Ewan was proud of it, placed it in a prominent position at the steading entrance, linked it to the burnlet at the back of the establishment by means of a somewhat precarious system of gutters, and used it principally as a cattle-trough. It also had been adopted as a convenient if circumscribed duck-pond by the grandmother of all the Corriemore ducks, and it was this old lady's agitated flapping and squawking at the plug end of the bath, added to the convulsive jerking of a pair of plump small legs that projected skywards at the other end, that was apparently responsible for Bally's present enthralment.

Without debate both Ewan and Mary began to run.

If the man had the longer stride, the girl was lighter on her feet, and the race was a dead heat. Panting, each grasped one of the kicking pink legs and lifted the gasping Ewanie out of the bath-water.

"My God!" his father cried. "For goodness sake—look at that! Och, saints alive—the little damned scoundrel!"

In the subsequent tug-of-war, Mary won easily. "Mercy me—my poor lambie, my little small rabbit, my pigeon! Did you get a fright! Did the bad water swallow you up . . . ?"

Over the opposite end of the bath young Kirsty's tousled head appeared. She crowed, and clapped delightedly.

Ewan pointed a shaking finger at his daughter. "What are you laughing at?" he demanded. " 'D'Almighty—what's so funny! I do believe you *pushed* him in . . . !"

"Ewan MacEwan!" the girl cried hotly. "You are a wicked sinful man. How can you speak that way to the darlings—how *can* you!"

"I . . . hell and damnation, I . . ."

"Dear God—swearing at them, too!" He was reaching out for Kirsty, but the young woman forestalled him. Clutching the dripping Ewanie to her bosom, she darted round and seized the little girl's fist. "Keep you your great hands off

21

them!" she charged. "You're not fit—you're not worthy to be having children, at all. Come you, my chickens." And off she swept towards the house.

"Well, I'm . . . well, I'll be . . ." Ewan swallowed. "Look you, Mary . . ."

But Mary was looking only in front of her, and going hard. Not till she was in the doorway of the cottage did she turn. "Go you back to your fences and your ditches," she called to the man who followed. "It's all you're fit for, whatever. *I* will see to these poor little foundlings!" And his own door was slammed in his face.

Even as the victim of cruel circumstance and feminine unreason stood staring, lips moving, the door opened again, momentarily. "If you're for doing the thing my father says, you'll be downbye this evening," his cousin announced cryptically, and disappeared once more.

Angrily Ewan swung on his heel, and strode off. And that was Mary MacEwan for you—Mary, that was supposed to be the kindly smiling helpful slip of a girl! The sooner that he had a decent respectful hard-working wife installed in Corriemore, the better, by Heaven!

So, with the cows milked early and his family immured securely, it was to be hoped, in its bedchamber under the roof, Ewan found himself down at his uncle's house by the shore that evening—and almost against his inclination and judgment. Or at least, not exactly at the house; he did not approach the front door—that nobody used—nor the side door that led into the Post Office, nor the back door that was the family entrance; he made for the pitch-painted oil-store alongside, in the smoky gloom of which, despite the fine evening it was again outside, he found the elders of Eorsa assembled in solemn conclave, sitting on upturned oil-drums and bundles of nets. He saluted the company with nothing better than a choking cough; the atmosphere of the oil-store, compounded of paraffin, thick black tobacco, creosote, dried fish, and collie dog, was less rarified than that of Corriemore up on its breezy hillside. He seated himself on a convenient fish-box, as near to the doorway as possible, and joined in the contemplative silence.

The uh-huhs, and ayes, and noddings eventually and decently over, and an erudite and authoritative series of pronouncements on the weather submitted and accepted, the way was cleared for the business of the evening. Finlay Sim, of course, led off.

"The good God made women for a purpose," he observed, profoundly, blowing a cloud of acrid smoke. "It doesn't do to be denying it."

There was unanimous concurrence.

"There are occasions when a woman can be a right help," he went on. "Practically a necessity. I've seen it many's the time."

"Aye."

"Surely, surely."

"A man has a duty towards his children, too."

"Och yes, indeed."

"Just that."

"And a duty towards the community in which the Lord God has been pleased to place him, whatever."

"You are right, then."

"My Chove, yes."

"Eorsa is needing the new blood." Finlay Sim looked surprisedly at his pipe, which seemed suddenly to have expired, knocked it resoundingly against his oil-drum, and glanced round the company, expectantly. He knew where to look. As shop-keeper, he was in a position to know who had bought tobacco recently from his store. "Aye, then. New blood, just. My thanks, Duncan."

"That is so."

"What else, indeed."

23

"There's women *and* women, of course. A man can easy make a mistake."

"My Chove, yes!" Finlay's younger brother, Hector the Boat, agreed fervently.

"Not considering the Erismore creatures, of course, or any Mull Macleans or Englishry, there's still them that a man would be wise to avoid."

"'Deed, aye."

"The Oban district's fair plagued with Campbells, they tell me," Murdo the Mill mentioned.

"Tut-tut," Finlay Sim declared. "Who would ever consider marrying a Campbell, whatever! Keep you to practical matters, Murdo. This is a serious question." He sought a match from his nearest neighbour. "There's these gold-diggers, now. There is some of these mainland women just out for what they can get and nothing else, I hear."

"Aye—and there's widows," Archie Grumach pointed out. "You have to watch the widows. A right menace they can be. . . ."

"Och, there's worse than a bit widow," Duncan Macdougall protested. "I mind . . ."

Finlay Sim frowned. "Widows should not be considered except if all others fail," he announced. "There's plenty without that, surely. But we do not want to be going to the other extreme, at all, either—no young bits of lassies."

"No, no—that would be no good, whatever."

"A woman of some sort of responsibility is what is wanted."

"Aye, *wanted* maybe, Murdo—but where are you going to find the likes of that?" Archie Grumach interrupted. "You fly too high, man, altogether. There's no use in looking for miracles, just. A sort of decent body, that's used with minding a house, with a bit way with the cows and the children, able to manage the butter and cheese and make a decent loaf of bread . . ."

24

"And with not too long a tongue to her!"

"One that's been in service, maybe . . . ?"

"Yes, yes," Finlay declared. "All that is right enough. We are agreed on the likes of that—just generalities, it is. More particular we've got to be, now. Time is the trouble, see you—there is only just the two weeks in it, or maybe three, with the corn to get in. No time for us to go traipsing about the whole of Lorne and Lochaber . . ."

"Us . . . ?" Ewan put in, there—his first contribution to the discussion.

His uncle ignored it. "None of you has anybody in mind at all? A likely woman that might be shortening the search a bittie? But no relation, mind . . ."

A gloomy silence descended upon the gathering, broken only by the tattoo of Ewan's knuckles on his fish-box.

"Wheesht, man—wheesht," Finlay Sim reproved testily. "This is a serious matter. Don't be playing with your fingers."

"Is yon Bella Farquharson still in the bit shop at Benderloch?" somebody wondered.

"Lord Almighty!" Ewan said.

"Och, she'll be a bit on the old side, Archie." Finlay shook his head. "A decent enough woman, she used to be, but old, old."

"Bridget MacColl died, did she not, or went to Edinburgh or something?" Murdo the Mill inquired. "Her that was the stewardess on the *Maid of Lorne* . . ."

Ewan all but choked. "Holy Smoke—Bridget MacColl gave up the stewarding while I was still at the school!" he cried. "That's near twenty years past."

"Is that a fact? Gracious me—the way the time goes in . . ."

"My Suffering Sam—what do you take me for, at all!" Ewan was exclaiming, when his uncle brought the meeting to order. He did it by knocking his pipe threateningly on his oil-drum, everyone watching its precarious contents with unconcealed alarm.

"Och, quiet now!" he ordered. "What way is this to be going on? Ewan Og—I do not like your language. I do not, by God! Near blasphemous, it is. You are not in yon Germany or Aldershot or any such place now. This is a God-fearing island, and yourself old enough to know it." He turned towards the others. "It looks like there is nobody just suitable comes to mind, then, at the moment. A pity it is. But we'll just have to be going and seeing for ourselves, with an open mind, as you might say. Monday's boat it will have to be. . . ."

"*We'll* be going! See for *our*selves!" Ewan burst out, discourteously. "And who the hell is *we*, whatever?"

Finlay Sim drew himself up. "Myself I was thinking of accompanying you," he announced, with dignity. "Two heads are better than the one, in a matter of this sort—especially when the one is a hot-head and something loose in the tongue . . ."

"No," Ewan interrupted him, and got to his feet. "If there's going to the mainland in it, I go alone."

"Tchach, man—do not be so stiff-necked at all. The Lord is ay against the stiff-necked and rebellious man. Myself, I could be a great help to you in your searching. Moreover, I could be keeping you out of the clutches of harpies and these gold-diggers and scheming women. That Lorne will be just full of them, all digging pitfalls for the likes of yourself. I know the ways of women, and . . ."

"Look," Ewan said, moving to the door, "it is myself that is supposed to be needing a wife, isn't it? It is myself that'll have to marry the creature? Me it is that will have to live with her. Well, then—I choose her, see you. Not a one else. I go alone—or not at all."

Finlay Sim frowned, tugged his beard, and shrugged. "Och, well," he said, "just as you say, Ewan Og. You are a . . . och, goodness me, just that, then. Monday's boat, then . . . and we will pray for you. You will be at the Kirk tomorrow?"

"I will not, no. I have too much to do, whatever." That smacked of ungraciousness, as well as impiety.

There was a shaking of heads, a sighing, and a clearing of dry throats.

"A drink we could do with, anyway," Hector the Boat declared, a trifle wistfully.

His brother did not seem to hear—and nobody else had any whisky.

Ewan MacEwan marched out into the sunset.

III

THE S.S. *Maid of Lorne* made her weekly call at Eorsa at the unseemly and depressing hour of six-fifteen in the morning. That she had been at Canna and Muck even earlier, was scant consolation. But at least, it meant that such of her passengers as were making for Oban and the temptations of the mainland, reached there in time for lunch, even in time to catch the south-bound train, should they be so foolishly inclined.

This arrangement meant an unconscionably early start for Ewan MacEwan—and for others too, of course, since practically the entire population of the island turned out to see him off. This was not wholly a tribute to his personal popularity, perhaps, nor to the commendable communal interest in the object of his journey; quite a large percentage was apt to put in an appearance each Monday morning when the boat came in—this being the principal item of excitement in the week—to dispatch their surplus livestock and produce, to collect their postal packages and mail, to discuss the week's landing of newspapers. Indeed, quite a few Eorsans found it seldom worthwhile to go to bed on Sunday evenings, so that Sunday nights had become established as *ceilidh* nights—after a Sabbatarian 6 p.m., of course.

Ewan, somewhat breathless and harassed, arriving down at his uncle's house about quarter-to-six, with the morning mists, an army pack on his back, and a complaining eye-rubbing child in each hand, found all satisfactorily astir. Finlay Sim, who obviously had not been to bed—as postmaster and harbour-master, of course, he had his responsibilities—was in a surprisingly mellow frame of

28

mind, with the aura of mature malt whisky about him like a halo. Excellent advice, from the ideal standpoint of both the man of the world and the pillar of the Kirk, flowed from uncle to nephew in a beneficent spate.

But Ewan, this misty morning, was lacking in appreciation. Advice was not what he desired. He wanted to disentangle himself from two wriggling and clamant youngsters, and to leave a variety of instructions and pleas with somebody who could be trusted to carry them out. He was a little concerned about Betsy, his black-and-white cow. . . . Disengaging his progeny from the Widow Macaskill's two piglets, which, tied together by a hind-leg each, were in process of postage to the butcher at Tobermory, he left Finlay Sim unkindly to his weighty and vociferous post-official duties, and entered the house proper.

In the low-ceiled kitchen, amidst the steam and the peat-reek, he found his Aunt Elspie stirring the porridge, a small quiet serene person, grave as she was gentle. Always a little tongue-tied and abashed with this retiring aunt of his, Ewan produced a loud and abrupt good-morning, a staccato observation that it likely would rain, and could think of nothing else to say. Elspie Cutach did not have anything to say, either, though she gave him a smile, fleeting, almost shy, and held out a meal-white small hand to the children, who ran to her like chickens to a hen. Pressing them to her side, she smoothed both unruly heads and smiled down at them, her lips moving to an almost soundless croon, and all the time her other hand stirred steadily at the futtering porridge above the glowing peats. The youngsters stared up at her, wide-eyed, adoring, their complaint stilled quite; always, that was the effect of Elspie Cutach on children.

Ewan sighed with relief. "Mary—is she about, at all?" he inquired.

His aunt nodded. "In the byre, she is," she said, and resumed her crooning.

29

Almost on tip-toe the man slipped out of the back door again.

The byre was warm with the friendly smell of the cattle and hay, and from it came the sounds of heavy-sighing beasts, the spurting milk lances, and Mary's singing. There was no end and no beginning to the simple air that she sang, a traditional milking song in the old language, and Ewan waited only a few moments before he cleared his throat. "Is that yourself, Mary?" he asked unnecessarily.

His cousin raised her head from the cow's broad flank, and smiled quickly, naturally—until she remembered. "It's you, then, Ewan," she said, and promptly creased that wide smooth brow into a frown. "You're on your road?"

"I am, yes." Heavily he said it, and hitched his pack higher on his shoulders.

"A long road, it's like to be, too . . . with some dirty patches on it, and an unchancy end to it!"

"Och, I'll not be away that long, at all," the man declared. "Just a few days . . ."

Almost she tossed her head. "Is that so!" she exclaimed. "No trouble at all, it'll be, for Ewan MacEwan! They'll be just falling over themselves to marry the likes of Ewan MacEwan! Just the answer to prayer, you!"

"No, no—not at all," he disclaimed. "It is not that, just. . . . There's a lot of these surplus women about, needing husbands, see you. It shouldn't be that difficult. . . ."

"Not if you're that easily pleased, maybe," Mary returned. "If it's all one to you what you get to give your name to so long as it's got skirts and, and . . ." She turned, and resumed her milking again, with enhanced vigour.

Ewan actually flushed. "That is no way to talk, at all!" he cried hotly. "I'll thank you to speak more respectfully about what is no business of yours, whatever! I tell you . . ."

But Mary was not to be told. Her auburn head was buried against the cow's blue-grey side again, the milk spears

30

drummed on the side of the pail, and she even recommenced her singing, if a little unevenly.

For a while the man stood wordless, tapping a toe on the cobbles of the floor. When it was apparent that the girl was going to continue with the noise, he spoke, and spoke loudly. "I've brought the children. I've brought the *children*, I say. They are with your mother."

She had no comment to make.

He frowned. "I am hoping that you will be good to them—look after them in some sort of fashion. . . ."

That stopped her singing. "My goodness," Mary cried, "d'you think I'd be letting the little ones suffer for the shame and sin of their father . . . ! Dear God—is that the way of it?"

Ewan swallowed. "Ummmm," he said. "Betsy will be needing a bit eye on her. She might be a wee bittie early. Early she was with her last calf, you'll mind." Warily he eyed her.

Whether she minded on not, Mary did not divulge.

"Aye. The other beasts will be doing fine. Bally will see to them. There's just the milking . . . !" He waited. "The milking, yes."

"I will not let the cows suffer, neither, if that's what you mean," she conceded shortly.

"Uh-huh. I'ph'mmm. Just that," he said. "The hens will do away, with Bally. It's just the ducks . . . och, you know how they are for getting away down the burn, at night. I wouldn't like the fox to be getting them. Yon Bally—I do not believe that he can count, at all." He looked at her out of the corner of his eye. "And there's the goat. There's no saying what it will be eating if Bally doesn't be keeping the doors shut . . ."

His cousin interrupted. "I understand, Ewan—very well. I am to look after Corriemore for you, while you go . . . go hunting women on the mainland!"

"Tut-tut," Ewan deplored. "Och, my, oh my." And in a different tone. "It was your father said, mind . . ."

"My father says too much, and says it too often!" the undutiful daughter proclaimed—which was not like Mary MacEwan, either. "But never fear—your croft will be looked after . . . but not for your sake, Ewan MacEwan, nor for whatever sort of a creature you're for bringing back with you! You can go with your mind easy—if not your conscience, whatever!"

"You won't . . . you'll not be away then, before I'm back . . . ?"

"Me . . . ? Away where . . . ?"

"To Glasgow, then."

"Oh, yes—to Glasgow." The other looked away, to her frothing milk pail. "Och, well—I've not just decided on the date, yet."

"Your father was saying you'd be for off soon. . . ."

She was very busy at the long-suffering cow. "My father ought to know then. He is the one for knowing things, is my father! He is so."

"You mean . . . ?"

"I mean that if I *am* away before you come back with your . . . before you come back, then, I will see that *somebody* is looking after your neglected cows and ducks and children. *They'll* not suffer, the innocents!" She got up suddenly, set down the milk pail in the aisle of the byre with a clatter that slopped some of the foaming contents on to the cobbled floor as a godsend to a swarm of lean and hungry cats, snatched up another pail and her little stool, and hurried to the next cow, all in less time than it takes to tell.

"Thank you," Ewan said, but doubtfully.

Probably she did not hear him, for she had started her singing again, and a shade higher, louder, than heretofore, as well as more evidently determined.

The man opened his mouth once or twice, but always shut

it again. Also, he said Aye a few times, or implied kindred sentiments. But it was heavy going, and short of bursting into song himself he was unable to compete on equal terms. The Eorsa Milking Song is like that—and there were two more cows to milk yet.

Five minutes of it, perhaps, or it may have been three, he stood, before, strident and unmusical above the singing, the sound of a distant siren penetrated. Ewan glanced up, almost with relief. "The boat," he said. "That's her."

Strangely enough the girl heard him this time. "Yes," she agreed. "Time you were on your way, then." She did not sing that.

"Yes. Och yes, I suppose so." This was not strictly true, of course; the *Maid of Lorne* had the kindly habit of blowing her siren when rounding the Ard, the northern tip of the island, and still a couple of sea miles from her heaving-to place in the bay, so that the Eorsans had fair warning of her approach, an arrangement much appreciated in inclement weather— especially by Hector the Boat, who was a man fond of his bed, and not apt to throw off the last blanket until he heard the hooter. So there was no real hurry. But the byre interlude was dragging, undoubtedly, and neither comfortable nor profitable. A pity. As well to go. "Well, I'll be away then, Mary," he decided.

"Yes."

"Aye, well . . ."

The Milking Song resumed.

Furrowed as to brow, Ewan went heavily back to the house to bid farewell to his offspring, found them entirely absorbed in plucking the morrow's boiling-fowl, and got not so much as a glance out of them. From his Aunt Elspie he got a light touch of the hand, a quiet word of Godspeed, and a curious perplexed shaking of the head, that might have signified sorrow or sympathy or a mild disapproval, or perhaps some inner doubt of her own. Her nephew did not seek

33

elucidation, and with a last rueful glance at the busy children, strode out.

The *Maid of Lorne* was like a water-beetle on the quiet grey surface of the sea. From his cottage window, Hector the Boat eyed it heavily, dispassionately, and yawned.

If Hector was backward, there were plenty who were not. Around the tumbledown stone jetty where Hector's ancient boat was moored, quite a throng was gathered, young and old, very much in the centre of which was Finlay Sim Mac-Ewan and his piglets, reinforced now, however, by a calf tied up to its neck in a sack, a crate of live poultry, and sundry sheep watched over by approximately one collie dog each. As the pigs were still squealing, the calf was lowing lustily, most of the dogs were barking at the complaining sheep, and a cockerel that had got its foolish head stuck through the bars of the crate was crowing itself into delayed strangulation, the scene and effect was stirring and vital, not to say distracting. The screaming of the gulls overhead, as well as that of the assembled children, was all but drowned in the clamour.

Ewan's reception was mixed. The men greeted him with a compound of sympathy, encouragement, and concern, but the women, strangely enough, without exception kept their distance and eyed him askance—which was by no means their normal. Even the elderly were affected. Not that he appeared to be concerned to seek any demonstration of support or interest—on the contrary. He moved down to the edge of the jetty, and stared out towards the incoming ship, as though he could not get away from Eorsa quickly enough. Such was remarked upon. His preoccupation was variously interpreted.

He was not allowed to stand in Napoleonic isolation, of course. The group around Finlay Sim gradually transferred its attentions to Ewan, its observations sober, responsible, and helpful. It was a fine quiet day for the voyage, yes. It might rain, though—it was to be hoped that he would not be having the bad weather for his ploy, at all; there was nothing damped the women's enthusiasm like the rain. Was he not taking a coat with him, one of these waterproofs, or maybe a bit of rubber-sheeting? Och, it was said that the mainland women were terrible frightened of catching the cold where they sat down. And what about him having his hair cut? Over yonder, it was said, there was a bit place, behind a shop that sold tobacco and those coloured picture postcards, where they took the hair off you, and sent you out smelling so that the women were fair fighting themselves to get at you. . . .

Tut-tutting a little at this last, Finlay Sim came down, to touch Ewan's elbow, circumstantially, authoritatively. "How are you about the money, man?" he inquired. "You will need the money on the mainland, mind. I have the wee box by me, and if you're needing something . . . ?" and he drew out of his pocket a battered tin box, of the sort that in another era used to contain a hundred cigarettes. Crushed within it was a creased and tattered collection of bank and Treasury notes. It was Eorsa's bank, that box, and was looked on with much respect by all—though it was seldom seen. How its contents should have been apportioned amongst the islanders was a problem to which, it was hoped, Finlay Sim knew the answer—for nobody else did. Money, as a medium of exchange, as it happened, was not used a great deal on Eorsa, save through Finlay Sim, his shop, his post-office, his agency for Messrs. MacBrayne of the steamers, and his representation of the Department of Agriculture for Scotland. There was a little black book that partnered the box, and was much more frequently in evidence, in which innumerable and complicated cross-transactions were recorded, Old Age Pensions set against bone-meal and ironmongery, Department grants against tobacco and sheep-dip, Ministry of Food vouchers against paraffin-oil and postage-stamps. The possession of and ability to interpret that little black book in no small measure accounted for Finlay Sim's unchallenged supremacy in Eorsa.

His nephew shook his head. "I have a bit account with a bank in the Oban," he declared. "I'll be getting the money, there."

His uncle knew about that account, of course, and disapproved of it. It was unnecessary, unsuitable, and looked as though Ewan perhaps did not altogether trust the island system of accounting. Like many another bad habit, it had started during the late war, of course, when, with Ewan a prisoner in Germany, a regulation-bound War Office had insisted on paying the incarcerated warrior's accumulated sergeant's pay into a bank account instead of into the wise and capable hands of Finlay Sim. The indirect consequences of war are frequently under-estimated.

The old man frowned, and snapped the box shut. "Is that so?" he said. "Well, then—see you that you do not get into any foolishness with your money. The proper use of the mammon of unrighteousness is a matter on which the Lord turns a jealous eye. Yes, indeed. I do not like you to be going alone, at all. Pitfalls lie in wait for the obstinate and the stiff-necked man, my God."

An antiphonal groan of agreement rose up to join the prevailing chorus.

Ewan did no more than raise a single rather sardonic eyebrow.

"You'll send us a postcard, maybe, Ewan?" Murdo the Mill suggested. "Just to let us know the way things are going . . ."

"And if you're needing a bit hand, at all . . ." Duncan Macdougall began, when he was interrupted.

"Tchach—Ewan knows where to come if it's a hand he's needing," Finlay Sim declared. "Where's that Hector?

Time it is that Hector was in it. Away you and fetch him, Archie. . . ."

"Aye . . . but I was just going to tell Ewan the kind of a woman to look out for—to have in his mind, just. We were after telling him, yon time, the kind he was *not* to look for, whatever, but not the kind he *was*. Myself, I've ay heard that ones with plenty to them across the small of the back were the best, with a good deep chest. Never mind about the weight. . . ."

"And keep you an eye on the feet, Ewan. A woman with bad feet's no sort of use at all. You'll be fetching in your own cows and digging your own peats before you know where you are!"

"And watch out for red hair, man, for any favour. I'd never marry a woman with red hair, unless, unless . . ." The rash individual who thus advised paused, blinking. It obviously had just occurred to him, by his darted glance at Finlay Sim, that that man's daughters both had hair that could only be described as reddish. "Aye," he ended. "Ummm. Just that."

"And there's the mouths," Murdo the Mill put in hastily. "You can tell a lot by the mouth—same as a horse. They say a good wide mouth, sort of thick lips, and fair-sized regular teeth is the thing, boy. Myself, if I was you . . ."

"My goodness!" Ewan burst out, "where in hell's Hector the Boat!"

"Here I am, then," a grumbling voice said, and his Uncle Hector came pushing through the throng, buttoning his reefer jacket. "What is all the hurry, at all?" He paused for none of them, but jumped down straight into the boat, his sea-boots clumping, stowed a package of his own under a thwart, took the cover off the engine, and stooped, muttering, to tackle the carburettor.

Ewan delayed no longer, but leaped down on to the floorboards likewise, off-shouldered his pack, and turned to

37

receive the cargo. The next five minutes were too full for the proffering or assimilation of further advice.

At length, with Finlay Sim's immediate responsibilities transferred from the jetty to his brother's boat, where, despite the effect of a draped net designed to counter their decentralising tendencies, Ewan found himself inevitably committed to the active restraint of the piglets and one in particular of the sheep, Hector started up the somewhat asthmatic engine. From the pier a last salvo of instruction, warning, and counsel, was launched, which however mainly failed to penetrate the formidable curtain of sound now emanating from the boat. Valedictory hands were raised, ropes were cast off, and Finlay Sim's shout rose almost to a scream.

"You'll mind it's the good of the island you have in your two hands, Ewan Og!" he cried, his beard jerking as though under independent control. "And the good name, too!"

His nephew shook his head, frowned, and shrugged in one, as Hector ground the engine into gear, and the laden boat drew away from the weed-hung stones of the jetty. Thereafter, necessarily, he devoted his attention to his onerous if unsolicited duties as supercargo. Only once did he glance back to the receding land, and then not to the jetty but towards the area behind it where the white-washed croft-houses dotted the green machair of the shore. And whether it was at what he saw or did not see, he sighed.

The steamer lay waiting for them on the gently-swelling bosom of the bay, the smoke from her squat red-and-black funnel drifting downwards in the still morning air to lie on the water's surface in heavy wreaths. Two or three pip-pips on the siren woke the echoes to speed their passage, but Hector the Boat knew Captain Angus Maceachan well enough not to take such seriously. With the tide making and the wind from the west, he swung in a wide arc round the stern of the ship to approach from seaward. There, a dark hole like a cavern already yawned in her side, with a white-capped mate and two or three seamen in the jaws of it. Despite the hour, a number of passengers lined the rail above, to watch the proceedings. Throttling back his noisy motor, Hector chug-chugged in under the ship's black side, whilst Ewan stumbled forward over net and livestock, to throw a rope to the waiting seamen above.

"Late again, Hector!" the mate sang out. "You are a terrible man for your bed. If it wasn't that I knew your wife . . . !"

Hector accepted that sally in the spirit in which it was made. "Och, man—there are some of us with more to do than sailing about the place with summer visitors, whatever!" This, for the benefit of the passengers aloft, largely islanders from Canna and Barra and farther out still. "It's not all of us have a life of pleasure excursions. . . ."

A stentorian voice hailed down to them from somewhere much higher. "Hector MacEwan—have you got yon you-know-what, I was telling you about?"

"I have so, yes, Captain—and the great trouble it has been, too. I'm hoping it will be appreciated. . . ."

"And the sea fair hotching with the stuff!"

"Catch it your own self, then. . . ."

During this shouted exchange, a small derrick had swung out above the motor-boat, lowering a steel cable with a stout net of ropework attached. Ewan unhooked this latter, bundled in haphazard a miscellaneous assortment of goods, packages and struggling animals, re-threaded the hook, and waved a hand. The tackle reversed, the cable tautened, the net changed shape, sundry projections, corners, and kicking legs stuck through, and the lot soared up and inboard and out of sight. Somewhere, in the noisome belly of the *Maid of Lorne*, when that net opened, there was going to be high jinks.

The piglets, protesting shrilly and refractory to the end, were the last to go, and then the process was reversed, as the outer world's weekly offering to Eorsa was disembarked. This did not take nearly so long, and soon Ewan was standing on a thwart, balancing himself, prior to making his jump. Hands stretched down, now near now far, to help him up. His Uncle Hector was conversing in a hoarse and penetrating whisper with the mate, who listened with round-eyed attention and portentous noddings. "You don't say!" he exclaimed. "D'you tell me that! My God—is that a fact?" He glanced at Ewan with interest, and more than interest. "My goodness—we'll have to be seeing what we can do."

"Just that," Hector the Boat agreed. "Aye—and the skipper was ay a knowledgeable one with the women." He nudged the dark-browed Ewan, and thrust his curiously-shaped package under his nephew's arm. "A bit salmon," he confided, "a cut for the Captain, too. A bit salmon can ay be a help with the women. Anything they can cook . . ." Hector, apart from Monday mornings, was representative of Lorne Salmon Fisheries Ltd., on Eorsa. "Try yon wee hotel on the Connel road—the Dunstaffnage Inn, they call it. Jeannie Grant'll not see you wrong . . . especially with the salmon. . . ."

Ewan nodded, only curtly it is to be feared, watched the rise of the swell, and leapt. Hands grasped his, and he landed easily enough, within the mouth of the cavern. Turning, he caught the pack that his uncle threw up to him.

The mate patted his shoulder, confidentially. "We'll fix you up, never fear," he cried. "You don't need to worry about a thing, b'damn."

His passenger eyed him with a woeful lack of appreciation or gratitude, and without a word or even a backward wave at his helpful uncle, strode on deeper into the quietly throbbing bowels of the ship. It looked as though he was setting out on his quest in a quite unsuitable spirit.

IV

HAVING delivered the captain's fish to a steward, and thereafter buried himself in the farthest recesses of the steerage accommodation, Ewan managed to maintain his privacy more or less inviolate during the ninety minutes or so of deep-water sailing between Eorsa and Tobermory. Thereafter, throughout the long criss-cross passage of the narrow Sound of Mull, with the ship calling at a series of little ports on alternate sides, her company was much too busy to inflict itself on any of its passengers. But once Craignure was astern, and the *Maid of Lorne* was nosing her way into the wide and almost landlocked basin of the Firth of Lorne, with a clear run ahead to Oban, Ewan found himself summoned to Captain Maceachan's cabin—and knew sufficient of matters maritime not to refuse.

He found something of a conference in session. The skipper and the mate were there, but also two others, the Area Inspector of Fowl Pests from the Department, and the Oban representative of a Glasgow firm of agricultural engineers. Captain Maceachan, large, jovial, authoritative, and forthright, hailed Ewan within in gusty benevolence, as the man that they'd got to find a wife for, and after introducing him in some fashion to the two other landlubbers, declared that it was time that they got down to business, and them into Oban in half an hour, no more.

Ewan's protests, that they were not to bother themselves with his small private affairs, went quite ignored.

The captain contended that the real matter they had to decide was—like every other problem—what port they were going to make for, and then the surest and quickest course to follow to reach it. It seemed to him . . .

The commercial gentleman interrupted to point out that it appeared to *him* much more a question of supply and demand. The essential factors were how much was the buyer able to put down, and what could he get for his money?

The Civil Servant demurred. Was it not all a matter of priorities? Priorities in availability, as against counter indications. They must categorise the classification, women and/ or girls, into the convenient sections—Type A, Type B, and Type C, with possible sub-sections A(2), B(2), and it might be, C(2). In the first, A, they might place such occupationally-suitable material as the unmarried daughters of farmers, crofters, and shepherds in A(2), those of Forestry Workers (excluding fencers and ditchers, which see hereunder). Then in B . . .

To hell with that, the captain thought, heavily. What they wanted was, where they were going to make their landfall— where they were going to start the lad off? Now, if it was himself, he'd be for trying the Plaza first—yon dance-hall behind the Free Kirk. Of course, Monday night would maybe not be the best for . . .

Nonsense, the agricultural salesman declared. Dance-halls were the wrong sort of place, altogether. It was a wife that was wanted, wasn't it—not a temporary convenience? The market was the thing. On market-day they had all the right sort of women coming into town. You had to study your potential buyers, and see that your commodity, properly displayed, reached the right public at the right time. Otherwise sales resistance would harden. That was elementary. . . .

The Labour Exchange, for a start, the Fowl Pest king decided. Undoubtedly. There you had the requisite information tabulated and available. This problem was occupational in the first instance. He would go that far with Mr. Turnbull. But the women coming to market would tend to fall under the category of settled labour, plus the sub-categories unemployable and superannuable. It was elsewhere that they must look for their material—amongst the classification Mobile Labour (Female), Seasonal and/or Occasional Workers (Women), and . . .

Damning his eyes and other parts, the captain indicated a lack of enthusiasm for the Ministry of Labour's categorisation. Also, market-day wasn't till Thursday. They couldn't just put the business into cold-storage till then. . . .

Mr. Turnbull pointed out that, while there was no harm in doing a little preliminary softening-up before then, there would be a great saving in time and travelling and on-costs generally by letting the customers come to the vendor, instead of the vendor going out to seek the customers.

The mate cleared his throat, and made his first observation—to the effect that yon Mollie that ran the ticket-office at the pier, there, looked like she had been needing a man, for a bittie. . . .

His senior officer requested him, och to hold his tongue. Mollie the ticket-office, indeed! Did he think punching tickets was the training for milking cows on a place the likes of Eorsa? The master paused, and a far-away expression came into his keen sea-blue eyes. That minded him. . . . Had they heard the one about the lady ticket-collector and the all-in wrestler? Och, then, they'd have to hear that one. . . .

They did, and were all but unanimous in finding it apt and very funny. And it reminded the commercial traveller of the one about the new bus conductress who asked the driver what happened when the wee bell was pressed *three* times. . . .

The representative of government tut-tutted a little at this one, more suited obviously to trade than to professional circles, and endeavoured to raise the tone of the discussion by

43

retailing an extremely subtle if complicated allegory concerned with the investigations of a certain high executive of the British Transport Commission into the vocational hazards of lady porters. This, of course, took a considerable time, and Captain Maceachan was straining at the lead long before he actually asserted his unchallengeable authority by producing a bottle and some glasses from a convenient locker and in the breathing-space thus achieved, adroitly proposing the toast of sweethearts and wives, which he coupled suitably with the one about the headmistress with the lisp.

Undoubtedly the refreshment had a good effect on their memories, for thereafter the flow and standard of relevant anecdote was greatly enhanced. So much so, that when presently a seaman knocked and thrust his head into the cabin, with Mr. Cameron's compliments and the information that they had passed the Dog Rock, it was to be dismissed with a nautical expression and no uncertain instructions as to what Mr. Cameron—presumably the First Mate—could do about it. Discreetly the mariner withdrew—but not before Ewan MacEwan had managed to slip out with him, fortunately without apparently giving offence, since indubitably his absence went quite unnoticed.

He eyed the rapidly approaching hotel-strewn coastline of Oban Bay with some doubts and misgivings, and went in search of his pack.

Unmolested, and with the gangway and the thronged and littered pier behind him, Ewan stood for a little in the centre of the pleasant crescent that made the water-front main street of the West Highland capital, below the endless circus of the screaming gulls. To turn right, left, or to go straight on? When face to face with the need for action, it became something of a problem to perceive the initial steps that should be taken in seeking a new wife in a strange town at approximately twelve-thirty of an August Monday. There were plenty of women about, admittedly, a bewildering assortment, of all shapes, sizes, ages, and charms—enough to fill a score of the Departmental gentleman's categories—staring into shop-windows, getting in and out of shiny cars in distracting fashion, gazing at the seagulls, the boats, and each other, just walking and talking, all talking. But Ewan felt instinctively that one couldn't just go up to selected individuals, inquire if they were already married, and if not suggest a quiet preliminary chat somewhere. Not in Oban. It was quite different in Eorsa, where everyone's background was known and no introduction was necessary. Anyway, nine-tenths of these women undoubtedly would come under the heading —since headings seemed to be important—of summer visitors or tourists, and so be unsuitable for his purposes at Corriemore.

A faint rumbling from within reminded him that it was seven hours since he had made his somewhat sketchy breakfast, and that probably he would feel twice the man he now felt and more able to face up to the demands upon him, after he had partaken of some lunch. He looked about him, accordingly. There was no lack, of course, of catering establishments in Oban—in fact, every second building seemed to be an hotel. But almost without exception, they were the sort of places that Ewan would no more have thought of entering than he would have done the first-class lounge of the *Maid of Lorne*, places where even his best brown boots and suit of hairiest dark-brown Harris tweed hardly would have looked right. However, round near the Auction-marts he descried a more modest establishment, dedicated to the cause of temperance, wherein he thought that he might possibly venture. When, after waiting outside in some doubt for perhaps five minutes, he saw a man in the dungaree garb of honest labour pass inside with complete nonchalance, he decided that the risk could be taken, and followed on.

45

Within, amongst a jostling crowd of small tables covered in off-white napery he found a space near the door, set down his pack and now rather moistly limp parcel of salmon, and waited in wary-eyed patience.

But his eyes were more than wary. After taking in the four other diners, the worn carpeting, today's menu chalked on a blackboard on the mantelpiece and the relics of yesterday's on the cloth before him, his speculative glance alighted on the two waitresses who had just issued from some inner sanctum to ply, with much expert twisting and sinuous undulation, between the tables. Both were young and well-turned, one rather more so than the other—though possibly that was only an illusion occasioned by the fact that the frock of black shiny stuff that she wore was two or three sizes too small for her. The resultant stresses and strains threw into high relief most of the major protuberances of her person, as well as opening a number of intriguing seams and fissures here and there at points of especial pressure. The eye-catching consequence was enhanced by the very distinct wiggle-waggle of a pair of noticeably spherical hips, an effect which she achieved either by the wearing of extremely high-heeled shoes or by sheer natural proficiency. Needless to say, Ewan had not a great deal of time for a proper consideration of her less tightly-encased colleague.

But by the time that this lady had swivelled her way to his table, ignored his polite good-afternoon, and actually interrupted his information that the rain was holding off, with a curt demand as to his needs, in a broad Glasgow accent that came with curious effect through jaws almost as rhythmically active as her lower parts, Ewan was quite disillusioned. He had never liked chewing-gum. As she tittuped away for his soup, he turned his regard in the alternative direction.

This nymph, now serving his overalled harbinger with mince and mash, though she gave a general impression of some internal sagging, rather like an old couch, at least did not masticate gum. And when she had eased her way back to the source of supply and announced the further order of steamed and custard, it was in the musical and familiar lilt of the Hebrides—Lewis, Ewan decided. And while he had no particular enthusiasm for scuffling carpet-slippers, he recognised that such must not unduly prejudice him at this stage—though, of course, it would be foolish to ignore the advice he had received on the essential subject of feet.

However, though he jerked his eyebrows, clattered his cutlery, and cleared his throat intermittently, he quite failed to attract this ministrant's attention—though not that of others. It was not until he was spooning up the ochreous residue of his custard, that she came to attend to a newcomer at a nearby table, a substantial and matronly lady hung about with shopping-bags and packages, who puffed.

Ewan said, sympathetically, "Good afternoon. It is a fine day, but warm for the running about. Bad on the feet . . ."

It was the red-faced puffing person who answered, looking at him sharply. "It may be warm—but there's nothing the matter with my feet, at all, young man!"

Ewan blinked, and coughed. "Och, it was not *your* feet, I was talking about," he protested. "No, no. There is nothing wrong with your feet, I'm sure. It was . . . it was this young lady's feet. . . ." He paused, and looked down. "I mean . . ."

"And what have my feet got to do with you, whatever?" the island maiden demanded, swinging round and paying attention to him at last. "It is bad enough to be after making a cripple of myself rushing about and waiting on the likes of you, without my feet being thrown into my face, good gracious!" It is surprising how the most pleasing lilt in any voice can be so effectively negatived by the tone behind it.

"Och, my goodness—I wasn't after saying that there was one thing *wrong* with your feet," the man disclaimed. "Your feet are fine, just fine. I was just saying . . ."

47

"They're *not* fine!" the young woman cried hotly. "They are not! They're bad, I tell you—just killing me." And she stamped one of them, just to emphasise her point, and moaned in consequent agony. "What do you know about it, at all? And what business is it of yours, anyway?"

"That's right, Chrissie," her Glasgow colleague confirmed, coming over to rest one of her hips on a convenient table-top, and transferring her gum from one side of her scarlet mouth to the other. "Whit wey's the guy shootin' oot his neck?"

"Damnation—I'm not for saying a thing, not a thing! I was just for passing the time of day. . . ."

"Swearing, now!" the stout lady pointed out loudly, and sniffed. "This is a right scandal!"

"Guy's nuts," the south-country waitress observed, suc- cinctly.

"I'm not caring if he *is* nuts!" her coadjutor insisted. "He has no right to be sitting there and criticising my feet!"

"Och, Holy Mike—what is my account, at all?" the man exclaimed, jumping to his own feet, and all but upsetting a series of tables behind him. "How much money?"

"Two-an'-four," he was told, between chews. "An' watch whit you're daein', you great muckle sumph. You needna think you can come in here, an' knock the joint aboot. . . ."

Ewan, scrabbling about amongst a handful of bent nails, .22 bullets, buttons, and pieces of string, uncovered a coin, which he threw down on the table. "There's a half-crown, my Chove—and you can keep the change!" he said. He was stamping for the door when he remembered his pack and his fish.

"Will you get a load o' that!" the Glaswegian demanded, indignantly.

"A girl should be protected from the likes of him," Chrissie asserted, tears in her musical voice. "It's not fair. . . ."

"Just one of these creatures from Mull, likely enough," the matronly customer suggested. "Never heed him."

48

"'D'Almighty!" Ewan choked, and reached the doorway. Within it, he turned and looked back. "Women . . . !" he said distinctly, and with profound feeling, and plunged out into the street.

His indignation and disgust carried him down to the High Street, right round the waterfront, and out to the end of the North Pier again, where he presently found himself staring almost longingly at the jagged Inner Hebridean skyline from which he had so recently issued. Nearby, the S.S. *Lochnevis* was taking on her last passengers preparatory to making her afternoon voyage to Tobermory, and Ewan felt himself strongly tempted to hurry aboard and be done with this whole uncomfortable and depressing business. Only the thought of his reception back in Eorsa, and the recognition that he had a reputation of sorts to keep up— hadn't he won the M.M. in the early days in France? —restrained him. Sighing, he retraced his steps to the town. The recollection of his difficulty in finding that half-crown drew him towards the substantial premises of the West of Scotland Bank.

Therein, embarrassingly, he found himself to be the only customer on view, and so the target for the concentrated regard of the bank staff. A young lady being present, he took off his cap and introduced himself. "It's not a bad sort of a day, at all, after the morning that was in it," he mentioned. "My name is Ewan MacEwan, Corriemore, Eorsa, and I'm wanting some money, please." He was afraid that that sounded rather aggressive.

There was a little general throat-clearing, and then the first teller nodded gravely. "Of course, Mr. . . . er . . . MacEwan. Anything you say. How much money would you like?"

Cautiously Ewan eyed him. "Well—how much have you got, at all? I mean, of *my* money. How much have *I* got?"

The teller glanced over the partition at his colleagues. "It's a problem, isn't it!" he said. "You, h'm, you haven't got a pass-book?"

"Eh . . . ? D'you need a pass, then, here?"

"No, no. It was just the book. . . . You *have* an account with us, I presume? Is it a current or a savings or a deposit account, Mr. MacEwan?"

Ewan rubbed his chin with the back of his hand. "Damned if I know," he admitted, and then glanced up a shade suspiciously. "*You* it is should know the likes of that," he charged. "You it is that keeps the account, isn't it?"

There was a faint stir in the back regions behind all the mahogany, and the teller frowned. With some professional hauteur behind it, he raised his voice. "Miss Ainslie," he requested, "kindly look up your ledger, and see if you can unravel this, er, client." He pronounced that "unrevel this clay-ent," and sounded daunting in the extreme.

The lady peering over the top of some handsome panelling disappeared, with a delightful giggle. "MacEwan, did you say? And Corrie-what . . . ?"

"MacEwan, Corriemore, Eorsa," Ewan said heavily. "It will be the only Eorsa one you will have, I'm thinking."

"Very likely," the teller agreed, with some significance.

"Let me see. . . . Yes, here it is," the clerkess announced. "E. MacEwan, Croft of Corriemore. Current Account." There was the sound of large pages being turned, and then Miss Ainslie herself, in her entirety, appeared in the doorway behind the teller, carrying a large leather-bound book. She took the penholder out of her mouth, and used it to indicate something in the book to her senior colleague. She was a tall and slender young woman, dressed like they are in magazines, and her hair might have been an advertisement for somebody's shampoo.

"Ah," said the teller. "M'mmm. I see. Hummm. Well, Mr. MacEwan—I see that your credit is, ah, quite shall we say, substantial. There is a balance of . . . let me see . . . of eight hundred and nine pounds, four shillings, exactly. H'rmmm. Mr. MacEwan—I say that there is a balance of . . ."

Ewan returned his gaze to the man, with difficulty. He had been assessing, not his balance, but the potentialities of Miss Ainslie, in as unbiased a fashion as he could, noting amongst other things that she wore no ring, but he had come to the honest if reluctant conclusion that, superficialities aside, she would be unlikely to measure up to the standards of Corriemore. Which was a pity, too, for she had notable eyes, and was using them now with considerable effect. But that willowy figure . . . He shook his head. "Er . . . thank you," he said.

"A pleasure," the teller declared, with some earnestness. "And how much will it be then, Mr. MacEwan?"

"Well . . . eight hundred, were you saying?" Ewan pondered. It might be as well to have a bit of money about him on this ploy. And on the mainland. Everybody agreed that next to dark wavy hair and a sort of broken nose, there was nothing the women paid more heed to than the money. The traveller-man on the boat, there, had been certain-sure that it was all a matter of supply and demand, that if the price was right the goods would be there. . . . "Och," he said, "I'll just take the half of it."

"Eh . . . ? Half? You mean . . . ?" The teller blinked. "You mean, four hundred pounds?"

"That's right," the client agreed. "That should be plenty. Damn, yes."

"Yes. Yes, I should say . . ." The other coughed. "And how would you like it, Mr. MacEwan?"

"Like it? Och, fine."

"I mean—how would you like the money? In what form? It's a matter of denominations. . . ."

"Denominations?" Ewan wrinkled his brow. "Man, I'm a member of the Church of Scotland—but what's that got to do with it, at all?"

51

"No, no. You misunderstand me. . . ."

The young woman's laugh was warm and understanding. "What Mr. Thomson means is how do you want the money made up, to take with you, Mr. MacEwan. Pounds, shillings and pence, you know."

"Och, it'll have to be in notes, see you. I could never be doing with all that in coins, no. Pound notes is the thing."

The teller swallowed. "Quite. Quite. But four hundred pound notes is quite a packet, Mr. MacEwan. Perhaps you should have some tens and twenties?"

"Pound notes'll do me, fine," Ewan was asserting, when the other placed a bundle of neatly-folded blue paper before him, itself made up of five smaller wads, all bound up in elastic-bands.

"That is *one* hundred," he pointed out. "And here's a ten and a twenty note."

"I'ph'mmm. Aye," Ewan said. He eyed the large-denomination notes without enthusiasm. "They're not worth it, to look at. I'll just take the pounds. They'll go fine in my pack." He off-slung that useful receptacle. "Och, I've plenty room."

The teller was writing, his pen spluttering a little. He peered over at the pack, and moistened his lips. "Just as you say, sir. Just sign here, will you?" Head ashake he compared the result with the specimen signature, and pushed over the polished counter the four tightly-packed bundles of paper. "You know best."

"That is so," Ewan agreed. He stooped to stow three of the packets away in his pack, and the fourth he thrust into his jacket pocket, where it bulged noticeably. "Aye, then."

"Nothing else I can do for you, Mr. MacEwan?"

"Not a thing, no." He was looking at the clerkess again. It was a pity about Miss Ainslie—just like a hazel wand, she was. He shook his head.

The young woman did not fail to observe his regard. She tittered. "I wouldn't mind helping you to spend that lot, Mr.

MacEwan!" she said. With a quick and half-defiant glance at the teller, she added: "If you need any assistance, you know where to come!"

Regretfully, Ewan sighed, hitched on his pack, and picked up his fish. "Kind, you are," he acknowledged. "But . . ." He shrugged, and put on his cap. "My thanks—and good-day to you."

A shaveling from the rear hurried round to open the door for him.

Out in the street, for want of any more definite plan, the man decided to take a walk round the town. It was a strange sensation to have no set programme, no unending series of tasks requiring more or less urgent attention. It was years since he had been in such a situation. He looked with interest on all that he saw—the shops, the hotels, the rail-way-station, the gas-works, the garages, even the churches. And, always, the people. All the varying types and sorts of people; though by no means a gregarious kind of man, hardly sociable indeed, Ewan always had been interested in, intrigued about, people. Eorsa was a little limiting in this respect. Now, more than once, he had to remind himself of the aim and object of his perambulations.

For all that, when an hour or so later, he found himself back on the waterfront, it was not without having come to certain relevant conclusions. He had decided that the Oban was probably not the place to begin his search; there was plenty of women about, of course—any amount of them—but by and large they did not seem to be the right type. They failed to give the impression of being made for the job. And they were not approachable; the one or two with whom he had tried, tentatively, to enter into conversation, had flounced off as though he had been going to eat them. This business was not so simple as it had seemed. It was the big-city atmosphere that was the trouble, undoubtedly. Time that he was out of here. Time, too, that he was getting rid of this salmon; its moisture had worked through the paper, and the package was tending to disintegrate under his arm. He would take a walk out towards Connel Ferry, see Hector the Boat's Jeannie Grant at the Dunstaffnage Inn, and unload his fish. It wasn't that far—only four or five miles.

It did not occur to him that he might take a bus. Taking the north road out of the town, past the park and the bungalows and the cemetery, he strode out, leaving Oban and its women, its auction-marts and its Labour Exchange, for possible future consideration. And he felt the better for the striding.

He found the place without difficulty; it was not really at Dunstaffnage at all, but up on the main road, near what was named a police-station, and about a mile west of Connel Ferry, where long Loch Etive opens out on to the isle-dotted Firth of Lorne. A small house, little more than a cottage, it bore a painted board intimating that Mrs. J. Grant, Proprietrix, was licensed to sell wines and spirits. Also bed-and-breakfast and teas. Pushing his way in, Ewan found an inner door marked Bar, and entered.

There was nobody about, so putting down his burdens, Ewan leant on the counter, and waited. He waited for quite some time, and presently grew impatient. He had discovered that he was thirsty. He knocked on the counter. There was no reply—though he heard movement in the room above. The ceiling was conveniently low, so he tapped on it with a handy tin tray.

This produced results, and footsteps on the stair heralded a striking lady with a yellow jumper and yellow hair, who eyed him without especial favour. "Well . . . ?" she demanded.

Ewan was somewhat taken aback. He had expected Mrs. Grant, as befitted a friend of his Uncle Hector's, to be different, somehow, and older—though this party was not exactly young, she was just at one of those indeterminate ages at which only a rash man would be apt to hazard a guess. He took off his cap. "You'll be Mrs. Jeannie Grant, likely?" he suggested, as though he was prepared to be convinced.

"No, I won't," the newcomer gave back. And with a glance at his pack. "And we don't want nothing, neither."

Ewan was still more surprised. The voice reminded him a little of that of his late wife, and had come a long way north to reach Lorne. "I am glad that you want for nothing," he told her gravely. "Myself, I should like a drink, see you."

She raised somewhat patchily plucked brows at him. "Then you should come at the right time," she said.

"Now, that is."

"No, it ain't." That was quite definite. "Not till five o'clock, it ain't. Didn't you ever hear of the licensing hours?"

Ewan *had* heard of licensing hours but had never really had occasion to consider them as realities. "Och, my goodness—it is just a drink I'm wanting."

"Five o'clock," he was told, inexorably. And with a kind of coy severity—for he was not a bad-looking young man in a saturnine sort of way: "You wouldn't want to get a girl into trouble, would you?"

A little surprised by the word girl Ewan disclaimed any such intention. "No, no—nothing of the sort, at all. No trouble. Just a small drink. A cup of whisky, just—that's all."

It was the lady's turn to blink. "A cup . . . ?" She swallowed. " 'Strewth—you a humorist? No use coming that stuff with me, chum. Out you go. Come back at five, if you're still thirsty," and she jerked a yellow head towards the door.

The man sighed. "A foolish business, this," he opined. On Eorsa, one drank by the thirst, and not by the clock. "But I'm wanting to see Mrs. Grant, see you," he objected.

Suspiciously she looked at him. "What for? What d'you want to see her about?" Her eye slid over to his pack again.

"Och, just a private matter." He paused. "A matter of business, whatever."

"Business . . . ? Well, you can't. She's out. Away to Oban. But she'll be back on the four-forty bus. Come back at opening-time, like I said, if you still want her."

Ewan sighed, and glanced at the jaundiced brewers' wall-clock, that said three-thirty-five. "I'll just wait," he decided.

The other frowned. "Well, you can't wait here," she pronounced. "This here is the bar, and it's shut."

"You sell teas?" the man suggested. "I'll just drink a cup of tea while I'm waiting. You see, I'm thirsty." That was mildness itself.

The lady tightened her lips, and drummed plump fingers on a table-top. "That's the next room," she declared discouragingly. "And I'll be a while making the tea . . ." A pause. "If you're all that thirsty, wouldn't a bottle of ginger-beer suit you?"

"Och, anything you like," Ewan conceded. "Can you be drinking ginger-beer before five o'clock, then?"

"A proper comic turn, ain't you! I'm splitting myself!" his companion observed obscurely, and swam across to the bar, lifted the lid of the counter, and inserted herself behind it. The man, if he considered her adequate proportions, did so with little objective concern or calculation. It was unlikely that those fingers could milk a cow.

Approximately half of the contents of a bottle were poured into a tumbler, and pushed over to him. "We only got large bottles," he was told.

"Perhaps you will help me to be finishing it, then?" Ewan proposed courteously, and attempted a smile.

He was considerably better when he smiled, and the other raised her brows, pursed notable lips, and then broke into an unexpected trill of fairly deep-throated girlish laughter. "I don't mind if I do," she said. "That'll be eightpence, ducks."

Gratified at this change of front, Ewan delved into his trouser pocket, and brought out his handful of utilitarian oddments—but apart from two pennies and a halfpenny, he could discover nothing commensurate with the demands of the situation. The lady's expression altered rapidly.

Sighing, he reached into his jacket pocket, and brought out his wad of notes. Slipping off the larger rubber-band, the thing fell into its five bundles of twenty, on the counter. His companion's eyes widened, and her breath caught in her throat and all but choked her. He detached one of the blue notes from one of the bundles, handed it to her, and stuffed the rest back into his pocket. "You will maybe have change?" he suggested.

The lady found no words at first, but busied herself in the till. When she had given him his pile of change, and sipped a little of her ginger-beer, she rested her elbows and her bosom on the counter, Ewan pushing aside his parcel of salmon to accommodate her, and eyed him thoughtfully. "What did you say your business with old Mother Grant was, ducks?" she wondered.

"Well . . . it's, och—it's sort of private," the man said. "But . . . how long have you been about this part, this Connel Ferry, at all?"

"Two years come March. Why?"

"Then, in a place like this, you'll be after knowing most of the girls that are in it, likely?"

"Girls . . . ?"

"Och, yes—young women that are not married, at all. Or, maybe, widows. Young ones. Ones that would not be missed, whatever."

Startled, his companion stared. "Strike me—and what d'you want the girls for . . . ?" she demanded, a faint quaver in her voice.

"I'm needing a woman, just," Ewan explained earnestly. "Where I come from, getting a woman is just a terrible

57

problem. Och, terrible. So they sent me over here, see you, to see what I could find. Maybe somebody like yourself could help. I would be very grateful. It's a job to find the right type, I tell you. . . ."

The lady was no longer supporting herself on the counter, but standing a little back from it—and from him—her mouth slightly open. Pursuing his advantage, Ewan leaned forward. "The kind I'm after looking for, see you, is between twenty and thirty maybe, strong and healthy, with good teeth and feet, and sort of broad about . . . och, well—broad about the seat of the skirt, just. They needn't be just beauties, mind, but it would be a help if they were not that hard to look at." Modestly he cleared his throat. "I can offer a good deal, in a sort of a way, too. I have the money . . ."

He stopped, struck by something about her expression, and the direction of her gaze. She was looking now, not at him but at his pack, where it lay on the floor against a table-leg. And, quite evident through the open flap at the top, the side of one of the four bundles of notes, and the corner of another, was to be seen. The effect was unusual.

The yellow lady pointed, and her plump finger trembled curiously. Her voice was tremulous, too, when she spoke, though nowise lacking in emphasis. "You . . ." she gasped. "You . . . scoundrel! You brute! Buyer and seller of 'elpless womanhood! With your foreign voice and your dirty money!" Both as to volume and tone, the pressure was rising. "You're a slave-trader, that's what you are—a batterer, a sucker of innocent blood . . . !" Suddenly the full horror of her position seemed to strike her, for her denunciation lifted up and up to a scream. "Help! Police! Police!" she yelled, and darting through the gap in the counter with remarkable agility in view of her dimensions, sped to the door. Still undulating, she passed from sight, if not from sound.

Ewan pensively rubbed his chin, finished his ginger-beer—and suddenly recollecting that he had passed a

58

cottage bearing the legend "Argyllshire County Police" only a hundred yards up the road, decided as suddenly that this might be a good place to get out of, just at the moment. Picking up his pack, he strode out into the lobby, perceived a back door standing as wide as the front, with a tangle of garden beyond, and the hillside rising directly therefrom. Up there was a black pine-wood, and it occurred to the man that that would be an excellent spot in which to find solitude and a little peace in an unaccountable and crazy world. The decision made, he wasted no time. Like one of the deer of his own hill, Ewan MacEwan made for his sanctuary.

It was not until he was safely within the dark anonymity of the trees that he realised that he had left his salmon behind on the bar counter.

V

EWAN'S cogitations thereafter, amongst the pine-needles, the busy ants, and the hopping rabbits, were gloomy and prolonged—even a little alarmed. His distress was two-fold; in particular, that the creature downbye should have such a wicked and stupid mind, and, more generally, the daunting thought that if women in the mass were as foolish and ungracious as he seemed to be proving them to be, how wise was he to contemplate tying himself up with another of them? Clear thinking was called for, both short and long term.

As to the former, he presently decided that, whilst he recognised the need for caution, there was no call to be unduly perturbed. Whatever foolishness this latest female might give tongue to, it was unlikely surely that any *man* would take her seriously—even a policeman. Ewan had not had much truck with the police. Indeed, apart from once asking one in Tottenham Court Road which bus to take for King's Cross, he had never spoken to a policeman in his life. The Military Police were different, of course—but one didn't speak to them, either. No, on deliberating, he did not think that he had much to fear from the police. He would give the woman a little time to simmer down, and then slip down later and have a quiet word with this Jeannie Grant. Likely she'd have a bit more sense to her.

It was this long-term programme that kept the man deep in thought in that dark plantation, for some considerable time. Obviously, there were a great lot of women that it would be most injudicious to marry, for one reason or another. What the proportion would be, to the total available, he could not know—but on present showing it looked high, high. He would have to watch his step, or goodness knows what he might find himself saddled with. It was advice that he needed. But he'd had so much advice already—too much, indeed. It was a woman's advice that was required—a sensible woman. But were there any such, at all? Look at Mary. He would have thought that he could have relied on Mary. Always they had been friends, himself and Mary; they had worked together, played together. She had written to him when he was a P.O.W.—the only one who had done—though she was only sixteen then. Och, they'd always understood each other . . . but maybe that was because they were cousins. He sighed, in tune with the woodpigeons that sighed above him. It was a great pity about Mary, altogether.

Well, he'd just have to see what this Mrs. Grant had to say, that was all. But not yet a little while. Give the dust time to settle.

Presently he moved down to the edge of the trees. There was no sign of activity down on the road, either at the police-station or at the inn. Indeed, apart from the small lonely figure of a man thinning his turnips in the middle of a field that sloped down to the shore, and a single car speeding towards Oban, nothing appeared to move in all that wide scene save the cloud shadows at their flitting over the hillsides and the unending play of sunlight on water.

And it was a wide scene, a vast panorama, that spread before him. Mountain and sea, inextricably commingled, as far as eye could see or imagination reach, colourful almost beyond belief. Before him, the blue firth, streaked with all the subtle shades of underlying sand and rock and weed, dotted with islands green and sepia, and rimmed by golden beaches and the reds and ochres of tangle and seawrack. To his left, the narrow Sound of Kerrera, in deepest violet, the yacht anchorage, the white terracing of Oban and its dark flanking woods, all backed by the tumbled brown hills of

61

Nether Lorne and Argyll, and the glimpse, down their long corridor, to the open burnished sea. To his right, the wimpling narrow waters of serpentine Loch Etive, the black span of the long bridge at Connel, the grassy levels and water-meadows of Achnacree and Benderloch, and beyond and beyond, to all infinity, the serried ranks of the great mountains of Appin and Glencoe and Lochaber, cloud-dappled, the deep purple of the burgeoning heather, veined by green burn-channels and scored by the grey gashes of the screes. The man, preoccupied as he was, could not fail to be affected by what he saw. That sort of scene had been coming between his people and their work for centuries. Ewan, finding a convenient fallen tree-trunk to sit upon, relapsed into something of the trance that has smitten the Gaels since ever they came out of Ireland.

He emerged from it, eventually, and decided that he might now suitably venture downhill. And Dunstaffnage, its inn and its environs, looked entirely peaceful.

Sensibly, he took the same way in that he had come out, by the garden and the back door. The murmur of voices from the bar, in which one high-pitched, feminine, and Cockney, persisted, gave him discreet pause at the foot of the stair. He was tip-toeing forward, for a peep round the door, when another voice, deep but authoritative, spoke from behind him, from above. He spun round, to find a square-looking elderly lady with a noteworthy moustache, eyeing him from the top of the steps.

"Well, young man—is it anything special you're after wanting, or just hide-and-seek you're at?"

There was a critical ring about that, but at least the voice was Highland. Ewan swallowed. "Och, I'm just looking for Mrs. Jeannie Grant. That'll be yourself, likely . . . ?"

"It might, then." That was cautious. "And who are you, at all?"

"Och, my name is MacEwan, just—Ewan MacEwan. I was

here seeking you a whilie back. I was for having a word with you about . . ."

"Mercy me—you're the birkie that was making all the stramash this afternoon!" Mrs. Grant charged. "You're back, are you! *You've* got a nerve, my brollach!"

"No, no!" Ewan disclaimed. "Not at all. Nothing of the sort. Just a misunderstanding, it was. I didn't say a word. It was the lady with the hair got me all wrong. . . ."

"Wheesht—or she'll be getting you wrong again," the other declared warningly. She had come halfway down the stairs. "You're the bright laddie that was after leaving the half salmon on the counter, eh?"

"Och, yes—just a bit fish for you," Ewan said. "But, see you—what I wanted to say to you . . ."

"Dear God—you've said plenty, I should think," Mrs. Grant interrupted him. "Take you my advice, laddie, and say no more, but just get away out of this as quickly as those long legs'll be carrying you. The police are after you!"

"Och, my goodness!" the man exclaimed. "Don't tell me that. They wouldn't be such damnation fools . . . !"

"Would they not, then! I tell you, the constable was in here not half an hour back, and asking plenty, too."

"Och—just the fellow from upbye, to quieten yon skirling woman . . ."

"He was for phoning Oban, anyway. And the Inspector's coming out, himself!"

"Holy Mike!" Ewan stared at her. "But what for, at all . . . ?"

"You should have thought of that before you were for taking up this game," the lady pointed out. "It is a risky trade you're in, whatever."

"Damned, I tell you I'm not in any trade, at all! I'm . . ."

"Quiet you—or you'll have the place about your ears. There's no . . . och, what did I tell you!"

Ewan did not have to turn to know what had happened.

The gargling yelp behind him was only too eloquent. In the bar doorway stood the yellow houri, supporting a tumultuously billowing frontage with one hand, and pointing at him shakily with the other, her mouth opening and shutting like a goldfish in a bowl. Behind her, three or four faces peered.

"Och, hell's bells, my goodness gracious!" the man observed, and swinging on his brown-booted heel, plunged for the nearest exit, the front door this time. It was a fine and easy establishment for getting in and out of, anyway, the Dunstaffnage Inn.

Outside, he turned right-handed—not wishing to meet any perambulating policemen from Oban or elsewhere—and ran clattering down the road.

Ewan MacEwan, like most Highlandmen, had a natural dignity that took but ill out of lumbering down even a quiet stretch of the public highway in the broad daylight of an early August evening, his pack jogging foolishly on his back. It was unsuitable and unseemly. If he was going to keep running, he would have to get off the road. To see whether he was indeed going to have to keep running, he looked back over his shoulder and his pack—and gulped to find a large car with a uniformed driver almost upon him. He swerved for the side, stumbled in the ditch, and was preparing to burst his way through a hawthorn hedge when the car swept past without a pause, and no more than pained surprise on the faces of the lordly chauffeur and the old lady therein.

This was still less seemly, and Ewan was for pulling himself together when another glance up the long straight road discovered a dark figure mounting a bicycle, and pedalling away from a group of people outside the inn-door, pedalling with a sort of heavy deliberation, and down towards himself. That was enough for Ewan. The chase was on.

He crossed the road, climbed the steep bank, threw his

legs over the sagging wire fence, and was on the lowermost slope of the same small hill that had given him sanctuary an hour or so before. It was rough pasture, coarse tussocky grass, bracken, and rabbit-cropped turf, and quite good going with the gradient not too steep. He started to run again, and a few cattle scattered away from him in stiff-legged alarm.

He did not look back until he was halfway up that hill. The policeman had not followed him up, but had dismounted and was standing at the fence, watching him. Ewan slackened his pace, gladly enough. But he kept on climbing, slanting slightly northwards. The further he put between himself and Dunstaffnage the better.

Which was all very well, of course—but when he got to the top of the hill, where the bracken had fallen back before the outcropping rock, he perceived that it was not so easy. He could no longer continue this northerly trend. To his right and front, the land dropped away in a wide sweep, following the curve of the coast and the mouth and southern shore of Loch Etive—and the road curved round with it. There was no escape that way, save across the bridge at Connel Ferry, and a man on a bicycle could reach that much more quickly than could he—and keep him in sight all the way from the road, too. He had no option but to move south-eastwards, in the direction of the mountains about the head of Loch Awe. Leading to the barren wilderness and the empty hills, it was not the direction that Ewan would have chosen, by preference. That was his geography of Lorne at fault.

Before, sighing, he turned to change his route, he glanced back downhill again—and his sigh ceased abruptly. *Two* policemen were starting to climb the hill towards him, leaving a large black car on the road behind them. And even as Ewan looked, it began to move slowly down towards Etive and the bridge. He swore explosively, and recommenced his running.

He had a little cunning to him. He ran on, on the same tack as before, until well over the crest of the ridge, and so hidden from his two immediate pursuers; it mattered not greatly that the car could keep him in view, so long as it could not communicate with the chase. And then, he turned sharply to his right, and plunged away downhill, almost at right-angles to his earlier course.

A tapering upland valley faced him, in which were two farmsteads, and along the rising ground beyond, the railway-line ran. Ewan considered both of these as he thudded down through the bracken and whins, as possible means of escape; he might hide among the farm-buildings, or he might make use of the facilities of British Railways; he had read about the singular convenience of train-jumping as an aid to escaping from policemen. But this involved the use of rolling-stock—not too quickly rolling either—and never in his limited experience had he seen a stretch of line less equipped with such. And as for taking cover in barns, it might be that the policemen would be more expert seekers than he was a hider. He probably would be wiser to keep right on.

At the foot of the hill, he looked back. The constabulary had not yet topped the ridge. He was across the narrow fields and the burn of the valley-floor, and climbing towards the railway, indeed, before they appeared. It looked as though they were less light on their feet than was he. Perhaps they had less practice at hill-climbing than he had. As he watched them come heavily down the braeside at a stiff-legged trot, Ewan cheerfully decided that he could leave them standing. Crossing the metals of the permanent way, and facing the moderate slope beyond, he proceeded to prove it to his own satisfaction.

For how long those upholders of the law followed him, Ewan never knew. He found another almost identical valley over this low ridge, this time with a single farm in it, and after that he was into wild country, of marshes and lochans and woodland beyond, with the woodland going on more or less indefinitely, around the northern slopes of the big hills. He saw them no more before he entered the trees, and thereafter he knew that he was safe.

Breathing deeply, but not otherwise distressed, he slowed to a walk, to a saunter. He even produced a distinctly patchy whistle—until the outraged wood imposed its own hush upon him. The fact was, far from feeling concerned, now, he was feeling better than he had felt all day, almost jaunty indeed. Stalking women was a weary business, but making rings round the police was a different matter altogether.

The rain that had been holding off all day came down presently, in a thin persistent curtain, to damp his ardour. But any Eorsan is used to more rain than fair, and it was the early dusk that it brought with it, rather than the rain itself, that sent Ewan downhill eventually, left-handed, towards the road. Not that he was for walking all night in the woods, anyway. He had a passable notion as to where he was, for he could see Loch Etive, grey now and cold, below him intermittently, and he knew that the road followed the southern shore as far as Taynuilt, where it struck off southwards by the River Awe through the Pass of Brander. He wanted to get across that river, and into the high wilderness beyond, where there were no roads and no policemen all the way up to Lochaber, and he had an idea that there would be a bridge somewhere in the neighbourhood of Taynuilt. It must be fully three hours since he had left Dunstaffnage Inn, and he could not have come less than eight or nine miles. So he could not be far from Taynuilt now. He swished down through the dripping birches and the soaking bracken of the foothills, to the eventual road, railway, and the water-meadows of Etive.

In the half-dark, he was not worried about the police car—even if it still was looking for him, which seemed unlikely. The headlights of any cars gave them away in ample time for him to dodge into the cover at the side of the road. But there were few vehicles indeed on that road that wet night, and no cyclists, no pedestrians; he and the wheepling oyster-catchers of the lochside flats seemed to have the evening to themselves.

Taynuilt is no metropolis, and Ewan was into it and almost out of it again, before he was aware of the fact. But he had passed no bridge, only the station-entrance and a dead-end that led down towards the loch; that would be the way to Bonawe and its ferry—but the ferry hardly would be running at not far off ten o'clock of a wet night. It was dark, dark for August, and not a soul about to guide him.

He trudged on for nearly half a mile, and then the road narrowed before him, and the sound of running water was as music in his ears. But when he was in the middle of the bridge, it was obvious that the stream below was a comparatively small one—not the River Awe, surely. Immediately beyond was a road junction, the hub apparently of no fewer than five roads of a sort, as far as the man could make out. And in the midst was a sign-post. Ewan marched up to it and stared.

Explicit and valuable instructions no doubt were there for all to read, but the man just could not distinguish a single name, screw up his eyes as he would. It was light enough to see the words, but too dark to identify the letters. He fished in his pocket for his matches, struck one, and held it aloft. But rain and wind were too much for it. Muttering, Ewan was striking another, when a crunching footstep on the road behind him swung him round. Simultaneously, a beam of white light flashed out, dazzled him for a moment, and then lifted up to the arms of the signpost.

"Can I be helping you, at all?" a companionable voice inquired. "A dirty night it is."

Blinking in the glare, Ewan peered owlishly. "My thanks,"

he said doubtfully. "It is just the bridge, I am seeking. The bridge across the Awe, that is."

"Bridge of Awe? Och, that is two miles more up the main road there," the Good Samaritan told him.

"Two miles." Ewan saw now that the sign-post confirmed that, with much other useful information. "That's fine then. I thought yon burn there was too small for it, whatever."

"Och, that's just the Nant. That's Glen Nant up yonder," he was informed. The electric torch described a sweep to the right, southwards—and silhouetted for a brief instant against its beam, Ewan perceived the peaked cap and black cape of the Argyllshire County Constabulary. "Not that much of a night for a walk!" it was suggested.

Ewan had a certain difficulty in finding coherent words. "No. That is . . . I . . . och, it is not so bad, at all." He drew a quick breath. "Not much of a night for standing at road-ends, either, maybe!"

"That is so," the other agreed readily. "I am just having a bit stroll, see you." He seemed to have some doubt as to what to do with his electric torch, apparently not wishing to extinguish it altogether and being too mannerly to actually shine it in his companion's face. In its gyrations round about, it lit up momentarily a bicycle a-lean against an adjacent tree-trunk—which seemed rather to invalidate the strolling statement. "Hiking, yourself, is it?"

"Well . . . sort of," Ewan conceded cautiously, and cleared his throat as the torch-beam, in one of its casual flourishes, flicked over his pack and costume. "Just . . . having a bit stroll my own self, see you!"

"Aye. Uh-huh. Just that," the policeman accepted understandingly. "Och, yes." And in an informative tone. "Yon Bridge of Awe is *just* a bridge, mind you, and nothing more. There is no place up yon road, beyond, till you're right through the Pass itself—and that is eight miles more. And late it is getting."

Ewan saw the point of that, and did some rapid thinking. "That is so. But, och—there is more than the one road round about the Bridge of Awe," he suggested. That was taking a risk, and he knew it.

"Ummmm," said the constable. "I'ph'mmm. There's the one back the other side, down to Inverawe and the loch-side, and the wee one this side of the river to Fanane, just. . . ."

"Just that," Ewan agreed heartily. "As you say. Och, well— I'll be on my way, then."

"Surely, surely," the other acceded, but without entire conviction. He scratched the back of his head, tipping forward his cap. "You wouldn't have called in, maybe, at yon Dunstaffnage Inn, in your walking, would you?" he wondered. "Och, no—I don't suppose so, at all."

Ewan looked thoughtfully into the night. "Dunstaffnage . . . ?" he questioned. "Would that be the place when you come over the Connel Ferry bridge, there? Just this side of the bridge?"

"No, no," the other declared sighing. "Not at all. The other side altogether. Nearer the Oban. Och—but I see you won't be knowing the place."

"I am not that well acquainted with this bit, at all," Ewan agreed apologetically.

"You cannot know every place," his friend acceded, generously. "Myself, there are bits I don't know. But I know Dunstaffnage Inn fine. Yon Jeannie Grant's a decent enough old *cailleach*, but yon Blondie Croker's a right card. . . ."

"Is that so?" Ewan said politely. "I knew a woman the name of Grant, myself, one time—but not Creaker, no."

"Croker," the policeman corrected. "Not Creaker." He sighed again. "Och, I mustn't keep you. But you wouldn't know anything about the salmon trade, now, would you? You wouldn't know where a man could get a bit salmon, at all?"

70

"Salmon, is it?" Ewan repeated, eyes widening. "Och, I saw a bit salmon in a shop in the Oban there, just today. But, man, the price! It was something wicked."

"That's it. A scandal it is. Myself, there's nothing I like better than a bit fresh salmon to my tea, but . . . Oban, was it? So, you didn't come over the Connel Ferry bridge, then, after all?"

Ewan swallowed. "Maybe it was Fort William where I was seeing the salmon, man," he suggested. "Och, you know how it is—a salmon looks much the same one place as another."

"That's a fact," his friend nodded. "You could easy get mixed up with a thing like that." His torch-beam left the branches of the birch-tree above, which they had both been studying intently, came down to the sign-post, lingered around their feet for a moment, and then slid up Ewan's back and pack, on its way to the tree again. "Man—that's a fine pair of brown boots you've got. It's not that often we see brown boots about Lorne, at all! Most of us just have the black, see you."

"Is that so?" The lucky possessor of the unusual footgear ran a hand over his mouth. "American boots they are, that I got when they let us out of the camp in Germany. . . ."

"Man," the other cried, "were you in that stramash? You'd be in the Fifty-first? Myself, I had a brother in yon ploy. In the First Seaforths he was—Ken Macleod, Mallaig, and as wild as a stirk. Och, but you put up a good show in the old Fifty-first." He slapped the hero's back heartily—or at least, his pack—in appreciation, and once again for good measure. "My Chove, yes—you were the boys." His hand descended once more on the pack, casually but rather more comprehensively this time. "That's the fine bag-full you've got there, man. Heavy it'll be, I daresay? What'll you be having in there, I wonder? Och, I wouldn't mind yon, stuffed full of pound-notes—I would not!"

Ewan opened his mouth, and shut it again, before he

71

rediscovered his voice. "My goodness—pound notes!" he exclaimed. "What a notion, that. I wouldn't mind that, my own self!" He achieved a sort of chuckle. "Then I wouldn't be walking this road, at all—I would not. I'd be wheechling along in a fine motor-car!"

The constable laughed, too. "Och, maybe, aye. Better you would be, too. It's going to be a right dirty night—no night for walking, at all. No, no." He paused, and patted Ewan's shoulder. "See you, now—why not you just come back with me to the station, downbye? Och, you'd get a bed there, and be fine and comfortable. Better than tramping on a dirty night, whatever."

"The station . . . ? You mean the railway station, at Taynuilt?"

"No, no. Nothing like that. They have no beds there. The police-station, just."

"No, thank you," the wayfarer declined earnestly.

"Och, you would be better, man. No trouble it is, at all. Come, you."

Ewan half-turned, to consider the other calculatingly, up and down. He seemed a large man, and solidly-built, but probably was not so large as his cape made him seem. "Kind of you, it is," he acknowledged. "But I think I'll be for the road, just the same. Another time, maybe."

"Mercy me, not at all." The constable's hospitable hand came down again on his companion's shoulder, and there remained. "Man, I just insist. A sort of duty it is, no less. . . ."

"I'm sorry," Ewan declared. "Very sorry about this. I am so." And his clenched right fist came up with explosive violence to that portion of the policeman's diaphragm directly below the meeting of the ribs. It met a fairly substantial target-area with entirely adequate force, and almost simultaneously his left leg thrust out behind the other's knees. His companion folded up neatly, winded quite, and staggering

72

backwards, fell over the outstretched leg behind, and the road all but shook to his downfall.

Stooping down, Ewan wagged his head. "Man—it's a great pity, this," he confided. "But you'll be fine in a wee while— just in no time. Myself, I'm for the road, like I said. Good-night to you."

He went great-strided across the road, changed direction at a thought, grabbed the bicycle, ran it over to the bank and trundled it down into the burn. Then he took to the wooded slope opposite with single-minded resolve.

It was seldom that his army training came in so useful.

VI

IT WAS very dark in the woods now, obstacles were frequent, and the ground rose and fell with all but complete abandon. With only the sketchiest idea as to the local geography in the first place, Ewan very soon was distinctly wandered; no Highlandman, of course, could ever admit to being lost anywhere north-west of Stirling.

This was right enough, as far as it went. If he was wandered, then it was likely that any pursuit would be wandered too—not that he had heard the sound of any such. He suspected that policemen weren't much use off the roads, anyway. So long as he kept away from roads for a while, he would be all right. Consequently, it did not matter much where he was.

Within reason, that was. He had no desire, however free and untrammelled the sensation, to spend the night daundering through dripping woods, struggling amongst clutching soaking bracken, and clambering up and down hummocks. Also, it was becoming increasingly evident that it was a long time since he had had anything to eat. His somewhat interrupted lunch at Oban had been only a depressing memory for hours, and he had no great regard for the nutritive properties of even the finest ginger-beer. Sooner or later it would be advisable to find shelter and provender—a house. But off the main road, Ewan thought.

In the event, he was much more fortunate than the circumstances seemed to warrant. His stumblings and gropings presently brought him to a steepish bank, apparently much deeper than the many that he had already negotiated, away at the foot of which he could hear the murmur of water.

74

Down there, presently, he discovered himself to be on a rutted track beside a fairly large stream. At a guess, he imagined that this must be the Nant again—which meant either that he had been trending round to his right during his wanderings, or that Glen Nant had made a bend to the left. The track, however, presumably led somewhere, and would be worth following. Downstream, no doubt, it led eventually to the crossroads and a district which he had already sufficiently explored. He turned left, up-stream. At one muddy patch, where he slithered and almost fell, he lit a match and stooped to investigate. No bicycle-tracks or footprints were visible thereon, other than his own. Cheered, he pressed on.

Round a bend in the dark glen, a yellow light gleaming steadily from amongst trees, beckoned him on. An iron gate, white-painted, that swung on hinges—obviously no croft or farm, this—brought him up to a cottage, from round and about which a great clamour of barking dogs greeted his arrival. A keeper's house Ewan imagined, and knocked at the door.

A woman's silhouette appeared at the window from which the light streamed, and remained there. Ewan stepped into the path of the illumination, touched his cap civilly, and made eloquent gestures towards the door. He had to keep up the performance for some time, before there was any apparent move in the desired direction.

And even then, the scrutiny was continued from the door, which was opened only to a chink.

"A poor sort of a night it is," the man mentioned, and then repeated it, more loudly, to outdo the chorus of the dogs. "I hope I am not disturbing you, at all?"

"Maybe you are," he was told, in the homely Scots of the Lothians. "It's a queer-like time this, to be chapping at the door. What d'you want, eh?"

"Och, I'm wondering if you could give me something to

eat, maybe, and let me sleep about the place, somewhere, ma'am."

"Guid sakes—is that all! And at this time o' night, too. You're no' feart, laddie."

"That is so," Ewan agreed, a little doubtfully.

The door opened perhaps an inch further. "Who are you, an' what—to be coming speiring aboot lodgings at this hour? Are you lost, or what?"

"I am Ewan MacEwan, Corriemore, Eorsa . . . and I am not lost at all, my God." That was distinctly and suitably stiff. "A man can be having the night coming down on him on the hill, whatever, without being lost, surely!"

"Mercy on us—hoity-toity, eh!" the lady cried. "What's the style of you, then? You don't sound like a tink . . . or a hiker, even."

Ewan frowned. "Can a gentleman not be walking on the mainland without being named things like that?" he demanded. "I have walked from the Oban this afternoon, and I could be doing with a bit food and shelter. If you cannot offer me them, ma'am, I'll be for moving on." Considering the dogs' hullabaloo, and the fact that he could not see to whom he was talking, that was not undignified.

"Dearie me—is that the way of it!" The woman laughed suddenly. "You sound perky enough to be honest!" She opened the door fully. "You're not a poacher, are you?" She still seemed misplacedly humorous.

"My goodness—I am not! I am just a man walking from the Oban to . . . to somewhere else. And I have plenty of money—och, plenty."

"Is that a fact! Well, well—just fancy that." The other stood aside, so that a little of the indirect light from the room revealed the lobby behind her. "I'm sure it's honoured I should be to have the chance to entertain such a well-trousered gentleman like yourself." She might even have been mimicking his Highland speech, there.

76

"Thank you," Ewan acknowledged, and shaking the rain off his cap, stepped within and past her, inclining his head courteously as he did so. "Not at all," he added.

"Watch your feet on the lobby gas!" his hostess said, mincingly, and then laughed again, full-throatedly. "Och away in with you, to the kitchen, and let's hae a look at you, for pity's sake!"

In the mellowly lamp-lit kitchen, they turned to inspect each other. Ewan saw a fresh-faced well-made woman of early middle age, with a direct eye which she was using on him at the moment with entire objectivity. She was in process of plaiting a long coil of black hair, her fingers busy. The room was pleasant and comfortable and not unnecessarily tidy. A gleaming range contained a wood fire, beside which a kettle steamed, on the rack above a pair of men's slippers warmed, and a stuffed wild-cat mounted over the dresser.

"Well—I've seen worse," the lady declared, out of her examination. "You're no' an *obvious* villain . . . but it's gey hard to tell, sometimes. Forbye, you've got a dour dark look aboot you, too. Am I safe wi' you, I wonder . . . or must I get a couple o' the dogs in, to protect a poor lone woman's honour?"

Ewan looked startled. "Och, my gracious me—what a thing to say!" he protested. "I assure you, ma'am, you are entirely safe. . . . Och, goodness, yes!"

Her eyelids drooped a little. "No need to sound all that definite," she objected, and flicked the long plait of her hair provocatively.

But Ewan was not looking. His regard was on the warming slippers, the shot-gun in a corner, and then the taxidermic feline above the dresser. The woman answered the unspoken question in his eyes.

"My man's oot, yes—I'm all on my lee-lane. If I take you in, it's an awfu' risk I'll be taking, too, is it no'?"

"No, no. Nothing of the sort, I tell you. I wouldn't hurt a

fly—I would not. But if you feel uneasy, ma'am, I will be away out of it, and find some other place." And he hitched up his pack higher on his back.

"G'away! Sit you doon, man, an' dinna haver," the inconsistent female ordered, indicating a chair near the fire. "An' take off your bag-thing. D'you think I wouldna' hold my own wi' you, if it came to grips?" She produced an extraordinary, if eloquent, sound, mid-way between a snort and a chuckle. "An' dinna keep calling me ma'am, for any favour— like I was your mother. I'm no' a' that auld, mercy me. Maybe I'm no' so much aulder than yourself!"

Ewan doffed his pack and sat down, obediently, but wary-eyed. "M'mmmm," he said. "Uh-huh. Just that."

From the other side of the table, she considered him, still plaiting the last strands of her lengthy tresses. The man noticed that it was only the one side of her head that was thus treated, so far, the rest was heaped up on the top of her head and pinned there. "So you've walked frae Oban, ower the hill, you're no' lost, an' you want food an' a bed . . . an' your name's Mac-something?" she summarised. "Mac-What was it?"

"MacEwan, just. Ewan MacEwan."

"Aye. Well, if you're a wee thing dry aboot the conversation, you're gey wet elsewhere, Mr. MacEwan. Wait you, an' I'll get you some o' my man's auld clothes, or you'll be dreeping all ower my furniture." She paused. "Unless you'd like to sit there in a dressing-gown, just?"

"No, no, thank you," the man assured hurriedly. "Och, do not trouble yourself. . . ."

But the lady had gone. Ewan considered his situation, found the glassy glare of a wild-cat somewhat daunting, and transferred his gaze to the fire.

His hostess was not gone half a minute. "Here you are, then, my mannie," she said, handing him a Lovat jacket and a pair of plus-four trousers. "Intae them, an' you'll be fine.

78

I'll hae you some supper on the table in no time." And as he glanced around him, the clothes in his hand, "Och, just put them on in front o' the fire, there," she directed. "It's warm . . . an' I'll survive. I'm no' a married woman for nothing!"

Doubtfully Ewan watched her bustle through to the scullery at the rear of the house, noted that she made no attempt to close the door, shrugged, and turning his back modestly, began to exchange dry clothes for wet.

"Better off wi' your shirt, too," he was counselled cheerfully, from behind. "A wet sark's a right coffin-filler."

Ewan decided to risk his coffin meantime, however—which was perhaps as well, for his benefactress was through with a large soup-pot for the fire before he had got her husband's trousering more than approximately into position.

"Nothing like a bowl o' soup last thing," she announced. Cocking her head, she added: "You're no' a bad figure o' a man. Just as well—my man's no' just a cripple, himself! Off wi' thae boots, and put on the slippers. The kettle's boiling, so we'll hae a cup o' tea. Will some cold roe venison suit you?"

A little overwhelmed, the man nodded, and did most of what he was told.

Presently he was sat down to an enormous plate of meat and cold potatoes, bread and butter, and strong tea, whilst the soup-pot was already beginning to steam on the welldoing fire. His companion stood before the range, set her own tea-cup on the mantelpiece, and letting down the unplaited side of her hair, commenced to brush it with rhythmic strokes. Ewan did not entirely succeed in keeping his eyes off the process, as he ate. There is something about a woman brushing her hair that tends to draw a man's regard.

"I . . . er, it's sorry I am if I'm keeping you out of your bed," he told her.

"Are you?" She smiled, but did not interrupt the measured sweep of her hair-brush. "Maybe you are. But, och—you're not doing me any hurt. There's little pleasure in a lonely bed. D'you no' agree, Mr. MacEwan?"

The man had difficulty with a crumb of crust. "H'rr'mmm," he said. "Oh, aye . . . i'ph'mm. I dare say." He kept his eye now on his meat. "Your husband . . . ?" he wondered. "Late hours he has, surely?"

The other sighed gustily. "He has so. It's thae poachers. Erchie's keeper here, an' the poachers are the bane o' his life. An' mine, too! He's after them near every night, an' here's me just aboot as good as a widow! He'll no' be home till near daylight, the creature. . . ."

"Poachers? At night . . . ?"

"Aye—it's at night they work, the blagyirds. This place is fair poached to death. We're ower near to Oban an' Fort William. There's gangs o' them, wi' cars, an' the black-market takes all they catch. They're a right pest."

"My goodness—poaching for money, is it!" Ewan was shocked. "It's a wicked thing, that. I don't see much harm in a bit something for the pot, now and again . . . but for money . . . !"

"Guid sakes—it's big business, nowadays. These boys'll make twenty pounds in a night, an' more. But, och, that's Erchie's affair—no' ours. Here's your soup ready."

When she had poured him a brimming bowl-full, the lady suddenly noticed his feet. "Man—you've never taken off your wet socks!" she cried. "Whatna sumph." And in a trice she was down on her knees, and removing his slippers. The man made an involuntary move, part-rising and part drawing away his foot, but her grip was strong, and as he collapsed back in his chair, she was peeling off one of his damp woollen socks.

" 'D'Almighty—you mustn't do that!" he protested.

Erchie's wife paid less than no attention. As his foot was

bared, it was revealed as just as brown as young Kirsty had made herself with the keel that day of the dipping—the rich dye of his fine brown boots. "Mercy on us—you're no better than a blackamoor!" she exclaimed. "You'll hae to wash those feet before you climb into any bed o' mine, this night!" She laughed heartily, looking up at him. "At least—you ken what I mean!"

Somewhat confused, Ewan assured her that he did, and cast about urgently for a change of subject. "My Chove, it's been very good weather, except for the rain that's in it," he declared, with conviction.

The other did not say anything, but went on working away at his feet. Glancing down, at her sudden silence, the man was struck with her very noticeable femininity, particularly apparent perhaps from this angle. He found words scarce, himself.

Looking up, and meeting his gaze, she came as near to blushing as the occasion demanded, but found it a help to lean on his knee in getting to her feet. "Well, well," she said, and stood for a moment or two, before moving over to the fireside for her cup. Bringing it back with her, she sat down at the table across from him, and sipped thoughtfully.

Ewan found the need for talk curiously compelling. "I'm after having a bit walk around the country-side," he informed, between a series of mouthfuls of soup. "Just sort of going from one place to another. It's all right if the weather keeps up. . . ."

"Are you selling something?" she asked, but with no great display of interest.

"Och, gracious me—no," he disclaimed. "I'm just having a stroll, and, and sort of keeping my eyes open."

The woman opened hers a little wider. "You're no' one o' these snoopers? These Government inspectors o' some sort?"

Ewan frowned. "My God—do I look like such a thing at all?" he reproached.

81

"No—I canna say you do. 'Deed, you wouldna be sitting there if I thought you were!" Directly she eyed him. "What is it you're at, Mr. MacEwan?"

"Och, well . . ." He considered his empty plate. "You haven't any more of that soup, have you, ma'am . . . I mean, Mrs. . . . ?"

"My name's Mary Munro. Aye, I'll get you some mair soup."

"Mary!" He wrinkled his brows. "Mary's a nice-like name." He sighed. "Aye."

"It's no' bad," she conceded, as she replenished his soup plate. "You dinna need to sound so cast-doon aboot it. What was it you were going to tell me you were at, wi' your walking?" Not to be deflected, she stood over him, waiting.

Ewan recognised that he had asked for this. It was his own fault. He had a foolish tongue. But, of course, he *had* been wanting advice from some understanding woman. "Och, it's nothing very much, at all—I'm just sort of looking out for a wife," he disclosed.

"A wife . . . ! Lord save us—what you talking aboot?"

"Just what I say, whatever."

She tapped his shoulder. "See you, Mr. MacEwan—I daresay I've got as good a leg as the next one. But I'm no' sure that I'd stand for you *pulling* it!"

"My goodness gracious—why would I be doing that!" he objected. "A man has to look around a bit before he takes a new wife, does he not? It's not a thing to be doing like ordering seed potatoes."

"Seed potatoes . . . !" Mrs. Mary Munro sat down abruptly on her chair, facing him. "Go on," she ordered, a little breathlessly.

Ewan went on, since he had no option now. A long story, he was not allowed to omit any of it. Undisguised interest, flattering attention, and shrewd questioning, had their due effect. Three re-fillings of the tea-cups were necessary, and each one brought the lady's chair a little closer to that of the man. Obviously, she found the subject enthralling.

In the event, Ewan did not have to ask for any advice; it was forthcoming quite spontaneously. He was detailing something of the disappointment that his Cousin Mary had been to him, when he was interrupted with surprising vigour.

"She sounds a bad one, that—a right wicked woman! Just as well you escaped in time. I ken her kind, wi' their claws oot. . . ."

"Och, no, no. She's not so bad as all that," the man protested charitably. "She's just . . ."

"You needna' tell me what she is, Mr. MacEwan—I ken my ain sex. I tell you, there's nothing worse than a designing woman." She shook her head. "Man—you're taking an awfu' risk, in this business."

"It is not so simple as it seemed on Eorsa," Ewan admitted. "There was a woman in a, a public-house I was in. I was telling her . . ."

"Heavens—dinna go near the likes o' yon! They're worse than harpies. They'll hae the breeks off you, an' into their pockets wi' you, quick as winking."

Her guest blinked, and drew in an elbow a little—the one that somehow was touching hers. "Well . . . this one wasn't just that way, maybe. She seemed to misunderstand what I was after. . . ."

"She'd misunderstand, all right. You've had a right Providential escape, so far. But you canna go on, this way. You need to be guided. Och, man—though you were married a wee while, I can see you know nothing aboot women—no' a thing. It's as well you came to me, I think." She laughed modestly. "As well, too, maybe, that I'm safely married myself, eh?" And his retreating elbow got a distinct jog.

"That is so," he agreed heartily.

She laughed again. "What you want is to be put wise aboot women, or you're going to be fair caught. Right practical advice, you want—an' you could hae worse than me to gie you it, eh?"

"H'mmm. Undoubtedly, Mrs. Munro."

"Just ca' me Mary, Ewan," the lady said. "It's mair hamely. You canna be awfu' stiff on a subject like this." She rose to her feet. "But come awa' ower to the fire—it's mair comfy. Sit you in the armchair—I'll get some water for you to steep thae feet, for the sake o' my sheets."

In a minute or so, then, Ewan, feeling distinctly self-conscious and not a little foolish, was sitting with his feet in an enamel basin of warm water, while his hostess seated herself opposite, hitching her skirt above her knees to give her greater freedom.

"Now, the first thing—what sort o' women are you partial to?" she demanded.

"Och, well—I'm not that particular. . . ."

"Havers, man. Dinna tell me a well-set-up chiel like yourself hasna any preferences! It's no' natural. Me, I've plenty, I can tell you!" And she looked him in the eye, with every appearance of frankness.

Ewan transferred his gaze to his big toes, which were wiggling.

"D'you like them fair, or nice an' dark, now? If you've any sense, you'll watch thae blondes." She sniffed. "You ken where you are wi' the dark—they're likely to have been born that way! D'you like them wee an' skinny, or decently-built wi' some substance to them? Is it a young bit ignorant lassie you're after, or a grown woman that kens something, an' can gie a man what he needs?" She smoothed her skirt a little. "A bit experience is worth a wheen girlish giggles, d'you no' agree?"

"Probably," the man admitted cautiously. "Och, I expect you're right. But not too experienced, maybe, see you—or she might be too managing, altogether. I wouldn't just want that."

"No woman is more managing than her man lets her be," his adviser mentioned pensively. "You've got a good strong jaw on you, Ewan man—I think you might master a woman quite . . . satisfactorily!"

Her guest coughed. "Aye . . . a right problem it is," he declared, with studied vagueness.

"Hae you no preferences, at all, man? Hae you no sort o' picture in your eye?" Her own eyes, after a moment, were down-turned.

"Well . . . och, if it was just a choice, maybe, I'd like fine a one sort of smiling usually, with red kind of hair—not just red, no, but reddish-brown—with eyes brown too, like, like a deer-calf maybe, and made supple and not fat, at all. With freckles, and not that old . . . maybe about twenty-five or six, just . . ." Ewan's voice tailed away into a sigh. "But that kind is not often found, whatever. . . ." He glanced up, to find Mrs. Munro frowning at him. "No, no—that's not the sort of thing to be looking for, at all," he ended.

"I should say not! Sounds like a right popsy to me. Calves-eyes, indeed!" His companion jumped up, stooped for the basin, and whisked it away from under his feet, slopping some of the amber water in the process. His heels on the mat, Ewan watched her hurry off to the scullery. He drew a hand over his chin.

But in a little she was back, bearing a towel, and all smiles again. "Och, you're a right tease, I can see that," she decided. She held the towel before the fire for a few moments, and then suddenly was down on the hearth-rug, half-kneeling, half-sitting, the towel in her lap. "See's that foot," she instructed. "Is yon a blister on it?"

Hastily, the man tucked his extremities under his chair. "No," he said.

"Dinna be daft, man—a blister's no joke." An authoritative

hand reached out to grasp his shrinking ankle. "An' better to see if yon stain'll come off on a towel, than on the bed-clothes."

Unhappily, Ewan submitted to the foot-rubbing. He was not entirely relieved, either, when the lady began to hum, or croon, some sort of song as she rubbed. He had a strong conviction that gamekeepers who were so preoccupied with poachers as to desert their wives night after night, were thoroughly blameworthy.

The clock on the mantelpiece whirred, and then struck a single note. The man glanced up. "Twelve-thirty," he announced, since something needed to be said. "Late, it's getting."

Mrs. Munro did not seem to hear him.

Ewan managed to get a slipper on to the foot that was now so adequately dried—though in the process his face came very close to that of his hostess, in fact, he jumped like a colt when one of her stray hairs tickled him. "Och, er . . . where am I to be finding a wife, then?" he demanded, with some concern.

She looked up. "I've been thinking aboot it. It's no' that easy. Maggie at Stronvair might suit you . . . or she might no'. An' you mightna suit her. I dinna ken you very well, yet, mind. If I kent you a wee thing better, I might could advise you better." She smiled at him sidelong. "I'll need to ken you better, I doubt, Ewan. How're we going to manage that?"

He assured her that he did not know—not in the time at their disposal. He also looked up at the clock again, and yawned earnestly.

"Are you tired, then? Wanting your bed?" she wondered.

"A bittie, maybe," Ewan admitted. "Four-thirty I was up, this morning. It's been a sort of full day."

Mrs. Munro drew a design with her finger on the re-maining captive instep. "Would you like to continue this discussion in bed then, Ewan?"

"My . . ." He all but choked. ". . . goodness! Mercy me, no—no thank you. Not at all."

"Och, hud your wheesht!" she ordered, laughing loudly, and slapped him on the knee. "A right terror, you are, an' no mistake. It's just the bed-closet's off my own room, and we could talk fine, wi' the door open."

"Oh. I see. Of course, yes. Just joking, I was. Fine that is. But, och—I'm not all that tired. No, no." He laughed too, if hardly as loudly. "A man shouldn't be tired just out of being up early and having a bit walk to himself. My Chove, it's nice here by the fire."

The lady sighed, but complaisantly, almost luxuriously. "Just as you like, Ewan. You say the word," and releasing his foot, she settled herself more comfortably on the rug, a proceeding which brought her person up against the man's knee, where she leant, at ease.

Ewan glanced at her head and shoulders, at the window behind them, and up at the mantelpiece. "Your husband . . ." he said. "He'll be for coming back. . . ."

"I told you—he'll no' be back till daybreak, the poor man. That's four hours yet, easy."

"M'mmmm." The man stared at the fire unhappily. Had he got to try to keep this up for four hours! He shook his head. "You were going to be giving me some good advice?" he said heavily.

"Aboot women," she nodded. "That's right. So I was."

She did, too. In the next twenty-five minutes, Ewan Mac-Ewan learned quite a lot about women that he had not realised before—and if the instruction tended to verge on to the practical rather than the merely theoretical, it was perhaps the more valuable for that, even if the student was less than wholehearted in his co-operation.

And outside the rain fell, and the trees sighed in the sad wind.

It was exactly two minutes to one when the dogs began to

bark. The man knew that, because he had been keeping a fairly close watch on that clock. He jumped back in his chair, at the uproar, almost upsetting his tutor. "Holy Smoke!" he exclaimed. "Your husband."

"Guid sakes—watch what you're at!" the lady cried. "It's no' Erchie—the dogs wouldna bark at Erchie." Nevertheless she got to her feet promptly enough, and her glance, towards the window, was less than serene. "What can it be, at this hour o' night?"

Three raps at the door only lent point to her question.

"Bless me—there wasna two o' you, was there?" she demanded.

"No, no. Just my own self . . ."

"Mercy on us—listen to that!" Mrs. Munro clutched Ewan's arm. The outer door was being opened obviously.

"Is that yourself, Mary?" a mild voice inquired. "It's me, just—Aeneas Mackay. Archie's not back, is he?"

"Och—Aeneas, is it! Man, you gave me a start." The woman hurried forward, but she was too late. Into the room doorway came a tall dark figure, to stand blinking in the light—a figure dressed in the all-too-prevalent uniform of the County Constabulary.

Ewan drew a deep breath, and forgot to let it out.

"My, my—is it visitors you have, Mary?" the policeman said. "Och, I'm sorry."

"It's just a, a gentleman that's been walking in the hills, needing the night's lodging. Mr. MacEwan the name is. This is Mr. Mackay, Taynuilt."

"Ummm," said Ewan. "Aye. A wet night."

"Evening." The other was looking at him keenly, curiously. "I'ph'mmm. Uh-huh." He spoke to the woman, though he kept his eye on the man. "I came to leave a message for Archie. I was to meet him and Ken down the river, at eleven, mind. But the Inspector from Oban was putting me on another ploy. A bad character, with a pack, and a lot of money. A right scallywag . . . aye, and a sight too free with his fists!" The constable's hand went up involuntarily to his upper abdominal region. "Aye," he said again, and ponderously.

At the mention of pack and money, Mary Munro's wide-eyed glance darted down to where the pack leaned against a table-leg, and then to Ewan's face, her mouth slightly open.

Ewan saw the doubt in the other man's eye; he had not seen him in the light, of course, and he was now somewhat differently clad. But he could not hope that this doubt would last. He darted a quick glance, to locate his effects, his boots, his clothes.

The newcomer was going on. "I've been scouring the countryside for him, this whole night. The Inspector's right keen to lay hands on him . . . but no keener than I am my own self, my heavens!"

"What's . . . what's he done, this man?" Mrs. Munro inquired.

"Och, I've not got all the details—but he's up to no good, I can tell you. He's in a right profitable trade, him! And he struck me—when I wasn't looking, b'damn! That's the sort of him. Assaulting the police in the execution of their duty, that is."

"Maybe . . . maybe it was just an accident . . . ?" the lady suggested.

"An accident! Lord—he knocked me flat on the road, and ran away! A desperate man he is, I tell you."

Ewan, out of the corner of his eye, noted where his jacket and trousers hung at the other end of the fireplace. He edged along towards them, on the hearth-rug warily.

But the move was his undoing. He had been standing in front of the centre of the range. Behind him, that area now came into view. And on the rack above the fire his boots were drying.

The policeman's hand shot out, to point. "Brown boots,

89

my God!" he cried. "That's him!" and following his jabbing finger, he came on.

Ewan acted swiftly, almost instinctively. He was much better at this sort of thing than at wordy discussion. Crouching, as the constable came round the table, he hurled himself headlong down at the other's knees. Mrs. Munro's screech was drowned in the crash of falling bodies. There was a confusion of flailing arms and legs, a certain amount of rolling, and then Ewan was out, on his knees, on to his feet. He was younger, lighter, and had not so far to fall—moreover, he had no flapping wet cape to hamper him. Quickly he knelt on and over the struggling man beneath, reached out for the table-cloth, and pulled. The lot, linen, tea-pot, bread, butter, and assorted crockery, came down on the unfortunate representative of the law. Grasping the folds of the cloth, Ewan flung it over the other's head, and wrapped and twisted it round. Jumping over, he tipped the table itself up on top of his victim. Stooping, he grabbed his pack, slung it over one shoulder, swung round to pick his boots off the rack, and bestrode the rug for his jacket. For only an instant he hesitated over his trousers, and then deserted them. Leaping the involved policeman, now on hands and knees, he pushed him flat again, and then made straight for the scullery door. And in the by-going, in all his grabbing, he grabbed the wrist of his bemused hostess, and pulled her along behind him.

"Back door through here?" he demanded.

She gave what was probably a nod, too preoccupied to speak.

Through the cluttered domesticity of the scullery they plunged, into a wash-house, and there was the back door. "It's all wrong," Ewan confided, gasping a little. "Just a mistake. Never a law would I break. Lord—no! Don't believe a word of it." In the open doorway, he remembered to release her arm, and thrust a hand into his pocket, realised that it was the wrong jacket, flung down the boots, and struggled out of it.

"Look," he said, fumbling in his own coat-pocket. "Take this for the damages . . . and all your kindness." He thrust a few notes at her. "Och, take it now. See you, I'm sorry about all that. I am so. The police are just terrible foolish. But . . . och, here he is, the great big stirk! Goodnight."

Ewan slammed the door behind him, in the lady's face, and clutching his boots, stumbled out into the darkness, whither he knew not, his gamekeeper's slippers flapping about his heels.

The night was a bedlam of barking dogs.

VII

IN a thicket of dripping birches not very far above the house, Ewan stopped, and listened. The dogs still were shouting their heads off, but he could hear no sound of pursuit; Mr. Aeneas Mackay might be feeling that he had had enough of him for one night, of course. Also, in the darkness, he would not easily be found. Unless those dogs were loosed, that is . . . But would Mackay be likely to do that, and them not his own beasts? And keepers' dogs, retrievers and spaniels, would never attack a man.

Anyway, he had to get rid of these damnation slippers, and get his own boots on. The things had been off half a dozen times already. He had no socks on his feet, but that couldn't be helped. Leaning against a birch-trunk, he effected the change, and laced up his boots thankfully. They had not dried sufficiently to be hard. The slippers he left in a crutch of the tree. Archie Munro would have to do with his stocking-soles tonight. Maybe his dogs would retrieve these for him, eventually. Anyhow, didn't the fellow come off best, with one pair of best Harris trousers, a pair of socks, and a perfectly good cap, in exchange for his wretched slippers and trousers?

Climbing up on the hillside, Ewan reached a small clearing, where he could look back and down. A light still shone from the open back door of the cottage, and he thought that he could make out two figures silhouetted against its radiance. What sort of a story, he wondered, was being retailed down there? Abruptly, he smiled to himself, chuckled, even laughed—and he was not a man over-much inclined to untimely levity. In that moment, he saw the whole business as permeated with a humour that had not occurred to him previously. It was all extremely funny, especially the policeman wrapped up in the tablecloth, and himself in another man's trousers—a gamekeeper's at that! But, b'damn—he'd nearly been in more than the gamekeeper's *trousers*! The thought sobered him swiftly—indeed, of a sudden, he felt an unaccustomed tightness round the collar. That had been a near thing, down there. That woman had almost had him. Good gracious—he was not a narrow-minded sort of man, whatever, but that one had just about had him beat. Married women, with husbands just down the road, were not his cup of tea, at all. If it hadn't been for that policeman coming . . . ! Gratitude welled up in Ewan's heart towards the unfortunate Aeneas Mackay of Taynuilt. Maybe he had been just a wee thing hard on him. And laughing at him, too . . . !

His relief like a garment about him, Ewan faced the hill in earnest.

His knowledge of his whereabouts and direction was general only. He still wanted to cross the River Awe and get away northwards towards Lochaber, into empty country. He understood that each county had its own police force, and the sooner that he was out of Argyll, the better, maybe the Inverness-shire lot would have more sense to them . . . or more to do with themselves. As best he could judge it, this Nant river must run more or less parallel with the Awe, with this ridge that he was now climbing in between. If he kept up and over, he ought to reach the larger river eventually. With the policeman behind him, this would be as good a time as any to get across the bridge, he reckoned. Though where his present line ran, in relation to the Bridge of Awe, he had no idea.

The hill was wooded all the way, and of no great height. Soon he was over the summit, and threading his way down through the sopping undergrowth. The rain had lessened to a drizzle but the trees dripped with a remarkable profusion and every bracken-frond was heavy with water. Soon he was as wet as he had been before Mrs. Munro took him in hand.

At the marshy foot of the brae, across a meadow wherein he disturbed a few shadowy cattle, the man found himself on a road of sorts, beyond which he could hear the rush of the fast-flowing river. Whether to turn left or right? This was no main road, little more than a rutted cart-track indeed. That policeman had said that the main road crossed the Bridge of Awe, and just a wee one continued on this side, to some place that he could not remember. This must be it, then. If he turned left, downstream, he must come to the bridge, sooner or later.

His reasoning proved to be entirely accurate. In no more than five or six minutes, his boots were clinking on the hard metals of the main road. And since he had not crossed any bridge as yet, patently he must now turn right. He did so, and in only a few hundred yards there was the Bridge of Awe. Thankfully but cautiously, the man approached it.

Obviously there was no-one on or at the bridge. Even on a bicycle, and going hard, he doubted whether Mackay could have got here yet. Beyond, steeply rising, lay the enormous bulk of Ben Cruachan, with the main road swinging away sharply to the right towards the Pass of Brander, and a side-road striking left towards the loch. Ewan crossed, clinging close to the parapet, and crouching low.

He was almost over, when the blaze of light burst upon him, blinding him—the powerful headlights of a car, evidently backed into some bushes where the road bent, not a dozen yards in front. Caught crouching there, he felt naked and entirely foolish—but only for a split second; he had other aspects of the situation to attend to. Even as he started forward again, at the run, he heard the car doors slam, the scrape of boots, and bellowed commands and instructions. He did not hesitate for a moment. Setting both hands on the coping of the parapet, he hoisted himself bodily on to the masonry, folded over it, and swung his legs over in a half-vault. For an instant he hung there, darting a glance downwards to see what lay below. But his eyes, dazzled by the glare of the lights, could make out nothing but stars and Catherine-wheels in an inky abyss.

An embryo prayer in his mind if not on his lips, he let himself drop into he knew not what.

Ewan's fall jarred every bone in his long body—because he only dropped three or four feet where he had expected to fall five times as far. He landed on a steep and apparently grassy bank, began to roll, and went on rolling. Shaken, his mind in as much of a whirl as his body, he could already feel the cold waters closing over his head, when he was brought up short and practically wrapped round the singularly branching and uncomfortable, if fortunately unyielding, bole of an alder-tree, one of a row that lined the water's edge. This fact was demonstrated to his somewhat wandering attention by the beam of an electric torch, shone down on him from the bridge above. Sundry shouts came down too, less helpfully. Disentangling himself and his pack from the clutching boscage, the man struggled to his feet, and went staggering downstream. The shouts followed him, but, after a little preliminary wavering, the light fortunately did not.

He had, he reckoned, perhaps fifty yards start—enough for him to show a clean pair of heels to any big-footed policeman, he was confident, a little dizzy though he might be; what troubled him was the road, the by-road that led down towards the loch this side of the Awe, the road which he had meant to take, himself. How closely it clung to the river-bank, he did not know. Bringing the car down that, they might head him off. . . .

A look over his shoulder in some measure relieved him.

The car was indeed on the move, but the beams of its headlamps were slanting away to the right, at a tangent to his, and the river's, course. Evidently the road swung out northwards. In a few moments the lights were level with him, past him, but well over on his flank, and still trending outwards. He had room to manoeuvre, at any rate.

Tripping and sliding on the wet, sloping and uneven bank, he ran. If there were footfalls behind him, the noise of the river drowned them. Quarter of a mile he may have gone, when a bridge loomed up before him, a railway bridge evidently. He wondered whether it was of any use to him—and decided against it, as being too obvious. Under its dripping girders he thudded.

Not far beyond, a narrow strip of plantation came down from the direction of the road. This was the sort of thing that he could use . . . and the sort of thing that the police might well expect him to use, too. He halted, and plunged into cover—not right, into the plantation, but left, into the fringe of the alders that still rimmed the river. Amongst the branches of one, he crouched, still.

He had perhaps twenty seconds to wait, and then two dark figures came pounding and slithering in his wake.

"Here's some bluidy trees," the foremost called. "Maybe he'll have gone up there."

"Maybe—but maybe no'," he was answered breathlessly. "Maybe he'll have carried right on. Away you up the wood, anyway—I'll keep along here."

"Right, Sar'nt." Not five yards from the fugitive, the first constable turned and started to climb the bank amongst the trees.

"See and don't give him a chance to hit you," the sergeant warned, as he came stamping past, panting heavily. In his hand Ewan could plainly see a drawn baton. The dangerous job they were on!

He gave them a minute or so. The sergeant's footsteps

soon were swallowed up, but the first man could be heard struggling up the brae, and cursing the entangling brambles. Ewan calculated that, with the car still manned, there were unlikely to be any more behind them. As the sounds faded, he stood upright, and turned to walk back whence he had come.

He did not go all the way back to Bridge of Awe. About halfway between the rail and road bridges, he started to clamber up the bank. Climbing a fence and crossing the railway, he was into a stretch of rough pasture, sheep dotted. Away over to his left, half a mile perhaps, the lights of the police-car lit up the night; it seemed to be stationary now, no doubt with reason. Ewan negotiated another fence, and found himself on the by-road. Across it, the vast mass of Cruachan towered abruptly. Cheerfully enough, the man set himself to the killing ascent. He quite liked climbing hills . . . and he did not anticipate any competition.

About fifteen minutes later, and perhaps four hundred feet above the valley, the man paused and looked back. Down there, the twin cones of yellow light that was the patrol-car, were moving slowly on towards Inverawe and the loch shore. Busy tireless men, the police, and conscientious, he decided. They must surely be greatly troubled with the white slavers in the Oban district.

Yawning a little, Ewan turned to move along the hillface, northwards. And in a short while, he began to trend downhill again, at a slant towards the long long shores of Loch Etive.

It would be almost an hour later that he came to the farm—only the second such that he had passed. It was nothing more than a footpath that he was on—there seemed to be no road up the eastern shore of the loch; transport for these isolated hill-farms must be by boat only. This appeared to be a small place, smaller even than his own place of Corriemore. He avoided the house, dark naturally at this hour, and made his silent way round to the dim range of steading in the rear—hoping that the farmer kept his dogs shut up at night, preferably in his kitchen. It would be a pity to disturb anybody, here and now.

He found a door, behind which he could make out a vague stirring, the occasional clink of a chain, and a contented sighing. Quietly he let himself into the byre, its pleasant warm homeliness welcoming him like a benison. If he knew anything about byres, the hay-shed would open off it. He moved along, feeling the way with toe and hand, his nose leading him to the aromatic scent of fresh cloverhay. As far as he could gather, in the pitch dark, there was no door between; the hay was stored beyond a partition at the further end of the byre itself.

On to its soft couch he sank, with a sigh as contented as those of the invisible cows, took off his pack, his wet jacket and his boots, and burrowed into the hay. Within its warm embrace, and with a cat coming to rub itself against him in an ecstasy of purring, he started to yawn again. It was a poor yawn, really—he was asleep before ever he had time to finish it.

Ewan awoke to a familiar and satisfying sound, that was so normal as to make his seemingly abnormal situation momentarily the more mystifying. It was the hiss-hiss of milk lances into a frothing pail. Frowning, Ewan stared up at the dusty cobweb-hung rafters above him, and scratched his head, tickly with hayseeds. Then he sat up, moved forward on his knees, and peered round the partition.

A young woman sat on a stool, not ten feet away, with her back to him, milking a raw-boned Ayrshire cow. She was dressed in a well-filled print wrapper, and not a great deal else at a cursory glance, and the sturdy bare legs that held the pail between them, ended in what, under an ancient encrustment of farmyard, looked extraordinarily like a pair of man's boots, unlaced. A number of massive hair-curlers decorated her hair, like steel-jawed traps around a pheasantry.

Ewan considered the scene for a little, only abstractedly critical, and then cleared his throat. "Good morning," he said. "A better day, it looks, than the night that was in it."

"Mother o' God!" the girl cried, jerking her head round. And at sight of him, "Merciful Mary, goodness me—what's this?"

Ewan could not really complain at that; in the circumstances, she might have said more. The cow had turned to stare, also, great-eyed, a protest emanating from somewhere deep inside her.

"I am Ewan MacEwan, Corriemore, Eorsa, and I have been having a bit sleep in your hay, see you," the man explained, reasonably, getting to his feet. "Late I was getting in," he added.

The other, a round-faced, red-cheeked, pleasant-enough looking creature, stared—as well she might—considering him from tousled head, by darkly unshaven face, crumpled shirt, plus-four trousers that hung halfway down bare hairy calves, to brown-stained feet, the whole liberally bedecked with stalks of hay and burr-like clover heads.

"Save us all!" she ejaculated. "You a tink, or what?"

The man drew himself up with some dignity. "My gracious me, I am not," he declared. "I told you—I am Ewan MacEwan, Corriemore, Eorsa, and I have a better bit farm than this, whatever! Here I was, sparing you the trouble of getting wakened up in the middle of the night, and you naming me a tinker, my God!"

Unconvinced, she gave one of the cow's teats a tentative tug, the milk missing the pail by inches. "What you doing here, at all?" she inquired.

"Sleeping, just," he reiterated. "I was having a bit walk. I came over the hill, yonder, and got here late, so och I just bedded in the hay, so's not to be disturbing the house. I was just coming over for a bite of breakfast, maybe."

"Walking . . . ?" she said doubtfully. "You don't look awful like a hiker. Where's your bag, then?"

He turned, and picked up his pack.

The sight of it seemed to reassure her, somewhat. "Och, well," she said.

"Just that." He nodded. "That is a nice cow you have there."

"Betsy, she is. And the other one's Flora."

"My goodness—is that so! Myself, I have a cow called Betsy—it is a small world, indeed. What is your own name, at all?"

"Och, just Maggie." She flushed, giggled, and looked down. The glance revealed to her that the milk-pail between her legs had the effect of exposing a deal of her ample thighs. Hastily she set it on the floor, pulled down her wrapper, and giggled again.

"Uh-huh," he said. "Oh, aye. Well, well."

There was silence in the byre for a few moments. Something niggled at the back of the man's mind. Maggie . . . ? He rubbed his bristly chin. "If I could be having a drop of hot water for a shave, before I come over to breakfast?" he suggested.

"I'll bring it over, yes." The maiden looked up. "But . . . but maybe I'd better be bringing your breakfast over too. My mother . . . och, she is not that fond of, of sort of travelling men about the place. . . ."

"But, damn it—I'm no tramp, or tink, or pedlar, I tell you!" Ewan protested. "And I'll pay for my food." He reached for his jacket, and produced a handful of rather wet pound notes from the pocket.

Maggie sniggered once more, and licked her lips with the point of a pink tongue. "Och, but I think I'll be bringing it over, just the same," she decided, with a remarkable

100

obstinacy for such an amenable-seeming creature. "My mother is a wee thing sour, maybe, in the morning. She . . . she is not that keen of strange men about me, at all!" And the giggle gave place to a sudden and brief high-pitched laugh, as, scarlet-faced, Maggie got to her booted feet.

"Ummm," Ewan said thoughtfully. "Och, well," he acceded handsomely, "I can eat my breakfast as well here as some place else. See you—I'll finish the milking while you go get it. I'll just be getting my boots on. . . ."

Whilst he worked, with his brow against this mainland Betsy's warm flank, he recollected. Maggie . . . at Stronvair, wasn't it? . . . was that gamekeeper's wife's tentative suggestion as a possible wife for him. Well, now . . .

He was stripping Betsy and ready to begin on Flora, when Maggie brought him his hot water, and the word that the porridge was on the boil. The man noticed that she had exchanged her boots for something considerably more feminine.

Shaved, washed, and feeling distinctly better, he was well into a mildly suspicious Flora, when the girl arrived back once more. Perhaps she thought that he *looked* distinctly better, too—at least her reaction was positive. As for herself, the wrapper had now given place to a jumper and skirt, and—was it?—yes, there was actually lip-stick encircling that liberal mouth. Also, the hair-curlers had gone. She had brought a milk-can of porridge, another of tea, a few thick slices of buttered bread, and she produced, with suitable modesty, two boiled eggs from up her jumper. This was all for Ewan, apparently, for, leaving him to set to, she seated herself on the stool that he had vacated, and went on with the milking—though now in a sideways position in which she could see and be seen.

The fine edge taken off his appetite, the man broke the operational silence. "You're not eating, yourself?" he pointed out, considerately.

101

"I'll have mine after—with my mother. Early it is, and herself not out of her bed yet. Just after seven, it is."

Ewan nodded—to himself, rather than to the speaker. Early rising—a good sign. And could cook decent-enough porridge. Farm-trained. A bit giggly . . . but weren't they all? "Himself . . . ?" he inquired. "Your father? Is he not up yet, either?"

"Och, my father has been dead five years." Even that provoked a titter. Ewan frowned in disapprobation—though, of course, maybe she was sort of nervous, for some reason.

"You run the place alone, then, do you—your mother and yourself?" he wondered.

"Och, we have a hired kind of a man, from Inverawe." As an afterthought, she added, with an incipient sigh, "Old, he is getting, though." And she caught his eye momentarily.

"Is that so." Ewan digested all this with his first egg. Used to running a bit farm. Solidly built. Good strong teeth. Plenty of substantial leg. "You aren't by way of being troubled with your feet, at all, Maggie?" he queried.

She seemed a little surprised. "My feet?" Looking down at them, searchingly, she shook her head. "Nothing wrong with my feet, is there?" That was anxious. "Och—those old boots, is it? I just wear them about the steading, some-times." And she blushed again.

Ewan waved that aside, and took a mouthful of the tea. Good tea it was, too—strong and sweet. "You're not mar-ried, at all . . . or anything like that?"

The question produced an immediate crescendo of mirth. "Mercy me, no!" she cried. "Och, dearie me—what next? You men are awful for the questions." For a beat or two she in-terrupted the rhythm of her busy hands. "Are you a married man your own self, maybe?" she got out, breathlessly.

"No, no . . . or, at least—yes, I was," he admitted. "I'm a kind of he-widow, just. My last wife died on me." And he shook his head, sighing.

102

She sighed, too, gustily, briskly.

"I have two small ones," he added heavily. "A right handful they are . . . I mean, for a man with no woman in it." That was a little hurried. "Och, they're fine youngsters—just splendid. They are so. A boy and a girl. And healthy—healthy as, as eels, whatever. No trouble at all . . . that is, to a woman, I mean . . ."

"Och, I like children fine," Maggie averred, looking far away. "I've never had one, at all, but—och, they'll be right cheery to have about the house."

"Aye—oh, aye. Uh-huh. Just that."

"Was it from Eorsa, you said you were?" she went on. "That's out beyond Mull, there, isn't it? My mother's from the islands, herself."

"Is that a fact?" Ewan sat forward. "My, that's a real interesting thing. There's nothing like the island people for sensibleness and making the best of things, whatever. What part is she from?"

"Och, it's just a small one—Erismore, the name is."

The man almost choked over the major part of his second egg. "Erismore . . . ? Goodness me—d'you tell me that! That's bad, bad. Och, what a pity."

Alarmed, the girl stared at him. "What's . . . what's wrong with Erismore, then?" she wondered.

"*Dhia*—it's a terrible place, that. Just wicked."

"Is it? I never heard that, before. But, anyway—she's been away from it for a long time now, see you."

Ewan shook his head. "Aye—but the blood is bad," he pointed out. "It's an awful handicap, that. And a lot of them are just Catholics, too."

Maggie produced her first frown—withal tempered by a pout. "I'm a Catholic my own self," she declared. "There's worse folk than Catholics, whatever."

"Aye. That is so, maybe. I'm not a narrow-minded man, myself," Ewan acceded. "I've nothing against Catholics and

Buddhists and Mohammedans and such-like, on principle, mind. But they're right particular on Eorsa. Still . . ." He bit into the last piece of bread. "None of us are just perfect, whatever."

"That's right," the other agreed, a little wistfully.

For a while the man munched, and cogitated, and the woman milked and darted glances and sighed. At length, he spoke. "They say there's good folk from all parts. This'll be Stronvair, maybe . . ."

"It is, yes. Campbell, Stronvair, Inverawe," she answered absently. "I was just thinking . . ."

Ewan jumped as though an adder had bitten him. "Campbell!" he yelped. "My God—did you say *Campbell*, woman?"

"Campbell, yes." Wide-eyed, she turned to him. "Campbell's not such a queer-like name to be finding at the foot of Cruachan, is it?"

Ewan was on his feet, swallowing. "Och, mercy on us— that's the end," he assured. "I'm right sorry . . . but, och, there's some things not to be considered, at all. No, no." He picked up his pack, and slung it on. "Time I was on my way, I doubt," he muttered. He held out one of his pound notes to the girl. "Thanks for . . . for my breakfast," he said.

Bewilderedly, dumbly, she looked at him, and wagged an uncomprehending head.

"Take it," he insisted, and stooping, thrust the note into the neck of her jumper. And at her blinking troubled-eyed dejection, he of a sudden impulse stooped still further, and swiftly kissed her tremulous lips. "Och, I'm sorry, Maggie," he said. "I am so. But . . . well, cheerio. And thanks again."

And he strode out of that byre into the young morning.

VIII

THOUGH the larks shouted, and the burns gurgled, and the sun, newly victorious over the bulk of Cruachan, poured its radiance on land and water, drawing forth its answering meed of praise out of the dancing wavelets, the humming bees, and the incense of heather and bog-myrtle— despite all this, and a full stomach withal, Ewan MacEwan was profoundly depressed, as he stalked northwards. Had not he reason to be? Had a single thing gone rightly for him since he set foot on Oban North Pier . . . since he stepped aboard the *Maid of Lorne* . . . since he crossed the threshold of his own house of Corriemore, yesterday morning? He wished to Heaven that he had never left Eorsa, and that was a fact! This Scotland that he had come to was chock-full of shrews, fools, scoundrels—and women that it was impossible to marry! Small wonder that they had let even the feckless English rule them for centuries! The sooner that he was back on Eorsa, and quit of this foolery, the better, by Chove—Finlay Sim be damned! It was all Finlay Sim's fault, anyway.

It was a pity about that lassie, back there. A mild kindly pleasant sort of a creature, enough. But a Catholic Campbell, out of Erismore! Suffering Sam—what a combination! It couldn't have been worse, it could not—unless she'd turned out to be some sort of a cousin of his, into the bargain! A narrow escape he'd had. Come to think of it, he had had one or two narrow escapes, now.

This latter aspect of his case presently began to temper his depression a little, and by the time that he had crossed the green levels at the opening mouth of narrow Glen Noe, his somewhat tuneless whistle was coming intermittently into evidence—without actually rivalling the joyous intensity of the larks.

It was an excellent morning for strolling up a loch-side, and there was a lot of such delectable strolling ahead of him. His route lay, as far as he could assess and memorise, on up Loch Etive-side for ten or twelve miles, then up the glen beyond the head of the loch, to the Lairig Gartain, which somehow or other ought to lead him eventually over into Glen Coe and so to Lochaber. He wished that he had thought of buying a map at Oban—it had not just occurred to him that he was destined for the trackless heather in this wife-hunt of his. It would have been a great help, for he was far from knowledgeable about these parts.

At least, there was nowhere to go wrong on the early stages of his journey—he had no option but to follow the footpath along the haughlands, mile after mile, between the steep hillsides and the sparkling water, fording a multitude of the streams that drained that great land mass, over and above the Rivers Liver, Kinglass, and Guisachan coming out of their glens. And he walked as naturally as he breathed or digested—especially once he had recollected that he had stowed a spare pair of socks in his pack somewhere; even if they were *only* socks and somewhat shrunk at that, and so left a hiatus between their tops and the foot of the plus-fours, they assisted his locomotion—and who was there to comment thereon in that deserted country? Two houses he saw, in all his morning, and at neither any sign of life.

By mid-forenoon he had reached the head of the loch, with the mighty trough of Glen Etive ahead of him between giant hills, and the twin peaks of Beinn Fhada and Stob Dubh beckoning him on. He could see that there was a road, now, at the far side of the river that ran into the loch, but he was unable to cross to it until, some distance up, near an impressive series of cataracts, he came to a bridge. At a

106

croft-house close-by, he received a lunch of milk and scones and honey, plus the information that the roadie there came from the *north*, not the south—in fact, it ended at the pier at the head of the loch, a mile or so further down. No car, police or other, could come up here from Connel or Oban. Northwards, it went on for some fifteen miles, apparently, eventually to join the Tyndrum-Glencoe road near Kingshouse Inn on the northern lip of the great Moor of Rannoch. There was no need, evidently, for him to climb over the high desolation of the Lairig Gartain Pass; this road would serve him famously. That, according to the crofter, there was only the one house, between there and Kingshouse, worried Ewan no whit. It was unlikely that it would be a police-station.

If his guide found the inquirer's costume peculiar, he was polite enough not to mention the fact. With a bag of stale scones and an entire comb of last season's sugary heather honey in his pack, for sustenance, the wayfarer stepped out, lengthening his stride.

It was a good walk that he had, a long walk, and entirely uneventful—over which the man made no complaint. All day he strolled through the scented valley, by the rushing Etive, under the frowning regard of Beinn Ceitlein, Maol Chalium, Fhada, Stob Dubh, and Buchaile Etive—and not a vehicle did he pass, nor a man did he meet, in all the long miles of it. Only the few sheep and the many deer, the circling buzzards and the mountain larks, had he for company.

He took his time. There was no hurry at all. This Kingshouse Inn place would suit him very well for the night, and tomorrow he would make his way north into Lochaber. Meanwhile, the day was his own—not a woman nor a constable to fret him. He gave himself a rest in the heather, beneath Buchaile Etive, in the early afternoon—and it was early evening before he awoke, to resume his pilgrimage.

But that did not matter, either—he could have only another five or six miles to go.

The weather which had been brilliant all day was changing now with the oncoming night, and soon all the soaring Glencoe mountains were glooming darkly as only they know how, under their cowls of scowling cloud. The rain began just as the man turned from the Glen Etive road into the wider trans-Rannoch highway. A signpost just light enough to read, this time—indicated Glen Coe and Ballachulish on the left, and pointed right-handed, by the old road, to Kingshouse Inn a mile away. Ewan, his last scone digested an hour ago, decided that it was far enough.

It was quite dark and unpleasantly wet before the welcoming portals of solitary Kingshouse—surely one of the loneliest hostelries in all Scotland—received him to comfort and refreshment. Two vehicles were drawn up before the door, a powerful shooting-brake and a humble plain van.

In the deserted dining-room, Ewan partook in solitary state of a repast adequate to his demands—the genial management of Kingshouse being entirely accustomed to providing substantial meals at the oddest hours, as befits an establishment serving some of the most celebrated mountain climbs in the country. For the same reason, no doubt, no eyebrows were raised at his costume, climbers being notoriously original sartorially.

In the lounge thereafter, however, he came in for a certain amount of inspection. The company there was divided into two severely separated groups—a monosyllabic couple of gentlemen in carpet slippers and correctly venerable tweeds, reading genteel periodicals before the fire, and a talkative party of five men in a tight bunch near the window, oddly assorted as to clothing and type, whose conversation varied from corner-of-the-mouth whispering to abrupt hoarse laughter—at both of which the pair by the fire raised well-bred eyebrows and shoulders. Each group, however, found

Ewan's entrance and appearance interesting. He took a modest seat near the door, pulled up his socks as far as they would go, and considered the toes of his mud-covered brown boots intently.

The whispering recommenced, and produced one or two very hearty laughs indeed. But after a few minutes and due deliberation, it was one of the fireside gentlemen who spoke up.

"Fishing?" he inquired.

Ewan did not realise that the remark was aimed at himself, for the questioner did not seem to have raised his eyes from his reading-matter. But when, after a pause, the word was repeated by the second reader, who at the same time transfixed the newcomer with a stern regard from over a pair of horn-rimmed spectacles, he perceived his fault.

"Me, is it? Och, no, no—not at all," he disclaimed. "I am just after having a bit walk to myself."

The two inquirers exchanged glances, grunted, and turned away in unison. A few moments later, one of them looked at his watch, yawned, and nodded to his colleague. Together they rose.

"Shut-eye," one observed. "Water should be good in the morning."

"Definitely," the other agreed. "Hope there's not too much, though."

As one they turned to sweep a disdainful gaze over all the non-fishing intruders, and passed on to their slumbers.

The party by the window now found it possible to raise its voice a little—but not quite out of the category of whispers. These travellers' inhibitions as to talk were scarcely paralleled in the realms of attire, however—which made their preoccupation with Ewan's legs in the worst possible taste, he felt. There were five of them, all comparatively young men, and three of them at least looked quite noticeably out of place in a Highland hotel in the wilds of Lorne. From glossy hair and incipient sidewhiskers, explosively-colorific American ties, nipped-in double-breasted suitings with over-wide trousers, to elegant pointed black shoes, they approximated to a mould, a pattern, more apt to Argyle Street, Glasgow, than to Argyll itself. Their two companions, very differently clad in a variety of ex-Service gear more suitable for hard wear in rough country, had distinctly less to say for themselves, as became tough customers of the great outdoors. Ewan surmised that they might have something to do with the hydro-electric developments in which the mainland seemed to have got itself involved.

One attempt he made at the civilities, for his own comfort of mind. "A very fine day it's been, and a small drop of rain at the end of it no harm at all," he mentioned reflectively to the room at large.

The glassy stare with which this reasonable summary was received seemed to indicate that the subject was not one on which the company was disposed to enter. Nor was any alternative subject for polite discussion mooted.

Ewan presently decided that his own company would advantage him quite as well as this, and he followed the anglers up to bed.

The hotel mattress and sheets were excellent. He was almost as comfortable as he had been in the Stronvair hay the night before.

But despite the respectability of his quarters, Ewan Mac-Ewan was rudely aroused—and after what seemed to be the briefest of intervals. A great hullabaloo was in progress somewhere nearby—shouting, swearing, the thumping of heavy boots, the slamming of car doors, the roaring of engines. Yawning and blinking, the man sat up in bed, seeking to collect his scattered wits. A whistle shrilled. Rolling over on to the floor, Ewan lurched to the window, tripping over his pack on the way. Drawing the curtain, he peered down.

His room was at the front of the hotel, on the first floor. Below him he could make out the shapes of two cars drawn up, and the red tail-light of a third disappearing rapidly down the gleaming wet road. Figures were running about down there, and in the streaming light from the open front door, he saw that two of them at least wore the wretched dark-blue and the diced cap-bands of the county constabulary.

That was enough for Ewan. Hurriedly he struggled anyhow into his clothes, not delaying to fully lace his boots.

Snatching up his pack, he opened the door. Authoritative voices from the foot of the stairway turned his eyes in the opposite direction. Along at the end of his corridor there seemed to be another narrow stair going up—which probably meant one going down as well. Forthwith he dashed thither, found a service stairway, and plunged down its steps three at a time. At the foot, a lady in a long white flannel nightgown and a hair-net stared at him open-mouthed from a bedroom doorway. Apologising breathlessly, Ewan sped past her, looking for a back door. He darted along one passage and then another, and heard strong voices ahead. Doubling back, he stopped at a window, flung it up, and throwing himself bodily over the sill, struggled through. His pack caught on the sash above, and held him. He wriggled like a fish in a net. Still it held. He tried to arch his body, and thus to raise the sash. But he did not have to. A large pair of hands lifted the window further to release the pack, and then came down firmly on the seat of its owner's borrowed trousers, but not to release *them*, while at the same time a stentorian bellow summoned all interested. Ewan, unfortunately placed, found himself with nothing more suitable to argue with than a thick pair of legginged ankles. He did what he could with them, but found them unresponsive and remarkably tree-like in their stability; all but rooted, they were.

The creature's unmannerly bawling quickly brought hurrying and substantial feet from right and left. Ewan was righted in no gentle fashion, and promptly frog-marched round to the front of the building with comprehensive propulsion. With three large captors, he decided that any struggling on his part would be undignified.

In at the open front door he was hustled, to the brightly lit vestibule, his original captor, a sergeant no less, shouting for the Inspector. That gentleman came hurrying along a corridor, accompanied by the distressed host.

"We've got one o' them, anyway," his escort pointed out, unnecessarily. "I doubt the rest got away in their cars."

"I told you to immobilise the damned cars, did I no'!" the Inspector cried. "If you'd done what I told you, man, instead of . . ."

"Och, Donal' was just at the immobilising when one o' them jumped on him, see you," the sergeant protested. "They must of had a guard on their bluidy cars. Donal's outbye there, wi' a cracked head. A spanner it was, likely . . ."

His senior officer, staring out into the soaking night, interrupted. "They went south, did they—over the Moor? We'll have to be after them. Get me Dalmally on the phone, Sergeant. Quick. They'll have to send a car up to Bridge of Orchy—there's no' a road they can turn off before that. We'll get them . . . or if we don't, we'll get their cars, at least." The Inspector, turning, considered Ewan, frowning. "You're sure there's no others left behind, except this crittur? This is a damned miserable haul, I'll . . . My God—the Man with the Brown Boots!"

His startled gasp was echoed by them all, as with one accord they stared down at Ewan's under-laced footwear. The wearer thereof cleared his throat.

"Och, this is a terrible carry-on, my goodness," he declared, with a nice mixture of sympathy and reproach.

112

"Whatna stramash! I doubt you've made an awful mistake, some way."

"We got him climbing out of a window, round the back," one of the constables informed.

"The pack, brown boots, and the stolen plus-fours!" That was almost a chant.

"Stolen, my heavens!" Ewan exclaimed wrathfully. "And me leaving him my best Harris trousers, my cap, and a pair of socks, b'damn! Yon keeper did right well out of me, I'm telling you."

"You admit to being the man who broke out of Archibald Munro's cottage in Glen Nant, then, and twice assaulted Constable Aeneas Mackay in the execution of his duty!" the Inspector charged him.

"Och, mercy me—not assaulted, no. It was yon one's own fault, whatever. He was ay making a grab at me. . . ."

"Aye, aye—man, you needna think that playing the daft laddie'll get you anywhere, now. We've had our eyes on you for long enough. That Dalmally, Sergeant? Right—I'll speak to them." The Inspector strode over to the telephone. "Dalmally sub-station? Inspector Cattanach, Fort William, here—speaking from Kingshouse Hotel. Is Patrol-car Five with you, still? Six . . . ? Well, Six then, damn it. Have it sent up to the road junction at Bridge of Orchy at once. Better go yourself—yes, every man you can get. This salmon-poaching gang's slipped through our fingers here—though we've got the leader. Aye, the guy with the brown boots. There's half a dozen o' them, in two cars—a big shooting-brake and a green van. That's right—the same lot we've all been after. Yes, they're crossing the Moor o' Rannoch now. Uh-huh. Block the road up from Bridge o' Orchy and they canna get out. Look—where's Inspector Mackendrick? He's no' back to Oban, is he? Oh—Tyndrum. What the hell's he doing over there? Och, never mind. Can you contact him? Good. Tell him to get all the men on this he can. Aye—and tell him I'm sending this Brown-boots geyser back to F'William, just now. Got that. Okay."

The Inspector came back to them. "There's one thing I canna just understand about this ploy," he mentioned. "I wonder at these baistards scramming off that way, and leaving their leader behind them. It's queer."

"It is not!" Ewan assured earnestly. "I am not their leader, at all, gracious me. Never did I set eyes on the creatures before this night. Och, it's just ridiculous, I tell you."

"He didn't come with the others, this one," the hotel-keeper substantiated. "He came alone, a good hour after I telephoned you."

"Aye—but he works on his own, this one. He's the boss—he co-ordinates these gangs. He's the paymaster too." The Inspector's finger stabbed at the prisoner. "You—do you deny that your pack's full o' bank-notes?"

"Och, well . . . no, not full, just," Ewan blinked. "A few there is, maybe—but they're my own. I got them out of a bank, see you. Och, a man has to have some money about him when he's . . . when he's sort of out for a bit walk. . . . But my goodness—I wouldn't have anything to do with salmon-poachers, at all. No, no."

"Are you saying, then, that you didn't leave half a salmon, weighing exactly nine pounds seven ounces, in the Dunstaffnage Inn, yesterday afternoon—tell me that, my mannie?"

"Och—that! That was just a bit present for Mrs. Grant—from my Uncle Hector, it was. . . ."

"Bah!" roared the Inspector. "Enough o' this! Maclennan—take him back to F'William, and lock him up. Better take Donal' Cameron, too, if his head's that bad. No—*you'd* better take him, Sergeant. We're going to need all the younger men—looks like there's going to be some bog-trotting on this Moor o' Rannoch, tonight. You take him, and Donal'. Better put the cuffs on him—he's a slippery customer. I'll take the other two cars after these blagyirds."

114

"But . . . och, my God—you've got it all mixed up, man. It's not salmon-poaching that I was after running away from. It was . . . och, it was just yon yellow woman at Dunstaffnage. She . . ."

"Quiet, you! You talk too much. If he's any trouble, Sergeant—knock him over the head. He's a dangerous criminal—committed two assaults already. Right—get cracking!"

Ewan found a pair of handcuffs clipped expertly over his wrists, and he was hustled out into the dark and the rain. Pushed into the back of a large black car, he was presently joined by a hatless and resentful constable holding a handkerchief to his head, who glared at the captive with a malevolence that could be felt even if not seen. Obviously, he looked on his fellow passenger as the ultimate author of his injury. As the engine came to life, and they backed, turned, and sped away north-westwards into the streaming night, Ewan had leisure to reflect that the Inverness-shire Constabulary were just as stupid as the Argyllshire lot—even if it was in fish and not women that their weakness lay.

IX

BEHIND the white brilliance of the headlights that made a tinsel glory out of the curtains of the rain, they roared and splashed their way, by Glen Coe, Kinlochleven, North Ballachulish and Onich, to Fort William and might never have left Rannoch Moor for all that Ewan, in his hour or so's run, s   of it. In a narrow street between dark houses, the car drew up, and he was pushed out, into a very functional building, down an echoing passage and into the first of a row of seemingly empty cells, examined to see that he carried no weapons, the handcuffs removed, and the door locked on him. It was his first visit to Fort William.

There was no light in the cell, but a lamp out in the passage provided a fair illumination through a barred aperture in the door. The place seemed to be whitewashed and starkly clean, the sole furnishings being a stone bench on which lay a straw mattress and three folded army blankets. Ewan, who knew something about prison conditions, found nothing to decry. He was philosophically removing his boots, preparatory to seeking a resumption of his night's rest, when the door opened to admit the sergeant and a new and yawning constable who carried a large leather-bound ledger—distinctly similar to that in the Oban bank—an ink-well and a pen. The door was left open, for the sake of light, and they seated themselves on the bench on either side of their prisoner.

"Aye, then," the sergeant said, wiping his mouth with the back of a large hand, while his colleague opened the ledger on his knees, and gripped the pen in a determined fashion.

"We got to get your particulars down. Then you'll maybe get a cup o' tea. You ready, Alec?"

The clerk squared his shoulders. "Aye," he said heavily.

"Right. Now, let me see . . . och, first of all, we'll have the name and address. Just a sort of a formality, that is, see you. You got your Identity Card?"

"Och no—nothing like that, I don't think. What is it, anyway?"

"Your *Identity* Card, man. The bit card with your name and address on it, that the Government gives you, to tell you who you are."

"I don't need the Government to tell me who I am—I know fine. We don't go in for such-like where I come from— we've good memories."

"You're supposed to carry it with you, look. There's a penalty for not carrying it," the sergeant declared.

"Is that so? Show me yours then, will you—so's I'll know what it's like."

The other coughed. "Och, well—we'll maybe manage without it, this once. What's your full name, man?"

"Ewan MacEwan, it is. Croft of Corriemore . . ."

"Na, na. Now, none o' that! Your real name it is, we need. This is official, see."

"That is my real name! What other would I be having?"

"Och, you might have plenty." His questioner was extracting a black notebook from his tunic pocket. "It's the right one, we want." He licked a large finger and thumb, and applied them to the pages. "Here we are. Michael O'Mahoney, otherwise Mike Mooney. That's it."

"What . . . ? What did you say?"

"Michael O'Mahoney, I said. That's yourself—your right name. I've got it down here."

"My Chove!" Ewan cried. "That's not a name, at all—that's an insult, I tell you! I wouldn't be found drowned with a name like that. I would not!"

117

"You mean it's a, a sort of a *nom-de-plume* . . . ?"

The constable intervened. "Alias it is, Sarg."

"It is not! Nothing of the sort. It's Ewan," the indignant captive declared. "Ewan MacEwan. And I'll thank you to stop making personal remarks, whatever."

The sergeant frowned. "Och, be quiet," he requested. "Just put down O'Mahoney, Alec—Michael O'Mahoney, alias Mooney, alias MacEwan. Got that? Now—the address?"

"Is it Ewan MacEwan's address you're after wanting—or O'Mahoney's . . . or even this Elias man's?" the offended prisoner demanded sarcastically.

"O'Mahoney's, of course—*your* address. And that's enough of your lip, my mannie. You're in Fort William Police Station, mind—not in the Glasgow Gallowgate, now!"

"Glasgow is it, that I come from, then? Well, well— you're the clever ones, my goodness. Man, if it's a Glasgow address you're needing for this O'Mahoney, put you down the Dumbarton Road—it's the best I can do for you."

"Dumbarton Road," Alec the scribe repeated, writing hard. "D'you spell it with an M or an N?"

"Och, please yourself."

"And the number . . . ?"

"You can make it nine-hundred and ninety-nine."

"999 Dumbarton Road, Glasgow—you got that, Alec?"

"Och, give me time, Sarg, will you. . . ."

"Aye. Well—are you a British subject, at all, do you know?"

"O'Mahoney? Not me. I'm a Displaced Person, see you . . . from Berwick-on-Tweed!"

"How d'you spell it?" the patient writer inquired.

"Spell what, man . . . ?"

"Och, be quiet, will you?" the sergeant said. "We'll want your age now, maybe."

"Twenty-one," Ewan confided. "Twenty-one today. Are you not wishing me a happy birthday, whatever?" He was getting into his stride.

118

The sergeant frowned again. "I'm inclined to think that last's an erroneous statement," he asserted ponderously. "There's a penalty for making erroneous statements to the police, mind you."

"Och, just put it on the account," Ewan requested. "O'Mahoney's account—with the salmon and the plus-fours and the Identity card."

"Aye, will we! Now—are you married?"

"Surely, surely. Och, every time."

"Wife's name and address . . . ?"

"Which one would that be? Three I've got just now, see you . . . but they all live together at 999 Dumbarton Road. . . ."

"Och, my God!" The sergeant got wrathfully to his feet. "I've had enough o' this—I have so! We'll leave the Inspector to deal wi' you, O'Mahoney. You needna think you'll get away wi' this. Come on, Alec—and see and don't put any sugar in his bluidy tea, either!"

"I told you—my real name's MacEwan—Ewan MacEwan, Corriemore . . ."

"Go you to hell!" he was directed, tersely, as the constabulary crashed its way out of his cell, slamming and locking the door behind it.

He had his mug of tea in bed, Alec apologising for the sugar that his wife had put in by mistake.

Except for the fact that they insisted on calling him O'Mahoney, Ewan had no complaints to find with the Fort William Police Station. He slept well, the food was good and plentiful, the plumbing facilities were excellent—better much than at Corriemore—and nobody troubled him. The young constable who brought him his breakfast and lunch, indeed, was entirely respectful. He did mention at mid-day that Inspector Cattanach and party were just back from the Moor of Rannoch, bringing at least one of the poaching gang with them. They had had a big night, apparently.

119

Ewan had found the night over-short, himself. He had some arrears of sleep to make up—the mainland was a terrible place for keeping a man out of his bed. His present situation provided a welcome opportunity to make up for lost time.

It was early evening before the threatened interview with Higher Authority materialised. The Inspector, evidently only partially rested and refreshed, arrived with the sergeant.

"I hear that you're being difficult, my man," he greeted the prisoner sternly. "Still denying that you know anything about these poachers? Well—we'll soon see about that. Come on—you're going along to the hospital to have a chat with one of the mates you won't recognise. Maybe he'll recognise *you*!"

"That'll be fine, just—I could do with a bit fresh air," Ewan thanked him.

"Is that so! Come on, then—and no funny tricks, or we'll have the cuffs on you. No need to bring that thing, man."

The captive, stooping to collect his pack, completed the operation. "There is so," he assured. "If *I* go, it goes. There's three hundred pounds of mine in there, that I'm not trusting to any policeman, I can tell you." And he slung the pack on to his back.

Inspector Cattanach muttered something, shrugged, and swung on his heel. The sergeant and a constable each took one of Ewan's shoulders, and followed on.

"Is this poor poacher-man in the hospital ill, or something?" the jail-bird wondered innocently—and received no answer.

In the now familiar patrol-car, Ewan was bestowed in the back seat between the Inspector and the sergeant, whilst the constable drove. His pack forced him to sit well forward, and provoked a certain amount of comment from his escort.

Fort William seemed to consist mainly of a single very long and narrow street, cramped between the hillside and

120

Loch Linnhe. It was crowded with visitors and shoppers, more so even than Oban, and the police car had to crawl and hoot its way through a maze of traffic and pedestrians. Ewan was not favourably impressed; with such a vast amount of open empty country all around, he failed to see why so many people wanted to cram themselves into this drainpipe of a place. They couldn't all be desperate to buy tartan souvenirs. Perhaps he was prejudiced.

The cottage-hospital lay a short distance out of the town. Their arrival created something of a stir amongst staff and patients, as they were led to a private room off a larger ward. Ewan distinctly felt the symptoms of half a dozen dire ailments manifest themselves in him as he ploughed through the heavy aura of disinfectants.

The small room contained another constable with a pile of illustrated magazines, and a much-bandaged individual on the single bed. Inspector Cattanach pushed Ewan forward, like a bashful bridegroom at the fatal hour. "Well . . . !" he said pregnantly.

The patient glared at him stonily out of the eye that was not covered with bandaging, and said nothing.

Feeling that something was expected of him, Ewan nodded his head. "Aye, then—it's been a fine day . . ." he was observing civilly, when he recollected that it was still spitting of rain, and amended skilfully, ". . . och, for lying in your bed, I mean. Are you fine and comfortable?"

The other varied neither his glower nor his silence.

Ewan nodded again. "Aye, aye. Just that," he said. "It's a pleasure to see you sitting up and looking so fit."

The victim muttered a single word, with conviction.

The Inspector spoke irritably. "Look here—you identify this man?"

"Well—it's not that easy," Ewan confided. "I don't just recognise the eye . . . but, och, the bandages look familiar!"

"Not you!" Cattanach barked. He jabbed a finger at the

121

patient. "You—M'Guigan, or whatever you're called—this man is Michael O'Mahoney, isn't he?"

"No' bluidy likely!"

"That's true. My own opinion, entirely," Ewan agreed.

"Quiet! You don't need to think you can trick us, M'Guigan. If this man is *not* O'Mahoney, who is he?"

"Hoo the hell should *I* ken?"

"Keep a civil tongue in your head, will you. Now—no more quibbling. I believe you know this man perfectly well. What's his name?"

"Search me! He can be the oreeginal Jock b——— Tamson, for a' I ken or care!"

"My goodness—that sounds awful like Glasgow to me," Ewan declared. "I knew a corporal in the H.L.I. one time . . ."

"Silence!" roared the Inspector. "Both o' you. Speak when you're spoken to—and speak the truth, or it'll be the worse for you. Now, you—O'Mahoney, or Mooney, or MacEwan or whatever your name is—are you prepared to swear on the Bible that you've never seen this man before?"

"Well . . . under yon bandages he's maybe one of the boys I was seeing in the hotel last night. I wouldn't put it past him. If you'd let me see his tie, I'd likely recognise it anywhere."

"Put it this way, then—would you swear that you'd never seen him *before* last night?"

"Och, yes—I'll do that. Bring out the Bible."

"M'Guigan—will you swear on oath that you've never seen this man before last night?"

"Sure. I never seen him—an' I hope the flamin' hell I never see the baistard again, neither!" And he threw in the oath there and then, gratis.

"Mr. M'Guigan speaks for the both of us, and that's a fact," Ewan asserted with dignity.

"You talk too much!" The bedevilled Mr. Cattanach

rounded on him. "Sergeant—take him away, back to his cell. I'll deal with this M'Guigan first, and him later. Away with him—and send the car back for me in half an hour."

"Aye then, Inspector. Come on, you."

"My goodness—that was a short visit to a sick man."

"Shut up!"

Threading Fort William's High Street again, Ewan chatted pleasantly to the unresponsive sergeant. He was beginning to appreciate the police; a pity about the Inspector—but it was much more comfortable in the back without him.

Near the southern end of that constricted thoroughfare, there is a brief, steeply-sloping side-street that leads down to the railway station and MacBrayne's pier. As the patrol-car reached this spot it came to a full stop—in which it was not alone, all other vehicles using the road having come to a stop likewise. The reason was apparent to the least observant—and vocal; a large number of sheep and cattle milled vociferously round a heavy livestock lorry that sagged drunkenly towards its off-rear as though a wheel had come off, its tail-boards down, slewed round and all but blocking the mouth of the side entry, whilst the ranked cars and pedestrians blocked either end of the main street. Vaguely in the centre of the boiling and steaming beef and mutton, a peaked and diced cap bobbed and floated.

"My God—look at that!" the sergeant requested, shocked. "Isn't that just wicked." Winding down the window, he thrust out his head. "What the devil is all this, at all?" he demanded, with authority.

Nobody told him. Indeed, it was all most confusing. All the circulating livestock could not possibly have come out of the unhappy lorry; whether they were on their way up from the pier, or on their way down thereto, was not apparent—though since Messrs. MacBrayne were now under the benign control of British Railways, it was quite conceivable that they were doing both. The matter was of only academic interest at the moment, however; impasse seemed to have been reached. Egged on by the barking of all the dogs of Fort William, as well as by the hooting of innumerable impatient motor-horns, the flocks and herds circled round and round the islanded vehicle as in a whirlpool, dizzy on the eye.

The driver leaned back confidentially. "Yon'll be Duncan, in there," he mentioned, and shook his head. "He's on this beat, the now."

"Well—don't sit on your backside, man, and sigh. Get you out, and give him a hand," the sergeant snorted.

His lips moving, the constable descended from the car and pushed his way forward, where he was able to watch the circus as it were from a ring-side seat. He took a skelp at a passing bullock, but otherwise refrained from positive intervention.

"Split me—just look at the big stot!" Ewan's companion exclaimed. "Standing there like he was a judge at a cattle-show!" He thrust out his head again. "*Do* something, man," he commanded.

His junior patted a sheep indecisively as it went past, and glanced backwards unhappily.

"Holy Smoke—is that not just the limit! And him on traffic-control for months!"

"Och, he needs a collie and a stick, whatever," Ewan considered judiciously. "The beasts don't recognise he's supposed to be controlling them."

"What . . . ?"

Raising his voice to penetrate the uproar, the prisoner repeated his observation, with the additional comment that it was no use scratching stirks' backs—you'd got to put your fingers up their nostrils and twist, if you were going to manhandle them.

"Is that so!" the sergeant snarled, ungrateful for this constructive advice.

"Yes. But, see you—if everybody would away home and have their suppers, the thing would solve itself in no time, at all, just."

"Hell's afire! Will you shut your mouth . . ."

The strident and incessant blaring of a new, more virulent and higher-toned klaxon from immediately behind, drowned the rest. His eyes protruding, the sergeant swallowed.

"Cut that damned noise!" he bellowed, and burst open the car door. "What the blinding bluidy . . ." His voice tailed away, and then resumed in a totally different tone. "My God—it's Glenspean! Och, my goodness me . . ."

Ewan peered out of the back window for a glimpse of the noted chief of Clan MacIvor. A purple-faced white-haired gentleman was leaning out from the driving-seat of an ancient Rolls Royce, gesticulating violently.

"You, Sergeant . . . !" he was saying, amongst other things. "What are you sitting there for? Do something, man—do something!" That is a woefully approximate and devitalised rendering of the remarks of a very fluent and patently widely-educated man. Ewan was much impressed.

So obviously was the sergeant. "Yes, sir," he said. "I was just . . . och, yes, indeed, sir. Right away." And he moved forward between the ranked cars, hurriedly.

Ewan's heart bled for him, and getting out himself he followed on.

"In a hurry, yon one . . ." he was sympathising, when the other rounded on him.

"Get you back to the car, at once," he ordered fiercely.

"Och, I'll just give you a bit hand," Ewan assured. "It's no bother." And reaching out, he caught a convenient bullock by its up-thrust tail, twisted that organ round in a vigorous series of turns, and brought the careering animal to a sudden and loud-voiced stop. Leaning forward, still clutching the cork-screwed tail, he thrust his thumb and first finger into the dripping and puffing black nostrils and gave the

125

whole snout a comprehensive clockwise turn. Blinking reproachful and suddenly tear-filled eyes, the creature stood still, amenable, and a long pink tongue came out and rasped over Ewan's hand, pathetically.

"There you are," he declared modestly. "*You* take it. Take it away. We'll soon get rid of the stirks, and then . . ."

"Get the hell out o' here!" the sergeant roared, backing away from the proffered livestock distastefully. "Get you back to that car, will you. . . ."

"All right. Just as you say," Ewan shrugged, offended, and released both nose and tail. The freed cattle-beast kicked up its hindquarters, thrust down its head, and charged off to join its perambulating fellows. Ewan stalked with dignity back whence he had come. At the patrol-car door he paused, looked thoughtful for a moment, shrugged again, hitched up his pack more comfortably on his shoulders, and strolled off down the street in a southerly direction.

He had not gone far when a shout, rather different in calibre from most of the others currently upraised, turned his head round. A tall man in civilian clothes, with a bandaged head, was pointing him out to a companion. There was something vaguely familiar about the expression. It was the malevolence. . . . Then he remembered. It was the constable, Donal', of the spanner and the night before.

Ewan took to his heels, darted up a narrow lane on the left, turned left again, and kept on running.

Fortunately there were few people about, the centre of attraction being presently elsewhere. Clattering along and bearing left still, he soon found another lane leading downhill this time, that brought him down to the main street again, but now on the northern side of the traffic-block. Slowing to a less kenspeckle pace, he thought that he could hear thudding footsteps from the alleys behind. Diagonally across the street was a cinema advertising untold delights. Plunging a

126

hand into his jacket-pocket for one of his pound notes, he strode thitherwards.

He was in such a hurry to get to the treat within, that he had to be recalled by the astonished lady in the box-office to collect his seventeen-and-ninepence change.

Thereafter, blessed darkness received him.

X

LED to a row of seats by an invisible nymph with an impatient electric-torch, Ewan commenced his halting progress towards the seat that he had paid for. It was a harrowing pilgrimage, sustained by blind faith only, and punctuated by a succession of gasps, growls, protests, and his own apologies, as he apparently stood on innumerable toes, entangled himself in an undergrowth of legs, and displaced sundry hats and coiffures in the row in front. All the same, he felt that such inevitable and minor concomitants of popular entertainment were scarcely worthy of the concentrated and vicious hostility that greeted his shrinking traverse—till he was made aware that his wet pack, in passing, was buffeting the face of each of his fellow patrons in turn. Much upset by this revelation, he commenced a sincere, eloquent apology to his informant and all concerned, but was promptly and discourteously subjected to a powerful barrage of shushes and hisses, and injunctions both to shut up and to sit down. Helpfully, he endeavoured to comply with both these requirements, as opportunity provided, but leapt up again in concern as the lady on whose lap he had eventually come to rest protested in abrupt if richly-metaphorical Gaelic. Stumbling on at enhanced speed, he tripped headlong over something that kicked violently, and coming to rest on hands and one knee, discovered that the space in which he found much of himself seemed to be blessedly devoid of other human extremities. Approximately righting himself, and turning to face the front, he sat down.

It appeared to be an extremely narrow and uncomfortable

seat, though the view of the screen was excellent—until a further outbreak from behind, and an unceremonial push, impelled him forward, and he perceived that he must have been sitting on the up-turned edge of the tip-up seat.

Amid giggles from one side and snarls from the other, he subsided thankfully.

This was by no means Ewan's first visit to a cinema, but the others had been in military camps, where the audience was more or less marched in and marched out again, under adequate lighting. The inkiness of the desired gloom was more than he had bargained for . . . though, on reflection, it only served his requirements the better; the police would need the second sight to find him in here.

When he was sufficiently relaxed to pay some appropriate attention to the screen, he discovered what appeared to be a most apt and topical drama in progress—an epic wherein a pleasantly-pugnacious young man of vaguely Irish aspect made rings round as stupid and ineffective a bunch of policemen as anybody could wish to see, in some ploy that continued to escape Ewan but with which he was in heartiest sympathy, whilst a spectacular young woman of remarkable apparent physical development—if limited vocabulary—who seemed to have something to do with a newspaper, complicated the issue with a composure that quailed at nothing, from indiscriminate embraces to equally indiscriminate corpses. Quite absorbed, Ewan followed his trans-Atlantic fellow-Celt from triumph to triumph.

So absorbed was he, indeed, that it was not until he had subconsciously moved his left knee to the right quite a few times that he became aware of a continuing and sideways pressure thereon. Still mainly in Manhattan, he put down a hand to clear the obstruction—and contacted what, upon continued manual investigation, penetrated to his preoccupied mind as a feminine knee, silk or possibly nylon clad. Withdrawing the hand as though it had been stung, he gulped an embarrassed apology. For a little, Manhattan receded.

The horrible and detailed death of a motor-cycle policeman who chose foolishly to interfere with the simple pleasures of the Hibernian hero was having its due effect, when the pressure began again. Assuming that the lady must have very long legs or cramp or something, Ewan leaned as far to the other side as was practicable, to give her space, only, there was a large woman planted there who already tended rather to overlap her seat, and who now began to regard him with heavy-breathing suspicion. In some perplexity as to the demands of good manners, he endeavoured to shrink in on himself, and stared ahead in concentration.

But when, presently, with an elbow projecting over the left plush arm of his seat and into his ribs, and a lot of extremely tickly hair lying on his shoulder and playing about his ear, Ewan glanced down and perceived the pale glow of considerably more than mere knee resting on his own thigh, the idea came to him that perhaps this patron was so emotionally carried away by the drama being enacted before them that she was unaware of her peculiar behaviour. As a mannerly man, he felt that the last thing that he could do was to embarrass a lady by acting as though there was anything unnatural or unsuitable about her attitude. Yet some move on his part, metaphorical since it could not be actual, seemed to be called for.

"It's a very fine picture, don't you think?" he said, pleasantly, conversationally. "Plenty of action."

There followed something that started as a titter and ended in a sigh. "Och, I'm just crazy about James Cagney—are you no'?" That was confidential yet apparently objective.

Ewan was unsure as to the precise significance of her statement, but was relieved that at least the lady did not sound even mildly hysterical. "Just that," he acceded agreeably. "Och, yes."

130

His neighbour sighed again, but not evidently in any distress. In fact, as she actually snuggled closer to him, the man began to consider whether she was perhaps not emotionally upset at all, but just a little bit lonely. That one could be lonely in a crowd he had heard and could well believe.

When, after a heavier sigh than heretofore, the lady's hand slid along his arm and into his own palm, he became practically convinced that his idea was accurate. As a sort of a gentleman, he felt bound to assist in whatever way he could, of course.

His somewhat halting co-operation was accepted by his companion in a nice spirit of give and take; indeed, her encouragement had a progressive quality that seemed to account his diffidence as of little matter. Ewan found the responsibility intriguing, the extra pressure supportable . . . but his concentration upon the filmic entertainment rather less easy. The thought crossed his mind that as a means of gaining introductions to possible brides he had overlooked the cinema.

He may have missed some developments, for the ultimate lead-filled climax caught him somewhat unprepared. But the triumph of two-fisted initiative over dull authority was entirely satisfactory, and Ewan was getting ready to applaud suitably when a comprehensive and evidently intuitive convulsion from the lady found her safely back in her own seat when the lights suddenly went on.

Less expert, indeed a little confused, the man turned to her—and his confusion doubled itself and changed to consternation. "Suffering Sam!" he whispered.

Though the contrast with the photogenic beauty on the screen was perhaps a little unfair to her, his companion, seen thus illuminated, was quite the least decorative female that it had been Ewan's lot to clap eyes upon hitherto. Details he did not really take in—though the teeth rather stood out—

but to his brief and startled glance the general effect was sufficient, excessive.

Swallowing, he looked elsewhere—to find the large party on his right eyeing him with marked disapproval. She also looked past him, to the lady beyond, and sniffed. Hastily, he transferred his gaze—backwards, over his shoulder, since his scope was becoming limited. And over the sea of faces, he perceived, standing beside the swing-doors, the insufficiently injured Constable Donal' and the uniformed driver of the patrol-car. Alarmed, he turned his head round two hundred and seventy degrees, to consider the other door, the one by which he had entered. There stood the sergeant. Switching his regard promptly to the front again, Ewan kept it there, deliberately.

None of the policemen had been looking in his direction. They probably had not seen him. But he could not expect to get past them. The trapped sensation was unpleasant. Almost, he could feel their eyes focusing on the back of his head, boring down into it. Was there any other door to the place? Down at the front, on either side of the stage, there was an Exit sign, but alongside one was marked Ladies and the other Gents. Could there be an access to the street that way? And if so, might it be unguarded . . . ?

The lights sank and died, and Ewan sighed with relief. So did his companion on the left, and lost no time in seeking to revert to the *status quo*. Embarrassed, the man sought to edge away. He might be a gentleman, but he was maybe not such a gentleman as all that! Besides, he was preoccupied now, with more urgent matters than providing comfort for the lonely.

It was difficult, however, to convey this tactfully and courteously—as difficult as it was to withdraw any further to the right without arousing the ire of the bulky lady. In a distinct quandary and an agitation of mind that was quite foreign to his nature, he played a losing battle with the other sex,

132

and weighed his chances with the police whilst seeking to appear to be enthralled with the saga of the Wild West currently proceeding.

The time came when he could stand it no longer. There is a limit to which even Highland mannerliness will stretch. With an abrupt goodnight to the astonished lady on the left, he got suddenly to his feet, begged the pardon of the lady on the right, and started to push his way along in that direction.

He could see now considerably more clearly than when he had come in, so that his progress was not nearly so disruptive as formerly. Also, as he had perceived during the interval, the central aisle was no more than half a dozen seats away. But despite this advantage, he cursed this increased visibility, which he felt must clearly show him up to the lynx-eyed police at the back. Despite the general gloom, he had seldom felt more conspicuous in all his life.

However, he reached the aisle without any authoritative hand descending on his crouching shoulders, and hurried forward and down, making for that magic word Gents. Head well down, he went, and prayed that his pack would not be silhouetted against the light from the screen. Along the very front of the auditorium, beneath the enormous distorted figures he turned, and knew what it must be like to be an aircraft pilot caught in a searchlight beam.

But the swing-doors received him at last, and he was through, out of that place of dancing shadows and straining eyes and eddying tobacco-smoke, of six-gun fire and thundering hooves, into a cool passage, that bent to follow the corner of the building. Part-way along, just before the bend, on the left, was another door, inscribed with the generic appellation of his kind. Passing it, Ewan moved cautiously to the corner, and peered round. At the far end, the passage terminated in another set of swing-doors, glass panelled. And outlined against an outside light was the bulky head and shoulders of a man wearing a cheese-cutter cap. Frowning, the fugitive turned back, and entered the lavatory. His eyes went to the window; but it was high and small, inadequate as a means of exit for anything much larger than a cat. With a sigh, Ewan examined the place, shrugged, reached into his pocket and found a penny, dropped it into one of the slots provided, and passed within to an inner sanctuary. And there, philosophically, he disposed himself as comfortably as he might, to await the passing of time.

Highlandmen are good at waiting.

He had noticed the cinema clock pointing to nine-twenty not long before he had felt himself impelled to make a move. By then the Western had been well into its stride, or its gallop. So he had perhaps three-quarters of an hour to sit listening to the muted rattle of small arms, thudding hooves, and twanging banjos—suitably accompanied by the recurrent sound of rushing waters from closer at hand—before the tinkling and thrumming hill-billy strains were succeeded by the inspiring chords of God Save the King, the opening of doors, the banging of tip-up seats, and the shuffle of feet. Only a few patrons looked in at his department on their way out, and fortunately none were in a mood for spending further money at this time of night. In a remarkably short space of time, silence had descended upon the establishment previously so productive of sound. Only the intermittent sigh of gushing water remained to break the hush.

Ewan did not stir, for all that; he was wondering just where all the policemen were now.

Suddenly authoritative footsteps sounded in the passage outside. He got to his feet, tense. It looked as though he might soon find out. The outer door opened. Ewan held his breath. There was a click, and the light went out. The door slammed shut, and the footsteps receded, as authoritatively as they had come. In the darkness, the man heaved a sigh of relief.

But his recent experiences had made a cautious man of

134

Ewan MacEwan. He waited where he was for another fifteen minutes at least, before venturing out into the lavatory, and then into the passage. A certain amount of light filtered therein from the glass panels of the outer door, presumably from some street lamp. He tip-toed thither, and found the swing-doors held shut by a brass rod. To raise it was the work of an instant, and the doors opened to his push. But beyond was a steel lattice-work gate, securely padlocked. There was no escape that way.

Back in the auditorium, inky black now, he lit a match, and by its wan glimmer directed his steps up the side aisle to the front entrance. He found the same security system in force there as at the back. He was trapped.

Not very hopefully, he felt his way down the central aisle, making for the lower left-hand exit. No light percolated along this passage, but otherwise the situation was identical— swing-doors held by a bar and iron trellis beyond. And that, Ewan imagined, exhausted the doorways to this thoroughly-guarded establishment. As an Eorsan, this preoccupation with locks and bolts struck him as morbid in the extreme; he didn't suppose that there was a lock that worked in all his native island.

Feeling back along the corridor wall, his hand encountered another door and handle. Striking a match, he lit up the word, Ladies. Of course . . . he had forgotten. Not that this was likely to be very differently planned from its opposite number on the right . . . except in minor details, that was. He had not much experience of Ladies' Toilets, as it happened, but . . . clearing his throat involuntarily, he pushed his way in.

The slightly less dark oblong of the window beckoned him—and he noted at once that it was larger and less highset than that in the Gents, for some reason or other. Modestly keeping his glance straight in front of him, he made therefor. A moment's manual inspection revealed that likewise it was built to a different pattern to the other—being, in fact, a normal sash-and-cord opaque-glass window. It was snibbed, but naturally from the inside. Ladies, evidently, were not expected to desire to climb out of their lavatory windows.

Slipping back the catch, Ewan raised the lower sash quietly, contentedly. It did not lift very far, but sufficient for his purpose. Taking off his pack, he pushed it through and dropped it. Then, climbing up and wriggling over, rather like a seal negotiating a rock barrier, he followed it. On some rubble-strewn waste-ground he got to his feet, recovered his luggage, and turned to close the window, his own man again.

Below him occasional lamps illuminated the gleaming wet metals of the permanent way. Beyond were the dark waters of Loch Linnhe. Down to the railway-line Ewan picked his way, to turn right-handed along it. He reckoned that he might be safer to journey along the sleepers than by the more usual highway. And journey he would—he was quite definite about that. He was going home, that's where he was going, as quickly and directly as his rather peculiar circumstances permitted. He had had enough—enough of the mainland, of its ways and complications, its policemen and its women, carpet-slippered, yellow-haired, grass-widowed, Campbell-blooded, and buck-toothed—he had so. Eorsa, from here, looked like paradise to him, wife or none.

This railway line, he believed, if he clung to it for long enough, taking a fork to the left-hand somewhere, would bring him to Loch Eil, Glenfinnan, Loch Ailort and the sea. It followed, indeed, the Road to the Isles. And that was the road for Ewan MacEwan, this night!

XI

WALKING along even a Highland railway-line in the dark tends to have a certain monotony about it—not unconnected perhaps with the necessity for taking identical and uncomfortably-sized strides. But Ewan made no complaint on that score, nor on any other; in fact he was quite content to go on walking thus as far as the sleepers would take him—all night, if possible. Once past the cleavage of the two lines soon after crossing the River Nevis, a mile north of the town, he knew that he could not go wrong. There were no branch lines, no crossroads and signposts, to complicate the issue.

And all night he did walk, unchallenged. Only one train passed him, early on, a goods drawing fish waggons to the railhead at Mallaig; unfortunately, though no express, it did not go slowly enough for the walker to jump aboard—though he had a try at it, achieving only a wrenched wrist and a bruised shoulder. Reluctantly he had to recognise that he did not come up to Mr. Cagney's standard, yet.

By Corpach Narrows and the long, long shores of Loch Eil he went, and, by half past two on the railway clock, had reached his first station after Corpach—Locheilside. He reckoned that he had come twelve or thirteen miles. There was no village here, nor anywhere since the service hutments of Annat. He imagined that policemen would be few and far between.

It was grey dawn before he reached his next station, Glenfinnan of history-book memory, with the lochside left behind him for the crowding shoulders of great hills. He was a little unsure of his geography, here—he had an idea that

Loch Shiel, whose head must be somewhere around, might bring him most speedily to the sea; but in the mist-shrouded dawn he saw no sign of a loch, and in the absence of a map he decided to cleave to the railway meantime.

The sunrise found him in a lonely glen twisting between steep craggy mountains, sharing its narrow floor with the road and a brawling river. He had done well over twenty miles on the sleepers, and was glad to leave them for the more comfortable surface of the road. Nevertheless, after an hour or so of the tarmacadam, with the watershed crossed and a new river beginning to broaden out into a long narrow loch, and road and rail parting company again, one to follow either shore, the man elected to transfer his allegiance back to the railway. Perhaps he was not entirely to be blamed for something of a preoccupation with policemen in cars.

The fine rain had stopped with the dawn, and now the morning was a splendour of slanting sunlight on gleaming water, glistening vegetation, and wet stone, rolling up the white mist wraiths out of every hollow and corrie and spangling the spiders' webs that decked each juniper and bracken-frond and birch-tree of the soaring valley-sides. Tired as he was, Ewan found occasion to whistle his way round the lovely isle-strewn waters of Loch Eil.

Beyond the loch, and round a wide curve in the long rift in the hills, he came suddenly on another small one-sided station—Lochailort. There was nobody about as yet, but the clock above the ticket-office said eight-forty, and nearby on the wall was a framed and glass-covered Ordnance map of the district. Ewan studied it with interest and gratitude, and discovered that though he could not actually see it, he was close to the head of Loch Ailort, itself only a long bent arm of his beloved Western Sea. No road but only a foot-track ran down its serpentine southern shore, the road and the railway trending away north-westwards for Arisaig and Morar and Mallaig. That foot-track would suit him nicely.

138

Cheerfully, if a little heavy-footed, he climbed the fence and said goodbye to British Railways—much maligned, after all, he was inclined to consider. And along the road he saw two houses, one a cottage and the other a small hotel. At the sight his drum-empty stomach all but convulsed, and he made thitherwards practically at a run.

Later, quite a little time later, fed, refreshed and locally informed, by the unique and motherly hostess of that place, he strode downhill towards salt water.

If Ewan still glanced behind him occasionally, at first, that forenoon, he very soon gave up the practice. Any worries he had about the police, he left behind for the meantime with the last house of Inverailort. Thereafter, the narrow stony path that he followed, now down at the sea-weed of the loch-shore, now high above it amongst the rocks and crags, effectively banished any possibility of potent pursuit by any but better hillmen than himself. And on this subject, at least, his complacency remained unpunctured.

Beyond a high pass, with the wrinkled loch far below and the rock-strewn hillside soaring on his left, he found a hollow behind a great outcrop of granite, and curled himself up to sleep in the smile of the sun.

Moidart was the sort of country in which a fugitive could sleep in peace. Charles Edward Stuart had found it equally so two hundred years before.

Ewan awoke, stiff, three hours or so later, and resumed his westwards trek, if not like a giant refreshed at least with a fair accession of vigour. His track dropped in a long decline down to sea-level again, and at the foot thereof, in a leafy setting of oak and birch, he passed his first house since leaving the road, the pleasant place of Alisary. The little pier and motor-boat nearby emphasised that any traffic hereabouts was apt to be water-borne.

All afternoon he trudged, beneath the towering peak of

Fros-Bheinn, round a score of little bays and headlands, with the opening sea ever beckoning him on. When, beyond the green promontory of Roshven, his eyes lighted on the unmistakeable Scuir of Eigg thrusting out of the azure plain of waters across the Sound of Arisaig, with the purple, jagged mountain profile of Rhum behind, the man's heart leapt in response. His islands—at least he could see them, now.

It was early evening, however, before, having circled Glenuig Bay and left Samalaman and its crofts behind him, he climbed the high ground of the knuckle-end of that long peninsula, and saw before him, in the face of the breeze and the westering sun, the wide Atlantic with, half-left, against the brazen glow, the black outline that was his own Eorsa.

Thankful, content, and suddenly tired—with forty miles behind him since Fort William—he saw a path that left his foot-track and slanted down over rough pasture to a couple of crofts by the rock-girt shore, and accepted its invitation.

At the first croft-house, beside a tiny strip of shingly beach above which nets hung to dry on reeling posts, Ewan gained no response to his knocking, despite the faint drift of peat-smoke from its chimney. Across a miniature valley with a chuckling burn and a plank-bridge, however, he perceived that he was being watched by two women from the second cottage doorway. Thither he bent his steps.

The women considered his approach with the frank and critical interest of a sex that has never taken good manners with any great seriousness. Embarrassed a little, especially over those short socks—which he had not had occasion to recollect, of late—Ewan touched a finger to his forehead as he came up.

"It is a fine quiet evening, but the midges are bad, bad," he greeted, warily polite. "Your turnips are looking real nice."

"They're no' bad," one of the ladies admitted.

"Are you after wanting a job thinning them?" the other wondered.

"I am not, then," Ewan disclaimed. "I am looking for a bit boat to be taking me over to Eorsa, just."

"My goodness—Eorsa! You don't want much, you!"

"You're a matter of fifty miles too far north, man," her companion told him. "Drimnin in Morven is the nearest the boat touches, for the islands."

"Och, it is not the steamer I'm wanting," the man explained "It's just a bit fishing-boat, maybe, to put me across."

They looked at him, speculatively, then at each other, eyebrows raised, and said nothing.

Ewan returned their scrutiny, doubtfully. They were both dark, almost swarthy, youngish women, of that Spanish-seeming type that has managed to persist along the Western seaboard since the Armada days, muscularly built and obviously sisters. One looked just a little older than the other—but he was not going to risk a guess at their respective ages, except perhaps to within five or ten years. They showed no grey hairs between them, amongst the raven black, even if they both had a sort of experienced look normally denied to the very youthful. That is the kind of youngish women they were.

"Are you a tink, or what?" the elder questioned. "I wouldn't think there'd be that much trade for a tink on Eorsa. It's an outlandish sort of place, yon."

"Is it combs and hairpins you have in your pack, there?" her sister demanded. "You'll sell not that many combs in Eorsa, I'm thinking." And, as an afterthought: "You wouldn't have any nylons in it, would you?"

Ewan sought to keep a steady and level voice, without complete success. "I would not, my Chove!" he cried. "Nor combs, either! And if there's tinks in it, there's some folk I can think of look more like tinks than, than . . ." He swallowed, and groped urgently for a return to the civilities. "Och, gracious me—can a man not be carrying a bit pack on his back without selling hairpins! I've just been a sort of walking-tour, in the north a bit, and am for making home to Eorsa. And what's wrong, at all, with Eorsa, anyway?" He glanced comprehensively about him, at the two humped-back cot-houses with their stone-hung reed-thatched roofing, the tumbledown outbuildings, the pocket-handkerchiefs of tilth scratched here and there on the stony slopes around, and he raised his own brows. "There's places I've been in, not that far from here, that Eorsa would not have on the island, whatever!" But at the ladies' stricken looks, he relented, as a gentleman must. "Och—but maybe it would be yon Erismore you were thinking of," he suggested, offering them a graceful way out. "It's a terrible place, that."

The younger sister nodded her head. "It's not been a bad summer, at all," she asserted hurriedly, whilst the other slapped a robust forearm heartily, and declared to her Maker that the midges were a sore trial, indeed.

The situation being thus satisfactorily restored, Ewan inclined his head towards the drying nets down near the beach. "You wouldn't have a sort of a boat about the place, maybe? I'd pay, see you, well enough. Och, yes." And he negligently drew from his pocket a most impressive handful of bank-notes.

He could hear the respiratory disorder of the ladies, but kept his glance turned modestly elsewhere, in order to allow them to recover their poise. The elder found her voice first.

"We've . . . we've only a bit rowing-boat, our own selves. You'd be needing more than that. . . ."

"Those nets, down there . . . ?" Ewan gestured, with his hand.

"That is Colin More's and Colin Beg's nets—our uncle and cousin. They have a coble, yes—but they are out at the fishing . . ."

"But they will be back," the younger of the two put in. "They'll be back before morning." She exchanged glances with her sister. "You could wait till then . . ."

"That's right—you could wait. With us. Surely. We could be putting you up. Och, easy."

"Yes—we could so. We could give you a bed in the room. Och, you'll be tired, likely . . . ?"

"And hungry? We'll get you a bit supper, in no time at all . . ."

"That's so. It will be no trouble, whatever. Come you away in."

"Yes, indeed. In with you. It's a pleasure to be sure."

"Just that. Come, now."

With a suddenly earnestly hospitable hostess at either elbow, Ewan, hustled within the cottage doorway almost at a run, was able to reflect on the curious and essential changeableness of womenkind.

XII

THE MAN'S reflections on this score only intensified as the evening wore on. From the suspicions and innuendoes of his reception, his benefactresses, named apparently Sara and Ailie MacNeill, proceeded through all the stages of social solicitude, to positively vie with each other in attentiveness towards their guest. Fed to the point of discomfort, his every want anticipated, their ministrations even became embarrassing to an inherently modest man—as, to some extent, did their thirst for information on personal data. Two to one, and with typical feminine directness, not to say unscrupulousness, by the time that the lamps were being lit and the fire stirred to a blaze, they had him into a corner, actually and metaphorically.

Ewan, though not ungrateful, was unable to avoid a certain feeling of alarm and despondency. For a man in deliberate search of a wife, it was borne in on him that he was perhaps less effective in coping with women than with, say, cattle-beasts, sheep, or policemen. One at a time was bad enough, but when there was two of them, and working together like well-trained collies on refractory sheep.

The simile alarmed him, and the man made an all-out effort to stop the rot, to regain the initiative, to raise the entire proceedings to a less personal plane—the more urgently in that, however efficiently the ladies worked together, and with their increasing cordiality towards himself, there appeared to be, strangely, a corresponding and growing unkindness towards each other.

Determinedly, if a trifle abruptly, Ewan plunged into

the meaty subject of Home Rule for Scotland, with special reference to the Small Isles, plunged and maintained.

It is an excellent subject, permissive of infinite arguments, interpretations, permutations, and pursuance of sub-themes.

Yet it was surprising how promptly his hearers had the general theme linked up with the individual, and how would Home Rule affect Eorsa, and, say, Mr. MacEwan's bit farm. Was it a decent sort of house he had on it, with up-and-down stairs, and a spare bedroom, maybe?

Ewan countered, that with their own government in Edinburgh, maybe they would get some interest paid to the food-producing potentialities of the Highlands and Islands generally, and an improvement on the transport facilities, the piers and the roads.

That was right, the ladies agreed. Was there a decent sort of track up to this Corriemore of his? Could you get fuel and seed and supplies up to the place on wheel, or had they to be humped on your own backs like here at Camisary? And what about the peats? Were they near at hand, and easy to win?

The man admitted that the peats were all right, and not that far from the house . . . but och, the electricity was the thing. A Scots Government, now, could be for giving them a bit grant to use their own water-power for the electricity.

Aye, water was the thing, the MacNeills acceded. Had he got a good supply—laid on in taps, or did he have to go to a well, just? Running-water was a great help.

Sighing, Ewan gave up self-government and the initiative, both. A stone-walling defence seemed to be the only tactics possible.

And even in this limited ambition, he had to concede failure before long. Alternatively beaming on him and glaring at each other, Sara and Ailie had him pumped dry of desirable information in a remarkably short space of time—

save for the jealously-retained primary object of his walking-tour and the less flattering items of the police persecution. The man had no confidence that even these were not in danger.

He envisaged a slight respite when, in response to considerable mooing from outside, Sara, the elder, fixed her sister with an authoritative eye and declared that it was ten o'clock and long past time when she ought to have shut up the cows for the night, and the poultry too. Avoiding action by Ailie—who evidently was the stock-woman of the croft—being firmly brushed aside, the latter counterattacked to the effect that Sara would have to go to the spring for water; the pails were empty, and the porridge not mixed for the morning. Ewan's immediate, even eager, offer to go for the water himself, was as immediately turned down by both sisters, with emphasis. Sara would go for the water—when Ailie came back from locking-up. No guest of theirs should be left churlishly unattended.

Reluctantly, Ewan sank back into his seat, and Ailie made for the door with backward and suspicious glances.

Sara did not sit down. The door shut, she came and stood beside the visitor, and her sigh held the tremulous urgency of deep feeling. "Aye," she said. "Uh-huh. Aye me."

The man kept his eyes straight in front of him. "Just that," he agreed, but with a lack of conviction, even some incipient agitation.

"I'ph'mmm. You'll be a lonely man, I'm thinking, Mr. MacEwan." That was a statement, and no question.

"Eh . . . ? Me? Och, not at all, no. At least—och, not what you'd call lonely."

She ignored that feeble disclaimer. "Aye—real sad it was about your wife. Loneliness is an ill thing—don't I know it."

"You . . . ? But what about your sister, there?"

"Ailie? Och, Ailie's a good girl enough—and a help with the croft. But, aye me, there's a loneliness even a sister cannot be after filling . . . and it's a lonesome place, this Camisary."

"But you've got your uncle and cousin, downbye," Ewan reminded her earnestly. He did not have anything against dark women as such and on principle, but thick black eyebrows like a bar across her face, and a noticeable jaw-line with a hint of the rat-trap about it, tended to make a cautious man of him.

Sara MacNeill flicked aside the Colins Mor and Beg contemptuously. "What use are they to me?" she demanded, tense-voiced.

"U'mmm. Och, well . . ." Ewan coughed.

"Och, but it's nothing like so bad for me as for the likes of yourself, Mr. MacEwan," she went on, in a different tone of voice—different, but no less purposeful, perhaps. "A widower's always a right pitiful thing, whatever. . . ."

"Pitiful!" The man had difficulty with his enunciation. "My goodness me—och, that's a bit strong!" he protested. "It's not as bad as all that."

"Is it not, then? I would have thought . . ." The other paused. "Well—a widower has *my* pity, at any rate."

"M'mmmm."

"Mr. MacEwan—you never thought of marrying again, did you?" The uncertain beginnings of a laugh went with that.

The man moistened his lips. "Well . . . not what you'd call seriously, maybe." He was a poor liar, at best. "Only just sort of vaguely, see you . . ."

Vaguely was ample for Sara MacNeill. "I'd say you couldn't do better, Mr. MacEwan," she asserted confiden-tially. "I would so. Goodness me, a man doing for himself is a sad thing to see." She glanced over towards the window, as though her time might be short. "A man shouldn't be milking cows and minding hens and keeping a house. Och, it's not suitable, at all. You'll maybe have someone in mind, though . . . ?"

147

"No. At least . . . och, it's not that important. . . ."

"But it is. A well-set-up fellow like your own self, with the fine bit farm you have and all, you're after having your responsibilities, to yourself and to the place and to the, och to the community, sort of. It's . . . there's nothing wrong with you, at all, is there? I mean . . ."

"Of course there's nothing wrong with me, my Chove!" Ewan said. "What would be wrong with me, just because I've not married again?" But his indignation was very much a flash in the pan. His eyes strayed to the door. "Late it's getting," he mentioned, producing a yawn. "A long walk I had this day."

Needless to say, Miss MacNeill ignored that. He felt her move the little bit closer that brought her into actual contact with his somewhat stiffly-held shoulder. "You'll need to look out for the right qualities in a wife, mind you," she advised. "You could be making an awful mistake. You'll want someone that's strong and healthy, used with farmwork and beasts, and can manage a house. And someone that's used with living in a lonely sort of a place . . ."

The door opened, and Ewan let out a lot of breath in relief. Her sister Ailie's glance was very sharp.

"That's the beasts in then, Sara," she announced, a trifle breathlessly.

The other frowned. "Well, what of it?" she demanded, with some asperity. "Are you wanting me to dance a reel, or something?"

"My, my—hoity-toity!" Ailie gave back. "Is anything biting you, at all?"

"Must you be bringing the manners of the byre back in with you, then?"

"My goodness—what next! The byre, indeed! Listen to me, Sara MacNeill—I'll thank you . . ."

Ewan MacEwan cleared a congested throat. "Och, it's a very fine night, out there," he observed. "The wind's dropped away entirely I'd think. Are the midges still bad, at all?"

"Midges . . . ? I can't say I was after noticing," Ailie looked from the man to her sister. "But Sara'll tell you when she comes back with the water!"

That lady sniffed, strongly. Then, abruptly, she turned on her heel, stepped over to a corner, picked up a couple of empty pails, and clanked out with them.

Ailie MacNeill emitted a brief titter, came and sat down in her chair opposite Ewan, and leaned forward in resolute fashion, her chin cupped in her hands.

"You're a right fortunate man, Mr. MacEwan," she asserted.

Ewan's eyes widened. "Fortunate, now, is it? Glad I am to hear it. . . ."

"Yes, you're the happy man, right enough, with the two little small ones that's in it. A boy and a girl, you said? Wee brollachs they are, I'm sure."

"Aye, they're that all right," the proud parent admitted dubiously. "Och yes—definitely."

"I just love children," his companion confided. Almost ecstatically, she entwined her fingers. "I reckon I was just one of Nature's born mothers." And she sighed deeply.

The man rubbed his chin. "Is that a fact," he said.

"Yes. And here's you with two of them—and not the least bit of interest in the poor little souls!"

"Och, good gracious—that's a bit steep! It is so," the guest complained. "I've plenty interest in them—b'damn, they don't give me that much choice . . . !"

"And yet here's you away on a long walking-tour, traipsing all over the country, and leaving them all alone; I tell you, my heart just bleeds for the poor motherless darlings out on that island, at the mercy of just anybody. . . ."

"No, no—you've got it all wrong, whatever!" the maligned father cried. "They're fine, and happy—happy as trouts, I tell you."

The lady permitted herself a small smile, of infinite compassion. "I don't really blame you that much," she revealed. "It's not just your fault. What you need is a nice motherly woman, not too old and not *too* young either, to look after the pair of them. Aye . . . and maybe yourself too!" And her smile flashing to real brilliance, she leaned forward and patted the fortunate man's knee.

Ewan attempted the answering gallantry which the situation invited, demanded, but with only moderate success. In fact, after the briefest meeting of glances, he switched his regard to the heart of the failing fire, and kept it there. Which was strange, too. The creature's eyes were far from repellent, and her general expression kindly to a degree; indeed, this one, whilst endowed with a distinct family likeness, was quite good-looking in her own way. And wasn't he here, on the mainland, for the express purpose of meeting such as herself? Presentable, strong, capable, croft-bred, fond of children, and seemingly interested—all these, wasn't she? Well, then. "Oh, aye," he muttered. "Just that. M'mmm."

The other sounded in nowise discouraged by his masculine slowness. "Such a one's not that easy come by, maybe. But I wouldn't say that there mightn't be a chance not that far from here, at all!" And she laughed heartily.

"D'you tell me that," the man commented. And after a momentary pause. "How far away is your well?"

"Eh . . . ? Oh, not that far, I'm afraid," she informed, with a sort of conspiratorial regret following her initial surprise.

"Uh-huh," her companion acknowledged, the regret less noticeable.

"Yes. I wonder, Mr. MacEwan . . . och, I think maybe I should just call you Ewan—it's more homely, isn't it! A nice name, Ewan is, too. Well, as I was saying, Ewan—I wonder, do you believe in Providence, at all? I'm a great believer in Providence, my own self . . . and it looks to me just like the hand of Providence that brought you. . . . Oh, damn!"

The clatter of a pail outside the door cut short the revelation of Divine purpose. As her sister appeared, the speaker, almost in the same breath, greeted her.

"My God—if those blessed pails are full, I'm a puddock!"

"Full enough for our needs," said Sara quickly. "And what way's that to talk, in front of Mr. MacEwan?"

"What's wrong with my talk, then, mercy me? Ewan's not been complaining—have you, Ewan?"

"Ewan, is it! Well, my goodness—just listen to that! If that's not brazen impudence, Ailie MacNeill . . . !"

"Och, hold your tongue, you great mealy-mou'ed yowe!"

"I will not hold my tongue. . . ."

Ewan MacEwan leaned back in his chair, and turned his eyes to the ceiling-boards.

It went on for quite a time, and indeed grew in intensity—long enough anyway for the man to come to a conclusion, to make up his mind. As to implementing his decision, it was not until there was a delayed and highly necessary pause for breath, that he was able to make himself heard.

"Yon boat you were saying you had?" he inquired patiently. "Is it a sort of half-decent thing? It doesn't leak, or anything?"

The required re-alignment of ideas occupied a few moments—and even then was most obviously temporary. Aye, it was a good enough boat, he was informed—and the difference of opinion resumed.

When next he got a chance, Ewan inserted another question. "Are you after using it much, this boat?"

That did not appear to register, and he had to rise to his feet and repeat his query before he got the answer that, no, they didn't often use the boat. Colin Beg, their cousin, used it sometimes, only.

"Have you ever thought of selling it, at all?" the man persisted.

At the word sell, a noticeable change came over the attitude of his hostesses. Suddenly he had their undivided attention.

"Sell . . . ?" Sara repeated. "You wanting to buy a boat?"

"I might, yes—if the price was right."

"It's a good boat," Ailie declared. "We've not had it that long."

"How long?"

"Och, three-four years, no more."

"And it cost, maybe . . . ?"

The sisters glanced at each other, their late antagonism evidently evaporated.

"Well . . . I don't just mind," Sara said.

"Six pounds. Not a penny less," Ailie asserted.

"That's right—six pounds," the elder sister substantiated, hurriedly.

"I'ph'mmm," Ewan nodded, one eyebrow raised. "Oh aye. Well—you've made a sale! I'll pay you seven pounds for your boat, oars . . . and what I owe you for your hospitality. Seven pounds."

"Well, now! That's . . . that's nice," Sara said, uncertainly.

"You must be awful needing a boat, Ewan," the other commented, more frankly.

"I can do with one, yes," the guest agreed, briefly. "I'd be better with a look at it, now, see you."

"Now . . . ? Och, not in the dark, surely to goodness!"

"It's not that dark . . . there's a bit moon in it, isn't there?"

"But it's no time to be looking at boats, at all. You will see it much better in the morning. . . ." Sara was protesting, when Ailie interrupted her.

"I'll take Ewan down and show him the boat," she offered, with prompt generosity. "Come, you."

Her sister frowned. "If you're that keen to see it . . ." she began, shrugged, and turned towards the door.

152

"No need for you to be coming, Sara," Ailie assured. "We'll manage fine."

The other threw up her head, and led the way.

Ewan bowed the younger woman after her, made a quick dart into a corner of the room, and then followed on.

It was indeed not very dark, a fine clear night with a crescent moon rising in the south-east and the wind gone. A well-defined path led the hundred yards down to the beach. Both ladies were suitably punctilious that their guest should not get lost, trip, nor miss his footing. The man ended by surrendering an arm to each, and thus maintaining equilibrium, and, as it were, the crown of the causeway. He did not let either of them get behind him.

The boat, an ordinary tubby dinghy, was drawn up on the shingle just above high-water mark, and tied to a rock. The oars lay along her thwarts.

"Och, she's a very fine boat, indeed," Sara decided.

"She looks all right," the purchaser allowed. "Is she heavy, at all—lie low in the water?"

"No, no. Och, nothing like that."

Ailie sighed gustily. "A fine night it is for a bit row, too."

"What nonsense!" her sister exclaimed. "You taken leave of your senses, Ailie MacNeill?"

"Never heed her, Ewan," that lady advised. "Sara never did like the water, at all. Sick, she gets. Me, now—I'm different. Och, I like a row, fine."

"We might be pushing her down, and seeing if she floats, at any rate," the man suggested, unhitching the rope.

"My goodness—what a ploy, at this time of night! You're not serious, Mr. MacEwan . . . ?"

But Ailie already had her not ineffectual shoulder to the gunwale, and when Ewan added his weight, the boat ran down over the rounded pebbles of the strand to the water, in fine style. The lady did not even seem to mind getting her feet wet.

153

"She floats, anyway," Ewan, at the stern, commented. "Is that a tin for the bailing, I see there?" He vaulted inboard, and still he managed to keep face-on to the women. "She'll do me, fine." Thrusting into his pocket, he drew out his handful of notes. "Seven, I said. . . ."

"Och, there is not all that hurry," Sara observed politely. But Ailie, though she agreed that that was so, held out her hand.

"One, two, three, four, five . . ." Ewan handed them over to her—and somehow managed to let the last two drop into the water. ". . . six, seven. Och, sorry I am . . . !"

"Mercy me . . . !"

"Good gracious . . . !"

Both sisters were stooping, promptly, peering into the dark water in the boat's shadow. Ewan stooped too, as promptly. He grabbed an oar, thrust it over the side on to the shingly bottom, and pushed with all his might. The boat forged forward.

"I've got one of them. . . ." Ailie cried.

"I'll get the boat out of your way," the man informed, hurriedly. "There it is. . . ."

"Ailie . . . !" Her sister straightened up. "Look—he . . . he's got his pack on!"

It was perfectly true. The boat, swinging round a few degrees to Ewan's pushing, silhouetted the man against the faint light of the moon. The pack on his back was unmistakeable.

"Yes," he agreed then. "I couldn't be leaving it behind, could I? I've had it a long time, this pack."

"But . . . where are you going?"

"To Eorsa, like I said! I'm for home." Sculling, now, he could hear the women's gasps. "Och, your boat will not sink on me, will it?"

"My God—you can't go, like that!" Ailie cried.

"I can so. It's a fine night for a bit row, as you said. . . ."

"But, Ewan . . . Och, this is terrible. . . ." Her voice broke.

Not so her sister's. "He's a blackguard, that's what he is!" she declared strongly. "A right scoundrel! Just a deceiver of trusting helpless women! We're well quit of him—we are so! A narrow escape we've had this night!"

"Och, it might have been worse," the departing guest gave back, philosophically. "You have your honour, whatever . . . and seven pounds!" He was twenty or thirty yards out now. Sitting down, he got out the other oar, fitted both between the wooden rowlocks, and began to row.

"Ewan—come back!" Ailie pleaded.

"Aye—maybe I will, one day. But not tonight!"

"Quiet, Ailie—I wouldn't cheapen myself with a man like that, my goodness! Come on. You got all those notes, now . . . ?"

"Goodnight, ladies," Ewan MacEwan called across the dark water, in his farewell to Camisary, to the mainland itself.

XIII

ROWING a small boat on a calm night and an empty sea is a soothing activity for a fit man, rhythmic, essential, unhurried, almost hypnotic in its effects on body and mind. Ewan sank into the steady cycle of it appreciatively, and thanked his Maker for many of His mercies.

For all that, he did not sink away entirely into any heedless unthinking Nirvana—nor even, for more than a very brief interval, into blissful self-congratulation on his cunning escape from the frying-pan, until he had ascertained the combustibility of the fire.

His assertion to the Misses MacNeill that he was for home, Eorsa, while substantially true, did not mean that he was fool enough to think of *rowing* there on his own. Eorsa must lie twenty-five miles at least west by south, and though the sea was quiet enough at the moment, and the weather looking reasonably settled, none knew better than Ewan MacEwan how swiftly conditions could change, how treacherous were those skerry-strewn waters, how unpredictable the pressure of the Atlantic swell on the sunken mountain-ranges below. His general aim was to pull down the coast some way till he could find fishermen who might take him at least part of the way, to the island of Muck, maybe. Moidart and Ardnamurchan had empty and barren seaboards, he knew, but surely there must be some townships along their coasts.

He pulled rather more south than west, then, over a smooth sea that heaved ponderously to the long slow swell that was the heart-beat of the vast ocean beyond. The water gurgled rather than slapped at his bows, the rowlocks creaked, and the man whistled through his teeth to the beat of his oars. Visibility was of that uncertain quality, not uncommon on a moonlit night, whereby features at a distance tended to be much more clearly defined than those close at hand. The black outline of the coast and the hills behind, between the wan glimmer of the sea and the deep blue vault of the sky, was distinct and clear-cut, whilst fifty yards or so was as much of the foreground as might be surveyed with any certainty.

Something of the same flaw in perspective was reflected in the man's mind's eye, in his musings on the situation. He was thankful to be out of that Camisary—he was so! But why? What was wrong with him? Wasn't that Ailie MacNeill the very sort of thing that he had left Eorsa to find? Was she not as suitable a candidate as he was likely to unearth—and keen, too? What for had he run away, then, as though she was poison? The other sister was a shocker, of course—but he wouldn't have had to take the two of them. Or would he, maybe . . . ?

He did not know, he did not know at all. But he had just had to get out of there, he just couldn't consider those women—either of them. He had to get back to Eorsa, to his own place . . . and to the devil with all women, whatever!

In that spirit he pulled at his oars, back and forward, back and forward, with long slow strokes that matched the lift and fall of the swell, while the crescent moon rose high in the blue heaven and the belt of black shadow that was the shore that he had left narrowed and dwindled. But the similar black shadow to his right, on the south, separated from the other by an indistinct gap which could be no other than the mouths of Loch Moidart—this other belt of shadow did not dwindle nor fail. In fact, look forward over his shoulder as he would, he could trace no end to it, thrusting westwards into the ocean. He had not realised that there was so much of the Ardnamurchan peninsula.

The night remained calm, though cloud gradually banking up from the south-west covered the moon. A smirr of fine rain brushed his right cheek, but did not come to anything. It was much darker. Deliberately the man pulled his prow a few points round into the west. Calm as it was, he was better to be well out into the open than closing that jagged and skerry-rimmed shore in the darkness. Unless the sea rose, he would keep out here, pulling due west until daylight. There were two lights to keep him right—one away north, that would be Arisaig Point, one dead ahead and low down, that could be nowhere else than on the island of Muck. Damn it all, he might even reach Muck itself, under his own steam!

That tiny pinpoint of light beckoning him on, Ewan pulled hour after hour into the night. He did not feel sore, nor yet tired; he barely felt anything—his conscious mind all but slept if his body did not.

It was the freshening breeze that rose with the dawn, rather than the dawn itself, that woke the man out of his trance. Quickly it lifted catspaws on the surface of the swell, as the sky paled wanly and his guiding lights faded, and leaden grey and slate succeeded cobalt and black. The loom of the land faded too, with the dim uncertainty, and only the tossing waste of drab waters remained, veined with dirty white.

The man, who realised that he was stiff, now, and cramped and weary-armed, did not turn southwards yet. He knew that a dawn breeze can drop almost as swiftly as it arises. With no landmarks to go by now, he sought to keep the small seas coming in on his port bow; with a south-westerly wind, that should maintain his general direction. The light boat tossed and dipped, slapping at each wave; but she was broadly-built and sturdy, and no trouble to handle. Ewan pulled on, only occasionally lifting spray from a roller with a tired oar.

Presently, he was satisfied that the wind, if not actually dropping, was at least not going to strengthen, meantime. Facing east, he watched for the sunrise.

Before that, however, the half-light had dispersed sufficiently for the Ardnamurchan coast to come into view again. Curiously enough, it looked more flat, hull-down as it were, farther away altogether, than it had done in the night. Of the Moidart shore that he had left, there was no sign at all, as yet. Depressed a little—the man was needing his sleep—he turned to look forward over his heaving shoulder. His heart lifted, and his depression fled.

Ahead, comparatively near at hand, much closer than seemed the long peninsula of Ardnamurchan, the serrated and uneven outline of an island stretched across the centre of his immediate horizon—the Isle of Muck. Three miles distant, it might be—perhaps even less. He could make out the white dots of individual cottages. With an access of vigour, he bent to his oars. He required all his augmented vigour, too, for progress became steadily more difficult. He could feel his craft being pushed in a north-easterly direction, and had to turn more and more into the south to counter it. Ewan recognised the cause readily enough; it was not the wind so much as the flow of tide and current. Hitherto the long promontory to the south had protected him, acted as a breakwater; now, though he was not yet level with Ardnamurchan Point, the tide driving in slantwise from the south-west and the open sea, was catching him in the wide gap. For a tired man after a night's exertion, it was trying.

Too trying, in the event. With the sun risen, dazzling the eye with its level yellow glare from between black bars of cloud, Ewan had to admit that he was making little or no progress against the tide—and his strength was failing. He did not think that he had drawn appreciably nearer to Muck in the last half-hour. With little option left to him, he changed his course. If he could not move south-west, he probably could move *north*-west. If that took him too far to the right, into the Sound between Muck and Eigg, at least Muck itself would then act, he hoped, as a breakwater, and he might be able to pull in eventually to its lee shore. If not, he would just have to run with the tide, and hope to fetch up on the south coast of Eigg. . . .

Swinging his bows round through perhaps 120 degrees, he dug in his oars again, the waves now half-astern. They were larger now, too, hissing a little as they rolled down on him and past, and occasionally a shower of spray drove in on him. But they were not vicious, and the man had no fear of them—only of his own flagging strength.

He was making progress now, however, and the next half-hour, grim as it was, brought him to not much more than a mile from the land. But it was nearing the northernmost point of Muck, under a narrow spine of hill that dominated that end of the place. If he kept on this course, undoubtedly he would miss the mile-or-so long island—and who knew just what currents the Sound of Eigg might hold for him? He turned in again, almost due west, directly for the nearest point of the shore.

It was better than he had feared. Already the bulk of the island was acting as a buffer to the tide. In a little while he recognised that he was going to be able to make the shore. But now, occasional patches of white water were becoming evident around him—skerries just below the surface. How close in dare he go? The shore was obviously rock-bound, and there were no houses visible on this part of the island, though he could distinguish a few cattle and sheep grazing on the green slopes. Instead of trying to land hereabouts, would he not be better to go as close in as he could and then seek to row south along the coast, looking for some sort of haven? The cottages which he had seen earlier were bound to have a landing-place, but they were some distance south of his present position.

When white water became too prevalent about him for any comfort, Ewan pulled round once more into the breeze and tide.

This was the choppiest and wettest part of his voyage, though by no means the heaviest pulling. Shallow jabbly waters kept the boat bobbing and plunging, but the main force of sea and wind was deflected. Watching the skerries with respect, Ewan worked his panting way southwards.

Round a headland, to which he had to give ample clearance, he came suddenly on a deep bay, a bight almost, into which the morning sun was streaming. In the glitter and dazzle on the water he did not notice for a little that as he entered from one side a fishing-boat chugged out from the other. When he did see it, and shouted and waved, it was too late. Evidently he had not been observed; the sun would be almost directly in the fisherman's eyes, of course. Disappointed, Ewan pulled on into the bay.

He saw that there were houses up at the deep head of it, under a rocky hill, blue smoke curling from their chimneys. At least, here he could find rest and refreshment. And then, coming out from the shadow that a hillock cast on the water, he found another fishing-boat, almost directly in his course. Drawing in his oars, he waited, thankfully.

Three men in the well of the boat eyed him curiously, throttling back their engine to his gesture, at their approach.

"A fine morning," the eldest mentioned—a father and two sons, by the look of them. "There'll be a shower or two in it later, though, maybe."

"Och, I shouldn't wonder, yes," Ewan agreed. "Uhhuh."

"Just that."

"You'll be for the fishing, then? Are you getting much, at all?"

"Little enough, man—little enough. Och, they're the kittle brutes, the fishes. Here tomorrow and gone today, sort of."

"That's it. There's little profit in it, whatever. You'll be for Maclean's Bed, likely—or the Birlinn?"

"We were thinking of trying Donald's Cradle." The fishing-boat was making a slow circle round him, now, to keep within polite conversational range. "There's been a fish or two lifted out of there, we were hearing."

Ewan's features lightened. "Och, that's fine. You'll get a boatful there, likely. A good bit, the Cradle." It was also the nearest to Eorsa of the three fishing-grounds mentioned, by a good four miles. "You could be making a bit pound or two in the by-going too, see you, if you were to be towing me behind you."

"Towing you . . . to Donald's Cradle!"

"You fishing too? In yon . . . ?"

"Och, no. Eorsa it is, I'm going to. I'm for taking this boatie back there. There's a pound if you'll tow me out that far."

"But, man—we couldn't be leaving you out yonder in a little small boat the likes of that!"

That was what Ewan thought, too. "Then there's another pound if you'll tow me just a wee thing further, to the mouth of Eorsa Bay."

The fishermen in the circling boat looked doubtful. Ewan somewhat apologetically displayed one or two of his pound notes, as if by accident, and hurriedly put them away again, as befitted a gentleman dealing with other gentlemen. One of the young men spoke.

"If we're not for taking you, how will you be getting to Eorsa, at all?"

"The good Lord knows!" the traveller admitted frankly. "Och, I've rowed from Moidart, there, and that's plenty." He yawned elaborately. "I'll need to have a bit rest, first, maybe." Glancing away, up towards the head of the bay, he added, "Maybe I could be finding out if the ladies of Muck are kinder than their men, whatever!"

162

His hearers eyed each other, quickly, and their decision seemed to be unanimous.

"Och, no need for that, at all," the eldest asserted. "No, no. Have you got a rope, see you?"

Ewan leaned back, picked up the coiled line which had moored his purchase to its rock at Camisary, and threw it across.

"Are you for coming aboard us, or biding where you are?" he was asked.

"Oh, I'll be fine and comfortable here," he assured. "And I'll keep the boatie in ballast. Go, you."

As the fishing-boat swung out of the bay and into the open water, Ewan MacEwan lowered himself stiffly down on to the floorboards, settled his shoulder against a thwart and sighed his relief. Before they made the southernmost headland of Muck, he was asleep.

XIV

IT WAS nearly three hours later before Ewan awoke. The changed motion of the boat it was, probably, that roused him out of the deep places of his slumber. For his towed dinghy was no longer lifting and curtseying into the tide and the breeze out of the south-west; it was rolling and pitching, now wallowing, now jerking forward, as the tow-rope slackened and tightened.

Or it may have been cold water in his face that awakened him, for the veils of spray were coming inboard now, from windward—and that was over the starboard side. For direction was changed, and more than direction; the wind had risen, and the sea with it, the short steep waves of the narrow waters super-imposed on the long swell of the Atlantic.

Ewan sat up, rubbing the sleep out of his heavy eyes. He was facing in towards an island, indeed—but it was in the wrong direction, by wind and tide and sun, and it was not Eorsa. The place was larger, harsher, consisting of wild towering mountains, stony screes, and beetling cliffs. Though it was not an approach with which he was familiar, there was no mistaking that island's profile; it was Erismore of the barbarians.

Frowning, Ewan cupped hands to mouth. "Ahoy!" he called. "That is Erismore. The wrong place, entirely."

From the chugging fishing-boat the older man waved back. "Aye," he shouted. "Too rough it's getting, for Donald's Cradle. We'll no' can fish there, in this. Or the Birlinn, either. There's a bit bank in the lee of Erismore, here, that'll have to be doing us."

The traveller got to his unsteady feet, clutching the

gunwale, the better to make his impression. "Eorsa it is I want. Och, Erismore is no good to me, at all!"

"Too rough," the Muck-man cried. "Getting worse. Here it is, or home."

Ewan omitted the civilities. "Damned inshore podlie-guddlers!" he asserted. "What's a bit wind! Your island's right well-named, my Chove!" This was an unkind cut, referring to the Gaelic word *Muc* or *Muchd*, of which Muck was the uninspired Anglicisation, and which meant the Isle of Pigs. Few men are at their most courteous when newly awake and being led astray.

His towers preserved a dignified silence—and their course.

The MacEwan dredged still deeper for effective insult. "Your money!" he enunciated distinctly. "I was paying you to be towing me to Eorsa! Pound notes!" Could a Highland-man and an Islesman say worse than that?

"Keep you your dirty money, my God!" the elder gave back, much moved, obviously.

"Lucky you are to be this far, I'm telling you," one of the sons amplified, whilst his brother spat with vigour almost halfway back to the dinghy, and against the wind at that.

Ewan, recognising obduracy when he saw it, sat down. What could not be mended must be tholed.

The fishing-boat beat round the northernmost headland of Erismore, giving the soaring precipices and their white-fanged skerries below a wide berth, into the quieter waters beyond, to the east, where the island's bulk gave them shelter. The dinghy bobbed along behind, its occupant wrapped in lofty disapprobation.

About half a mile down the savagely barren east coast, the Muck-men swung in towards a thrusting buttress of rock, and then, evidently selecting their position with care, they put a buoy over the side and began to pay out their net. At the same time, one of the young men untied the tow-rope and flung it back to its owner.

"It's all yours!" he called, with a comprehensive gesture, eloquent as it was offensive.

Ewan, staring from the jagged and inhospitable coastline to the slowly circling boat, declared his shocked conviction with some detail. And then followed it up with indignant inquiry. "You're not after leaving me here!" he charged, unbelievingly. "My goodness—you wouldn't do a thing like that!"

"Fine and near the shore, you are," one young man called.

"Row, you," his brother advised briefly.

"We're for fishing this bank," the father declared. "Do you as you like, whatever."

"But . . . damn it, I'll not can row to Eorsa in this wind! And I'll not can land on this coast, here. . . ."

"Then pull you back round the head, there, and into the bay that's in it. There's a bit pier."

"Och, my Suffering Sam—what would I want to land *here* for! It's a right useless place, Erismore."

"Please yourself," the unfeeling Muckerach shouted. "You can go, or you can wait. If the wind drops, we might be giving you a bit tow again . . . after we're done here."

And with that Ewan had to be satisfied. Since to row back round that great headland and into the teeth of the wind and tide that would meet him there, enamoured him no more than to try to land on this iron-bound cliff-girt and deserted eastern shore, he decided that dignity could be purchased at too high a price, and that discretion and patience would probably pay the better dividend. So he got out his oars, and pulled over to the buoy, tied his painter to it, to use it and its nets as a sea-anchor, and settled down to wait.

Fortunately, like all his race, he was good at waiting. And even Muckerach, he hoped, might be subject to the better impulses, on occasion.

Actually, he had not so long to wait as might have been

expected. The fishermen, having let out their net to its curving limit, were filling in *their* time of waiting with line-fishing, when Ewan, rocked by the swell into a doze, was aroused by a shouted exchange. Looking up, he found the trio pulling in their net at speed, with something not unlike panic.

Turning to stare in the direction of the men's glances, Ewan perceived that three more fishing-boats had rounded the thrusting headland, and were heading down towards them. And he obtained the swift impression that they were more heavily crewed than was usual; certainly they contained more than three men apiece. It looked as though the Muckerach had suddenly decided to go fishing elsewhere.

Ewan was prepared to recognise that they might well be wise in that—wiser indeed never to have started to fish this bank at all. The Erismore borachs had a rough reputation, and might conceivably feel that their private fishing grounds were being blatantly poached. He was sure that no Eorsan in his right mind would have dreamt of fishing Erismore waters—not in daylight, anyway.

The Muck-men got in that long net in double-quick time, hauling it aboard anyhow. But even so, net-lifting is not a speedy procedure, and the oncoming boats were within hailing distance before the last dripping coils were being dragged aboard, and the buoy after them. The flotilla's crews were hailing, too, in no uncertain fashion, a most unseemly hullabaloo. Ewan, weary as he was, knew some small excitement.

"Damned—I told you Erismore was an ill useless sort of a place!" he reminded the panting, soaking Muckerach, now quite close to him, with just a hint of the satisfaction of the man whom events have proved right.

But any satisfaction was wiped off his face very promptly as he perceived what was afoot. The buoy being now aboard, still with Ewan's painter attached, one of the young men had grabbed a small axe, and with three or four strokes, where the rope crossed the larger boat's gunwale had severed the taut strands.

"My Chove!" he cried. "You're not . . . you wouldn't . . . och, mercy on us—you wouldn't leave me here!"

Unfortunately it was only too apparent that they would do just that. The three Muck stalwarts made no reply, did not even look at the objector, their preoccupied attention elsewhere. With a trail of white foam boiling behind its agitated screw, the fishing-boat surged away in a north-easterly direction, its engine abruptly flat-out.

"Devil blast and blister you!" Ewan ejaculated, with sufficient feeling to shake a fist after them.

The howls from the approaching armada rose to a crescendo. Two of the boats swung away to port, after the fleeing Muckerach, but the third came right on towards the lonely rocking dinghy. Ewan looked from it to his so ineffective oars, shrugged, and resumed his waiting.

The boatload that drew near might not have seemed so very different from any other such group of Hebrideans, to the average eye, but to Ewan MacEwan they were clearly without the pale. Unmannerly, noisy, hybrid, heretical, little better than tinks—and as like as not Campbells to a man! He did not grace his hatchet-face with any beam of courteous welcome.

The Erismore boat came bumping alongside, and a man with a boathook secured one of the dinghy's thwarts, almost pulling Ewan out of the way in the process.

"My goodness!" that man complained. "What is this, at all? Watch you, with that bit stick!"

"That's enough out of yourself!" the man with the boat-hook advised, a black-avised desperate-looking character— almost as dark as Ewan himself.

A substantiating chorus came from his colleagues. But they did more than that. Two limber fellows vaulted lightly over into the dinghy, wobbling it perilously, and Ewan

168

found himself gripped unceremoniously, one on either side. The lack of ceremony was indeed very noticeable, and enhanced by the wild swaying that thereupon took place, as three men in a violently curvetting small boat endeavoured to maintain their precarious balance, and one at least, his dignity.

"Och, to hell with this!" the outraged MacEwan cried.

Hands from the fishing-coble grasped the dinghy's side, and sought to steady it, and Ewan found himself propelled from the rear by a knee under his posterior, towards the other craft.

"In with you!" he was urged, rather unnecessarily, as all three more or less fell over the two craft's gunwales. A certain amount of miscellaneous hauling completed the transfer, and boarding-party and prisoner sorted themselves out on the fishy floorboards of the coble.

"Holy Mike—if it's a stramash you're wanting . . . !" Ewan struggled to his knees and his unsteady feet, his fists clenched, before he was tipped back into ready and plentiful arms.

The squat gorilla-like individual at the tiller, clad in patched dungarees, a blue jersey, and an ancient green felt hat, spat thoughtfully, and spoke with heavy deliberation. "Quiet, you!" he said. "Or is it the swimming for you, maybe?"

Ewan MacEwan, as has been indicated surely, was a reasonable man at base. Looking round him, now, he perceived the need for reason writ large on seven deplorable Erismore faces. He swallowed his wrath, sighed away his indignation, and shrugged. "M'mmmm. Aye," he said. "Uh-huh. Just that," and relaxed, to some advisable extent.

The steersman nodded briefly, his associates indicated just how wise was the captive, with illustrations, and the coble swung round in a great arc, chuffering its way back towards the headland, the empty dinghy dancing in the rear.

Away to starboard, three fishing-boats arrow-headed into the grey north-east.

Though Ewan, still reasonably, held his tongue for a space, there was no lack of talk in that boat, strong talk, and not so incoherent but that he gathered something of what the Erismore vigilantes intended to do to such unprincipled reprobates as dared to steal their very bread out of their mouths. From what was said it appeared as though this was not the first occasion that they had been so insulted . . . though, even so, they were making a most unseemly fuss about a bit fish or two, whatever. Ewan was not sorry that he was so transparently innocent in the matter, just the same.

Even in such company, presently, however, the Eorsan felt that the occasion warranted at least an allusion towards the civilities . . . even if a well-deserved coal or two was thereby heaped. "A pity about the wind that's in it," he observed judiciously. "But, och, it's not been that bad weather, at all."

A profound silence greeted this balanced and philosophical declaration.

Ewan sniffed into the wind—they were just rounding the Point, into the face of it—and nodded, authoritatively. "A fine evening, it'll be, and the wind dropped."

The squat man at the helm sighed gustily. "Shut your face, my God!" he mentioned, with a sort of melancholy abstraction.

That was Erismore. Ewan relapsed into contemplative quiet.

He still was contemplating when, after negotiating with quite deceptive ease a boiling fearsome gap in the jagged reef of protecting skerries, and crossing the comparatively placid waters of the bay beyond, the coble drew in to a tumbledown stone jetty, and it was forcibly impressed on him that he should disembark. A collection of women, children and old men was awaiting their arrival. He eyed them a little askance, naturally; this was a sight that he had never looked to see. He insisted on retrieving his pack out of the sternsheets of the dinghy before being landed.

The askance looks were more than mutual. Ewan, in the circumstances and out of the standard of conduct and intelligence that might be expected hereabouts, was prepared for a certain amount of misunderstanding of his own position; but not for the volume of hostility, invective, abuse, and even expectoration with which he was greeted, from all quarters. The women were particularly eloquent—a peculiarly inexcusable state of affairs to a man from Eorsa, a civilised island where they had long had their womenfolk well in hand. The fact that a fair proportion of these Amazons were somewhat striking as to appearance only made their conduct the more disgraceful.

Ewan was hustled along till he was face to face with an aged man with a flowing white beard and the air of a degenerate patriarch, who, whilst seeming to be more concerned with the firmament of Heaven, squinted at him out of the corner of a rheumy eye and combed his beard with claw-like old fingers, incredibly dirty.

"Is this all, then?" he wondered, in a querulous high-pitched whine. "Blessed Mary of Mercy—is this the size of it?"

Ewan did not like his attitude and tone of voice, at all, and was about to say so, when the ape-like helmsman answered him with quite ridiculous and unsuitable respect.

"No, no, no. Och, not at all, Fergus Conn. Others there were in it, and them away like the devil was under their tails! Fergus Og and Murdo are after them. This one just was buoy-man for the net. Those others were . . ."

"My Chove—I was not!" Ewan interrupted strongly. "Nothing of the sort, my goodness. I was just after getting a bit tow. . . ."

"Hush, you!" the old man said, petulantly, addressing a

sailing cloud-galleon. "Mother of God—a man cannot be hearing himself speak for you!"

"Well, I'm damned!" the prisoner gasped. "I tell you . . ." A hearty dunt on pack and shoulder-blades brought that to a choking conclusion.

"Hold the clattering tongue of you!" he was advised, with some acerbity.

"Muckerach again, it would be?" the ancient suggested.

"Just that," the steersman agreed. And added objectively, "The flames of hell roast them!"

"I'm no Muckerach," Ewan croaked, having difficulty with his tonsils. "Damn, no! I'm from Eorsa. . . ."

"Eorsa!" The patriarch's gaze turned still more acutely heavenwards, and he went through the initial movements of crossing himself, before spitting noisily. And all around him throats were cleared and spittle spat.

A little taken aback, Ewan cleared his own throat, and spoke into the sudden silence, jerkily. "I'm from Eorsa, yes. On my way home, I am. I've been on the mainland, sort of travelling just. I was after rowing out from Camisary in Moidart last night. I got to that Muck this morning. Yon boat was leaving for the fishing, and I got them to be giving me a bit tow. Tired I was. They were for fishing Donald's Cradle, and they were to put me over to Eorsa first. For money, it was. But the wind in it changed their minds on them. They came in here. I said no. I told them . . ."

The murmur of disbelief that accompanied most of this grew loud enough to drown the rest. Ewan stopped, and shrugged once more.

The deliberate squat fellow from the boat began to speak. "To Eorsa? In that little small boatie . . . all the way from Moidart . . . ?" But the old man stopped him with a gesture, strangely commanding for one so indirect and so derelict.

"This one is a great liar, or he is mad itself," he declared to all the dome of the sky. "Which, we will be deciding later, when the others are back. Angus—lock you this up till then . . . and do not be losing him, in the name of God! The fish-house will be best, I'm thinking." And with supreme indifference towards anything further that might be said, the patriarch turned away and went shambling off.

Ewan drew a long quivering breath, preparatory to really disposing of this nonsense once and for all—and promptly found himself being propelled forwards, part-run part-carried in a species of frog-march, in a northerly direction. What he said, in fact, was no more important then than it is now.

Presently, after stumbling amongst tussocks and crunching over a section of stony beach, he was thrust briskly into a cold, clammy, and odoriferous vault, and a heavy door banged upon him, and was barred. Listening to the heavy footsteps dying away, Ewan MacEwan let out the residue of that long breath that he had taken. "Erismore!" he said, bitterly, and scratched his black head.

XV

WHEN, after a space, his equilibrium was sufficiently restored for him to take an objective interest in his surroundings, Ewan made an examination of his quarters. Not that any prolonged inspection was called for. He was in a cavern-like cell hollowed out of the solid rock, part-natural part-hewn, sealed with a heavy oaken door that looked as though it had come from some substantial wreck of long ago. The actual fit of the door into the aperture was far from perfect, however, and from a variety of gaps and chinks thin beams of light penetrated, illuminating the rocky interior with a wan glimmer. That light was sufficient to reveal the steeply-sloping floor of shingle, the naked uneven stone walls running green with moisture, and the rows and rows of rusty hooks, hung on wooden batons, that lined them. The fish-house, that old miscreant had called it—and it was not difficult to perceive its use; its chill damp atmosphere would tend to maintain the freshness of fish even on the warmest day. Also, its security as a place of detention was equally apparent.

Ewan tried the door, without any hope. These borachs were unlikely to shut him up in any place out of which he could break easily. It felt, indeed, almost as solid as the rock itself. The massive hinges were mortared deep into the walling, and not one of the crevices and chinks was large enough to offer any purchase. Without an axe, or a crowbar at the least, he was as secure as he had been in the police-station at Fort William.

Sighing, the man sought for the driest corner of the uncomfortable and unsavoury floor, and sat himself down.

174

That Fergus Conn—the Fergus Conn MacCallum, undoubtedly, that he had heard ill tales of at his mother's knee—had said to lock him up until the others came back, blast him! Which presumably meant, the crews of the other two boats. And how long might that be? When last seen, they looked as though they were prepared to follow the intruders right back to Muck, if necessary. They were more heavily-laden than were the Muckerach—there was no reason to suppose that the pursuers would be likely to overtake the pursued. All of which seemed to indicate that he might well be immured in this objectionable cave for hours. It was now early afternoon; three hours it had taken on the outward journey, and now the seas were rougher and the wind strong. That could mean anything up to six or eight hours—possibly more. With something like a groan Ewan reached this conclusion. A woefully empty stomach by no means exalted his morale.

Misjudged, imprisoned, uncomfortable, threatened with further unpleasantness, hungry—what assets remained to him? It says much for Ewan MacEwan's native philosophy that he could still recognise two such—the righteousness of his case, and an excellent and unimpaired capacity for sleep, with vast arrears to make up. Committing the one to the other, the man went to some little trouble to scoop hollows out of the shingle for his shoulder and hip-bone, and laid himself down, head pillowed on his pack, knees up to his chest to counteract the gnawing of a stomachic void.

Lulled by the rhythmic sigh of the waves on the strand outside, he sank into satisfactory unconsciousness.

Sleeping came natural to Ewan, and once started he found no difficulty in keeping it up. He had no idea for how long he had lain, when, shaken by the shoulder, he sat up, to find his squat captor and two others standing over him with some food. By the rosy bars of light that came levelly from the cracks around the door, he blinkingly perceived that it must be evening; the cave faced seaward of course, due west into the Hebridean sunset.

His gaolers pointed to the food, and appeared to be about to depart without any sort of remark. Ewan, confused as he was with sleep, felt bound to voice his protest, however incoherent.

"Mercy on us—this is a scandal!" he asserted. "A right scandal. It is so. What . . . how the hell . . . och, my gracious—how long is this nonsense going on?"

The trio paused on their way to the door, and stood, unanswering. Ewan could not see their expressions, but they had an undeniable and infuriating air of impassivity about them.

"How long are you for keeping me in this damned hole?" the captive insisted. "That old . . . old man—he said till the others came back, just. Are they not back yet, my goodness?"

"No," he was told, baldly, by one.

Another stooped, picked something up, and tossed it to him. It was an old and torn plaid. "Och, you'll be fine," he mentioned, and they all laughed, and moved to the door.

"My Chove!" Ewan gasped. It was obvious that he was being left for the night. "Confound you—you'll not can get away with this, whatever! Goodness me, I tell you . . ."

The flood of gold and scarlet from the opening door, and then the solid slam of it, was his answer. The bar he heard being fixed in place, and then the footsteps crunching away over the beach. He had had his goodnight.

Ewan was perhaps unreasonably angry—but wrath seldom can stand before hunger. Before long he had turned to the provender. It consisted of a can of milk, a couple of hard-boiled eggs, and a considerable pile of stale scones. No hungry man was going to find fault with such. Without more ado he got busy.

Thereafter, though he tried conscientiously, he could not quite recapture the full flower of his choler. He brooded, of course, and ruminated, and recognised himself to be a much injured man. But that is not the same thing as being a really angry man, and he knew it. He thought about that for quite a while, and wondered. He wondered, and yawned . . . and yawned. . . .

Ewan had not intended to fall asleep again there and then, of course—or he would have chosen a more comfortable position than hunched forward with his chin on his knees. But that is the position in which he awoke in due course, cramped and stiff with cold. It seemed to be quite dark.

Even in his heavy state of mind, he knew that something had wakened him, something quiet, furtive. He sat up, almost creaking in his discomfort.

There . . . ! Yes. Plainly, from beyond the door, came a faint sound, the noise of a shoe clinking on stone. And following it came another sound, quiet too but clear.

"Hisssst! Are you there?" a voice said, a soft woman's voice, whispering.

"I am, yes," Ewan assured. To add, slightly unnecessarily, "Myself, it is. Who's there?"

"Och, it's just . . . just somebody." A slight pause. "Ailie MacCallum."

"Is that a fact."

"Yes. Look—you said you were from Eorsa. Is that the truth?"

"It is, yes. Eorsa."

"And you were on your way to Eorsa? You weren't after fishing, at all?"

"Right you are, entirely."

"The boat—the ship—calls at Eorsa every Monday, does it not?"

"Yes. . . . But I had this dinghy to fetch back, see you. . . ."

"Look," the voice interrupted, and now it sounded distinctly breathless. She must be very close to the door.

177

"Can you sail your boatie from here to Eorsa, your own self?"

"I could, yes. Though the wind that was in it was bad. I was . . ."

"The wind has dropped," she said. "What I . . . och, would you keep a promise, whatever?"

"My name is Ewan MacEwan, Corriemore, Eorsa, and I keep my promises!" that man declared, formally, into the darkness.

"Yes. Well, then." Her heard her swallow. "Will you take me to Eorsa with you in your boatie, if I let you out of there?"

"My Chove!" It was Ewan's turn to swallow. "I . . . I will so, my goodness. You're not joking . . . ?"

"Och, where would be the joke in that? I am wanting to get away from here, from Erismore, see you, and they will not let me. For long I have been trying to find a way. You will take me—tonight?"

"Surely. Och, it will be a pleasure, just."

"And I will be getting the big boat from Eorsa, on Monday?"

"That's right—first thing Monday morning. You couldn't do better."

"Wait you, then, and I'll be back. I'll not be that long—I have to be getting my things."

"Are the other boats back? The two that were chasing the Muckerach?"

"They are, yes. They have been back two hours. They didn't catch them. They hadn't that much oil. . . ."

"M'mmm. What time is it?"

"Eleven, about. If I am a wee whilie, it will be me waiting on my mother to go to her bed."

"Good, then." Ewan laughed softly. "Och, I'll not run away, Ailie!"

To the waiting man it seemed quite a wee whilie indeed

178

before he heard quiet footsteps on the shingle again, and a fumbling at the bar of the door.

"My gracious," he said. "I was thinking you were after changing your mind, woman."

The door creaked open, and he saw the slight figure of a young woman holding a bag, silhouetted against the faint luminosity that came out of the cold heart of the northern sea.

"It was my grandfather," the woman said—she was a girl only, obviously. "He wouldn't settle. But he's sleeping, now."

They looked at each other in that negation of light. Features were not to be discerned, but the man was struck anew by the youthful aspect of his rescuer. An uncomfortable thought occurred to him.

"You . . . you wouldn't be under twenty-one, would you?" he asked, a little anxiously.

"Och, no—I'm twenty-three past." There was an incipient giggle there, vastly reassuring.

"Good." Ewan sighed with relief, and smiled into the dark. "I wouldn't like the police to be after me for anything, see you!"

"No." Miss MacCallum, not unnaturally, promptly sounded anxious again. "Come, then. Your boat is still at the pier. We can be getting along the beach."

"Wait you, a minute," Ewan told her, and went back into the fish-house, to emerge again with the old plaid. "It will be cold in the boat, likely." He shut and barred the door behind him. "Let's see your bag," he said, and took it from her.

"Kind, you are," the young woman acknowledged, and they moved off soft-footed along the sighing shore.

It was no more than three hundred yards to the jetty, and there was the dinghy drawn up on the strand, fortunately still with her oars aboard. To push her down to the water's edge did not take long, the girl assisting—though the noise

179

of its keel scraping over the pebbles had Ewan looking anxiously up towards the nearest crofthouses. But no light showed, nor sign of life, on all Erismore. And the noise of the waves would cover them.

They were launched and aboard with only one of Ewan's feet wet. And despite the blister on his left palm, the man was happy indeed to feel those oars in his hands again.

But it was by no means a case of all being over bar the shouting. Erismore was ringed by a girdle of the most vicious skerries in all the Inner Hebrides, and none worse than those enclosing this central bay. To try to take a boat through them without exact knowledge and in the darkness, was to court inevitable disaster. It might be that the girl had not thought of that . . . or perhaps she knew the gaps. He put it to her, now.

Ailie MacCallum knew the gaps, yes—in a sort of a way. But she did not think that they should attempt to work through the main skerries. There was a better way. They should row northwards, along the shore of the bay, until they were close under the Rudha nan Altair, the big headland. There was a narrow passage round the base of that, between the skerries and the cliff-foot, that was all right at half-tide and more. The tide was just past full, now. And beyond it there was an easy place to get through the reef.

Ewan was pulling round to port, northwards, even as she spoke.

The sea here, within the breakwater of the reef, was not high, and the wind undoubtedly had dropped satisfactorily, but the continuous roar from the line of the skerries seawards was a frightening thing. To its grim accompaniment the little boat pulled along parallel with the shore, and ever the din grew and deepened as the horn of the bay swung out towards the headland and the skerries drew closer. There was no conversation in the face of that clamour.

180

It was light enough, in that northern summer night, for the bold precipice of Rudha nan Altair to stand out clearly against sea and sky, and around its dark base the phosphorescent glow of breaking waters gleamed eerily and ominously. But the girl directed Ewan to pull as though directly for the foot of it.

Soon the commotion of waters became alarming and unpredictable, and the noise awesome. Ewan pointed out his difficulty, though such was scarcely necessary. But Ailie MacCallum insisted that he pull straight on, right under the black soaring wall of rock. Now they were both rolling and pitching hazardously in the sea's onset and backwash, rising and falling dizzily with the ebb and flow of the swell, that lifted and sank ten or more feet with every surge of the tide. The inner rim of the skerries was no more than thirty yards away, on their left, and the great impending palisade of cliff closer still on the right, amplifying and throwing back the roar of the tortured waters as from a sounding-board.

Ewan had to trust that the girl knew what she was doing—though, with the turbulence of the seas, he was too much occupied in keeping the dinghy on some sort of a course to consider anything else very coherently. Drenched with spray from both sides now, and the night lit up all around them by the wicked greenish glow of phosphorus and white foaming waters, they lurched on. It must be a deep-water channel; anything else would spell suicide. . . .

The young woman was shouting something to him, now leaning forward to pitch her voice against the tumult. "Pull over . . . a little more towards the skerries!" she cried "There's a bit sticks out from the cliff. It's narrow. We're nearly through. . . ."

Panting, the man nodded, and pulled on his port oar—though it went against the grain to draw any nearer to the gnashing fangs of that reef. But a swift glance behind him showed him the urgent need. A flying buttress on the cliff, split from off the face of it, almost halved that narrow corridor. His heart in his mouth, he pulled still further seawards.

Now high, now low, with the skerries so close on their left, now a jagged black barrier of streaming rocks, now a white cauldron of spume and spray, they surged forward into the gap. Ewan had a vision of the towering pinnacle of the buttress almost directly over his head, but veiled in spindrift, and knew a terrible moment of panic as an oar scraped on rock. And then they were through. The cliff receded abruptly, and he could pull hard away from the mouthing skerries.

"My God!" he said, and again, "My God!" And that was as good as any anthem of praise.

But they were not yet finished with Erismore's jealous guardians. Though the rise and fall swiftly grew less dramatic, they were now having to cope with actual breakers, regular, white-crested, and hissing. The reason was not far to seek. These were the surface combers of the great Atlantic swell, and that they were coming through thus in their entirety, must indicate a break in the wall of the skerries, or at least a lowering of the level of the reef. Even as the man realised this, his companion directed him to pull hard round, seawards, taking these snarling waves on their port bow. For the first time, spray from rollers breaking on their boat and not on rock, came inboard, but that frightened the oarsman infinitely less as he drew round ever more closely into them.

And then, there was a minute perhaps of peculiar swirling and stalling, with the dinghy jerking and shaking unaccountably, and the oars making little or no impression. Dipping crazily into a great and suddenly-opening trough, they climbed out steeply, the little craft shaking her forefoot gallantly. And each succeeding comber was smaller, less broken, and then the steady rollers of the wide ocean received them.

Ailie MacCallum clapped her hands, in an access of relief. "We're through!" she cried. "We're through, whatever!"

Ewan nodded, breathless but thankful. She had guided him over what must be a deep depression in the reef. "Bless you, woman!" he praised, hoarsely.

And pulling round directly head-on into the run of the long seas, he lengthened the sweep of his oars, and settled down to steady rowing.

So, for the second night in succession, Ewan MacEwan rowed his cockle-shell westwards across the waste of waters. Or south-westwards—at least, he hoped that he rowed south-westwards, in which approximate direction lay Eorsa, five or six miles off. But it was a cloudy night, and there were no stars to guide him, and fairly soon even the bulk of Erismore had faded into the gloom behind them. The wind was light, now, but fitful and not to be trusted; only the direction of the seas themselves could he rely upon, which almost invariably ran in from the south-west on this seaboard. It suited him, too, to keep his prow directly into them—but the direction of even the most regular seas offers scope for a fairly wide margin of error. Five or ten degrees divergence might never be noticed.

Ewan, naturally, kept his navigational doubts to himself.

They talked a little, now—not volubly, for the man required most of his breath for the task on hand, and the girl seemed to be of the quiet sort, and with a suitable tendency to reserve. But she did reveal something of her story, in bits and pieces— how she had a young man, in Inveraray, whom her parents and grandfather would not allow her to marry. She had met him when she was in service on the mainland—he was a forester on the Duke's estate, with a house and a widowed mother. When her people had heard about him, they had fetched her home to Erismore, at once, for Dougal was not a Catholic. Twice he had come trying to get her away—but Erismore was as ill a place to get into unwanted, as to get out of. Now she was going to him, and nothing was going to stop her.

Quite right, too, Ewan agreed. Erismore struck him more than ever as a place to be detached from, at all costs. He was just a little relieved, too, to be thus assured that this young Erismore female was not likely to involve him in any of the complications that seemed so inevitably to arise with her kind where he was concerned. Though, too, the thought did occur to him that, if it had not been that she was from Erismore, she might not be the least suitable of the creatures that he had come across on his pilgrimage—a thought that he was able to dismiss with no more than token regret.

He inquired whether she had heard tell of a Mistress Campbell, at a place called Stronvair on Loch Etive-side with a daughter called Maggie? She informed him that that would be her own mother's Auntie Ada, but did not pursue the matter further.

After that, conversation flagged, and presently, wrapped in the ancient plaid, Ailie MacCallum slept.

The man, left to his own thoughts, was not any too happy about his direction. There was a mighty lot of sea, and it would be an easy matter to pass Eorsa in the dark. He reckoned that he had been rowing for nearly three hours, perhaps; it ought to be at least looming in sight, by now. Though, with these head seas and the wind against him, his speed would be very low, of course. He wondered how much drift they were making . . . ? He wondered rather a lot, as he went on rowing, rowing like an automaton.

It would be *more* than five or six miles, of course. It was that distance from the north-east tip of Eorsa to the south-west tip of Erismore. But they had not started from that tip; indeed, they had left the northernmost point of the island. And Erismore would be three miles long, at least. That made a difference. Why hadn't he thought of that? Maybe he would be wiser to be turning a peg or two into the south . . . or into what he hoped was the south. . . .

With no enthusiasm or certainty upon him, Ewan

MacEwan fought his battle with doubt and the night and the sea.

The grey dreich eventual dawn taught him nothing—save only that he was not very close to any island. Empty heaving waters surrounded them, with nothing more solid in sight than their own frail timbering. Worried, Ewan contented himself with keeping the dinghy's head into the waves, rather than wearily forcing her onwards. It looked as though he would have plenty of rowing to do still in due course.

It was a dull morning, and the man waited with growing impatience, not to say agitation, for visibility to improve, foolishly envious of the girl who slept so soundly curled up in the sternsheets.

When, at last, with the brightening light of the east, he saw land, he was much shaken. It was not the land that he had looked to see, and it was not anywhere that he had looked to see it. Actually, what he descried was the jagged lofty peaks of Erismore catching the first flush of the sunrise—but they were far away, and far east by south.

Hurriedly he turned to look over his right shoulder, for Eorsa. There it was, away to the south of them, miles away— further than it was from Erismore itself: Groaning almost, he pulled round his bows, practically through ninety degrees, to face it. The wind and the seas must have been much more westerly than he had bargained for, and the drift to the north strong, strong.

There was nothing for it now but hard back-breaking rowing—hours of it. But at least he could see where he was going. And the sea was levelling.

Ewan MacEwan sort of hoped that that young woman would not wake up for a bit, after all. He had just his share of natural-born pride, the man.

185

XVI

IT WAS mid-forenoon before, bone-weary, jaded, and maybe a little light-headed with his exertions, Ewan grounded the dinghy on the steep strand of a little sandy cove on the north shore of his own Eorsa. It was by no means the first or nearest spot on which he could have chosen to land—but he had had plenty of time to think the matter over, and it had occurred to the returning prodigal that there was no need for him to advertise his home-coming unduly, blatantly, by pulling right into the main west-facing bay of the island; it was a very obvious sort of bay, under the windows of nine-tenths of Eorsa's population, and he modestly felt in no need of a reception committee to mark his return, in the circumstances. That at his departure had been bad enough. Undoubtedly, his passenger would tend to feel the same way, he decided.

He was just a little bit disappointed with Ailie MacCallum, actually, in broad daylight—a not infrequent male reaction towards the opposite sex met for the first time under the kindly veil of night. The cast of features, the figure, and the voice, were good—that he had been able to perceive in the darkness; the effect, now, was hardly borne out by the expression, complexion, and general appearance. In fact, she appeared to him, this dull sunless morning, as a very ordinary sort of young woman, mousy-haired, somewhat pasty-faced, and a little dull. Perhaps he had romanticised her in his mind, a little bit, as a result of the night's ongoings; certainly there was little romance to help them on their way over this morning's sombre miles of hostile waters. Ewan, of course, was typically and masculinely unfair; no woman

186

can be expected to look and sound at her best after a night in a storm-tossed open boat. Had he been able to glance in a mirror, himself, he might have more suitably recognised the need for charity.

The grinding of keel on gravel, however, was a grateful sound in the ears of both of them. Ewan, getting to his feet, found his knees so stiff as to barely unbend. Like an old man he got himself over the side into shallow water, and started to haul the boat up on to the shingle, his arm muscles so limp as to make a woeful task of it, and handed out the girl and her bag. With little word between them, he moored the dinghy securely, shouldered his pack, and directed Ailie MacCallum to face the lift of the empty braes. Perhaps his thankfulness at his home-coming was too deep for words.

Eorsa, roughly crescent-shaped to enclose the afore-mentioned bay, rose to high ground all around the eastern perimeter, with steep hills and beetling cliffs dropping dizzily into the sea—a similar pattern to Erismore, in fact, but on a lesser scale. On this inhospitable area mankind unanimously turned its back; no house nor haunt of man relieved its loneliness. Ewan, though it entailed a four mile tramp over country trying to a tired man—not to mention a tired woman—decided that it provided an excellent and seemly route for an unostentatious fellow to return quietly to his hearth and home.

They saw no soul on that high-level trudge, only some deer and a scattering of Ewan's own sheep. Lower, he was amongst his hill-pastured cattle—and happy to be so. And presently they stood at the stony edge of a bracken slope and looked down on the birch wood, the infields, and the steading and house of his own Corriemore.

It seemed a long time since he had left it, a long long time. There was no sign of life about the place, so far as he could see—that overgrown scoundrel Bally would be sleeping somewhere behind a wall! Farther down, at the foot of the white ribbon of his road, lay the scattered crofts around the sickle of the bay. The man's eye fastened moodily on the larger house and outbuildings that belonged to his Uncle Finlay Sim. It was all just as he had left it. Nothing had changed in . . . in . . . goodness gracious—in five days! This was Saturday, only, and he had left on Monday morning, just. It didn't seem possible, at all. Frowning, he moved downhill. All but forgotten, the girl moved after him.

The poultry were pecking about the steading as they passed through—which was normal and satisfactory enough. The goat, too, tethered in the stackyard, was as it ought to be. He had seen, from above, that the milkcows were in the infield, and Betsy had not yet had her calf. Och, the place had not been just entirely neglected, then. . . .

He rounded the gable to the front of the house, and there was the door standing open. Mercy—if that was Bally, asleep on one of the beds . . . !

Inside, however, there was no sign of his monumental employee, and everything seemed to be in order—very much, excessively, in order. The place looked unfamiliar, uncomfortable, with everything in its proper place. Everything, that is, except for two full baskets of berries that stood in the middle of the kitchen floor. Considering these thoughtfully, the man recollected his wilting guest, instructed her to sit in the more presentable of the two sagging armchairs, and went out again, to round the further gable, and face his fruit and vegetable plot beyond.

Mary MacEwan, her slender back to him, was stooping amongst his currant-bushes, another basket over her brown arm. And she was crooning a song to herself as she worked.

For a good minute Ewan watched her, words lost to him. When at last he spoke, it was out of due care and consideration. "Busy are you, Mary," he said.

She whirled round, spilling some of the fruit, and catching her brown skirt on a neighbouring gooseberry bush in the process. "Ewan . . . !" she gasped. "Ewan! I . . . I . . . och, bless me!" She took a single step towards him, and stopped. Perhaps that was the gooseberry, again. "Where . . . now . . . och, what d'you mean by creeping up on me like that, my goodness gracious!"

"Creep . . . ? Me! My Chove," the man expostulated. "Who's creeping? Aye—and who's stealing my berries, more like!" Which was not what he had meant to say at all.

"Stealing, is it! Here's me tearing my fingers to the bone to save the fruit that's just rotting in wicked waste on your wretched bushes, and that's all the thanks I get!"

"Well, now. I'm sorry about your fingers, Mary—I am so. But what were you going to be doing with the berries, once you'd saved them . . . ?"

"I was going to be making jam and jelly for a graceless ill-mannered boor, and with *my* sugar, Ewan MacEwan—that's what I was going to do!" she cried. And that was shattering enough for any man, tired or not.

"Oh," her cousin said. "Och, well." Actually, he was not very interested in the destination of his soft fruit. He was just realising what it was that had been wrong with each and all of the women that he had had dealings with on his travels—they were none of them remotely like his Cousin Mary.

"Well, indeed! And where is she, then?"

"She's in . . . Eh . . . ? What's that?"

"Where is she? Your new . . . woman. Mrs. Ewan Mac-Ewan of Corriemore, to be! What is she like, at all? Have you got her in the house, there?"

"Och, damn—no! No. At least . . . Och, what a thing to say, Mary! That's no sort of way to talk . . ."

"Indeed, and is it not! Isn't that what you went for? Don't tell me you haven't got one, after all! Don't say that none

189

of the mainland hizzies would have you—Ewan MacEwan himself! Or is it you've just come back first, to get the house painted up for her, maybe? That'll be it—you'll be wanting me at the cleaning. . . ."

"No—nothing like that, at all." Ewan rubbed his unshaven chin, frowning. This was difficult. He had been remembering Mary MacEwan, all this time, as a gentle laughing happy creature—not a flashing-eyed wild-cat, spitting and snarling. He had rather forgotten that she had been like this a little, when he went away. "Och, there's nothing just fixed, at all," he assured.

"You mean . . . ? Not just fixed? You have a one, then? What's she like? Is she big or small? Fat or thin? Is she young—younger than me . . . or older? What's her name, the, the . . . Och, I can't wait to meet my new cousin . . . Ewan's choice!" And she swallowed, and nodded her auburn head vigorously to emphasise her eagerness, blinking.

Her companion eyed her from under one down-drawn eyebrow. "You are too fast, Mary," he told her. "I was just saying that there was nothing fixed. There is not just any *special* one. . . ."

She interrupted him, firmly. "Have you got a woman, Ewan MacEwan—or have you not?"

He sighed. "I have not, no." He all but glanced behind him. "That is . . . not for me, no."

There was silence for a few moments. "Well, now," the young woman observed at length, on a long exhalation of breath.

"It was . . . och, there was none of them just suitable, you see," Ewan explained. "With one it was one thing, and with another it was another, if you see what I'm meaning. Some of them were nice enough, but . . ."

"So there were *some* of them, were there!" She took him up quickly. "One and another! You tried them out—but they didn't come up to your standards, just! Is that it?" ·

"That is so," the man agreed. "Or . . . och, well—sort of. You see—a man can't just be marrying *anybody*."

"Is that a fact! It's taken you a while to be finding that out. . . ." She paused. "Or has it? You seem to have learned a lot in three-four days, Ewan. Quite a lot. I'll be interested to hear the details—I will so. Or maybe, are they not just fit and suitable for a girl's ears, whatever?"

"T'st, t'st . . ."

"And that's another thing. How *are* you back so soon, at all?" She glanced down over the empty waters of the bay. "The boat's not due till Monday morning . . . ?"

"I rowed, just," he told her, with the simplicity of the strong man.

"Rowed . . . ! My goodness me—you didn't?"

"Well—not all the way. I was buying a small bit of a boat in a place they call Camisary in Moidart, and rowed out as far as Muck. Some Muckerachs at the fishing towed me from there to . . ."

"You rowed to Muck!" she cried. "Ewan—you shouldn't have done that. That was wicked . . . dangerous! You might have been drowned."

"Not me," the man declared strongly. "Och, no. You'll not drown Ewan MacEwan that easy."

"Ewan MacEwan will drown as easy as the next one— once the wind's been let out of him!" Mary asserted severely. "What for couldn't you have come home decently on the *Maid of Lorne*?"

"Well—it wasn't convenient, just. I . . . I had got up into Moidart, see you, and . . ."

"And what were you doing up in Moidart? It's uninhabited, just about—you'd not be finding many women waiting on you with open arms, in Moidart!"

"You'd be surprised," Ewan mentioned, mildly. "Och, I hadn't *meant* to go there, at all. I was sort of forced into it as you might say. . . ."

191

"Who forced you? Some horrible Moidartach Jezebel . . . ?"

"No, no. Not a bit of it." He wrinkled his forehead, in an effort to make a tired brain work more nimbly. "Actually, it was the police that was the trouble. . . ."

"The police! Dear God—what have the police to do with it, Ewan?"

"Nothing—nothing at all," he assured earnestly. "It was just a sort of a mistake, see you. The police are terrible stupid—och, you wouldn't believe it."

"That's likely enough, anyway!" the girl agreed, and shook her head. "Well . . . ?"

"It was all the fault of a woman in a public-house at Dunstaffnage," he explained. "Yellow hair she had, and nails, and . . . and . . ."

"Ewan MacEwan!" Those fawn-like eyes were remarkably resolute and direct, their laughing mildness only a memory, as she came out from the fruit bushes towards him. "You'll tell me just what you've been up to! You will so, and at once . . . or I'll never so much as speak to you again!"

He could not do that, of course. It was out of the question. There was so much that might not be properly understood, even by the sensible and level-headed, at the first go-off— much less by a woman. And the effort was beyond him, at the moment, he felt. Also, he was getting a little alarmed about that Ailie MacCallum. He would have to be saying something about her, and soon. She might be appearing round that gable, any minute.

"There's a . . . there's a bit girl . . ." he began, and stopped, wagging his head.

"There is, is there? Yes?" she took him up. "You told me a whilie back that there was not. Which is it? You'd better tell me the worst, Ewan."

"Och, not just now, Mary," he objected desperately. "I'm tired, a bit, you see. Rowing's a right tiring business.

192

And . . . look at the blisters on my hands!" That might be a good line, and he thrust them forward for her inspection, hopefully.

The girl pursed up her lips, but whether that was meant to signify sympathy, distaste or mere disapproval, he did not know.

"Damn it—I haven't been in a proper bed since, since I left home! At least, I had an hour or two in one at a hotel on Rannoch Moor, but that wasn't much of a rest. . . ."

"D'you tell me that!" his companion said ominously. "I can well doubt the properness of the beds you've been in, and that's a fact. Aye—and I can believe that you're tired, too!"

"It's just lack of sleep I'm tired from—and tramping the heather day and night!" the man declared indignantly. "I tell you, the only other sort of a bed I've been in was in a cell at Fort William Police-Station. . . ."

"You've been in the cells—in prison! My goodness—what next!" She pointed an unsteady finger in the direction of the bench at the front of the house. "I think we'd better be sitting down, while I hear the worst."

He shook his head wearily. "No. Not now. Another time, maybe. I'm . . . I'm hungry, see you. I haven't had a bite to eat since my supper at Erismore." Almost he got his voice to break.

That had its effect. "You mean—before you started your rowing? Good grief—you are an awful man, Ewan. You shouldn't be allowed off this island—you should not. There is nothing much at all in the house, here—if I'd known you were to be back, I could have had something for you. You'll have to come away downby, and get something at home. Mother will see you right."

"Och, no need for that," the hungry man disclaimed. "I'll do fine here. I'll make myself a bowl of porridge and a couple of eggs."

"You'll do no such thing. A decent meal it is, you need. You'll come away down."

"No, no. Not just now. I'll come later, maybe. There's no hurry, at all. . . ."

"Is that so! You're in no hurry to see your poor motherless bits of children. You should be ashamed of yourself, Ewan."

He had completely forgotten about the children, and that was a fact. Life was just full of complications. "Och, well," he sighed. "I'll come."

"Are you not going to ask how they are, then, the wee lambs?"

"Och, they'll be fine, those ones. Just indestructible, they are."

"Well! A fine father you are. I don't believe you've so much as thought about them, all the time!"

"I did, yes," he told her seriously. "More than once. But, och—I knew they'd be all right, with yourself looking after them. I knew everything would be all right, with you, Mary. My goodness, I wish . . ."

"Yes . . . ?" she asked, mild again.

"Och—what's the use of wishing, whatever!" He shook his head. "See—I'll dump my pack in the house, and then I'll come downby with you."

She sighed a little, and then all but choked, her finger raised to point, helplessly.

Ailie MacCallum stood in the doorway, looking at them, somewhat diffidently. "A fine day, it is," she said, to Mary.

Ewan found his throat to be in need of considerable clearing. "Och, goodness gracious—here's me just about forgetting Miss MacCallum, altogether!" he declared, with sudden heartiness. He laughed, too, with much amusement— his first laugh that day. "Mary—meet you Ailie MacCallum, of Erismore. This is my Cousin Mary, just."

194

Miss MacCallum mustered a small brief smile—in which she outdid Mary MacEwan considerably. Emotions were chasing each other too swiftly over the latter's features to allow of any room for smiling. She opened and shut her mouth twice, indeed, before words would form. She looked from Ewan to the girl, and back again.

"So . . . so this is it!" she said.

"Och, I was by way of giving Miss MacCallum a bit lift in my boat, see you," the man explained, with entire frankness. "She's on her way to Inveraray, of all places—there's no accounting for tastes, whatever!" He had another good laugh at that one.

Mary shook her head. "You don't . . . you mean . . . ? A lift, you say?" She sounded unconvinced, to say the least of it.

"Just that. She was for getting off that Erismore—and I'm not blaming her, my goodness. Och, she got me out of a sort of a hole that I was in, on Erismore, and that's a fact . . . so I brought her across with me in the boat, just. Didn't I, Ailie?" He beamed, as he recollected. "She has a young man she's after wanting to marry, at Inveraray. Monday's boat, she's for getting. Isn't that right, Ailie?"

Thus urgently appealed to, Miss MacCallum nodded. "That is so."

Mary MacEwan still looked less than entirely reassured. "Erismore . . . ?" she wondered. "What were you doing on Erismore, at all?"

"That was just as far as the Muckerach would take me. They towed me there. We had a, a sort of a misunderstanding with the Erismore people . . . about the fishing, just. And, well Ailie here got me out of it. The least I could be doing was to give her a lift. You see, her folk are not that keen on her marrying this one at Inveraray, so . . . so . . ."

"So you abducted her, as you might say!"

"Good gracious—no!" Ewan waxed righteously reproachful. "Not that polite, are you, Mary, to a, a guest on Eorsa!"

"Mercy me—I'm sorry!" The gentle Mary bowed low, even if her eyes gleamed. "My apologies to Miss MacCallum. Och, my *deep* apologies! And to you, too, of course, Ewan. Surely."

All three of them looked at each other askance.

"Oh-huh," the man said. "Oh, aye. Just that."

"And what were you thinking of doing with your guest, with Miss MacCallum . . . *while* she is your guest, Ewan?" That was politeness itself.

"Well . . ." He glanced at her sideways. "I had a sort of notion that maybe yourself . . . that maybe Aunt Elspie would put her up. Just till Monday morning, that is . . . ?"

"Indeed! I see." Strangely enough, that curious young woman sounded a degree or two less frigid. "Well," she said. "Come on, then." And turning about, she started off down the weed-grown garden-path forthwith.

Ewan looked after her, biting a lip, eyebrows raised, picked up Ailie MacCallum's case, gestured with it, and followed on.

So they walked, not side by side but almost in Indian file, down that white sandy road that led to the grassy levels of the shore, and they had not much to say to each other. Indeed, the girl from Erismore dropped noticeably behind—though it was not the two in front that noticed it. The heather was blooming richly purple on all the hillside now, with a beauty that was almost painful to the eye, the bracken, like the strips and patches of corn around the crofts, was beginning to turn to gold and the birch-leaves to delicate lemon, the cropped turf of the machair was emerald green against the gleaming white of the cockle sand beaches and all the blues and violets of the sea. The man saw it without consciously noting it, and was glad to be back in his own place. But he was dissatisfied too, profoundly, almost hopelessly, and the pleasure of his homecoming was curdled within him. It was the girl in front's fault, of course, and yet he tended almost to blame the girl behind . . . along with circumstances. And those circumstances tended to crystallise and derive from one source.

"Your father . . . ?" he said, at length. "Finlay Sim. He will be downby?" That was heavy.

"Yes," she agreed, without turning round.

"Aye. I'ph'mmm. Uh-huh. Och, he will be well enough, I'm sure?"

Almost Mary smiled. "Never better," she admitted.

"Aye." He was very gusty. "He's fit, fit, for his age."

"He is," the daughter nodded. She walked a little more slowly, examining the head of a wayside thistle which she had plucked, so that her cousin came up almost level with her. "He's not going to be so pleased about you and . . . about you coming home sort of empty-handed, my father," she mentioned, tentatively.

"Damn your father!" the man said. And there was nothing tentative about that sudden outburst.

Surprisingly enough, in view of all the previous reproof and reproach, the young woman let that pass. She commenced to pull her thistle-head to pieces.

After a little while, he glanced at her out of the corner of his eye. She did not seem to be frowning, or anything. He commenced a tuneless whistling beneath his breath. "Och," he declared abruptly, "I wish I'd never gone, Mary."

"I wish that too, Ewan," the girl concurred quietly. "But then, I'm always wishing things."

He considered that. "Are you, then? So am I. But—och, what's the use of wishing!"

"True." But she shook her head instead of nodding it. "What indeed? Wishing . . . and hoping. You can waste a lot of time at them, whatever."

He echoed her sigh. "Hoping's different maybe," he put to her. "You've always got a chance, with hoping. But when it's just wishing . . ."

197

They had come to the last of Ewan's well-tied-up gates, at the edge of his land. Mary negotiated the hurdle, out of long practice, with her admirable adroitness, and turning round, became aware again of what she had almost forgotten—that they were not alone. "Och, we've . . . your guest, Ewan," she pointed out.

The man, about to step over, paused, "Mercy me, yes," he agreed. He put the other girl's bag over, and turned to wait for Ailie MacCallum. "You all right—coming along fine, Ailie?" he inquired, with sudden solicitude.

"Och, yes," she assured, and declining the proffered hand got herself over the gate efficiently enough, if without Mary's flair. She looked at Mary quickly, and then away. "I wouldn't want to be any sort of trouble to you, at all," she said, in a rush.

"Nor will you," the other young woman assured, and her voice was kindly now. "Don't you be worrying—about anything, see you. You will be fine. My mother will look after you, and you well out of the hands of that great borach there. . . ." She stopped, blinking. Ewan, overcoming the obstacle in turn, was in process of throwing his long legs across the sagging wire fence alongside. Mary became aware of the self-same limbs, for the first time—which was only tit-for-tat, after all.

"Mercy goodness—what sort of things are those you've got on, Ewan?" she exclaimed. "Those are no trousers of yours. And bare legs, too!"

The man also had forgotten his trousering. He coughed deprecatingly. "They're just a pair I had off a keeper's wife, one place. I hadn't the time to get my own ones back. And . . . and och—haven't you got bare legs your own self!"

Woman-like, Mary eschewed inessentials. "A keeper's wife! And what was a keeper's wife doing with your trousers, Ewan MacEwan? Tell me that."

The man groaned. They were back where they had started,

again. Discreetly, the other girl moved on down the white track. "Drying them," he explained ponderously. "They were wet. Raining it was. She gave me these while they were drying. . . ."

"And why did you have to leave them . . . your ones? Why did you come away, like this?"

"It was the police, see you. A policeman arrived at the house. He was after me . . . for poaching salmon. . . ."

"Poaching salmon . . . !"

"Och, it was just a mistake. I hadn't touched a salmon. It was Hector the Boat's salmon. . . ."

She shook her head, helplessly. "Then why did you have to run away?"

"Well . . . you see, I had sort of knocked the man down, a wee whilie before."

"You'd . . . you'd knocked down a policeman!"

"Och, maybe knocked's not just the word. *Put* him down, just gently, you know. He was for taking me to his cells. It was this bit salmon. . . ."

"But why on earth didn't you explain it?"

"I didn't know that it was the salmon, then." Ewan once again cleared his throat. "I thought it was something else, altogether. . . ." His voice tailed away.

"Something else! Goodness me—what else *had* you been up to, Ewan?"

"Nothing, at all. It was just this woman at Dunstaffnage— the yellow one. She thought I was for . . ." He glanced down the road after the Erismore girl, and lowered his voice unhappily. "She thought I was sort of doing a kind of trade in women and girls, and started skirling for the police, the great silly lump of a creature!"

"Dear God!" Mary swallowed, struck dumb. She could only stare at him, appalled.

The man went on, hurriedly now. "And after that, they were after me all the time. It was this salmon. Och, yon mainland's just thick with salmon poachers. It's a roaring trade. And the police are a right menace. . . ."

"Ewan—if the police were after you on the mainland, they can come out here seeking you?"

He shook his head. "Not them," he decided. "It's not Ewan MacEwan they're after looking for, at all. They think I'm a creature the name of Michael O'Mahoney, good God, out of Glasgow!"

Wordlessly, the girl wagged her head.

"Och, they wouldn't listen to anything about Eorsa," he went on. "They need an Identity Card, before they'll believe your name, over there—terrible suspicious, they are. It's only my description they'll have—that's why I wasn't wanting to come home on the *Maid of Lorne*, and the boats watched, maybe. Och, no—the police'll not come to Eorsa."

"I hope not. My, oh my—it sounds a terrible place, that mainland."

"It is so," her cousin agreed. "Don't you ever go, Mary—it's . . ." He paused. "But . . . I forgot. Weren't you to be off to Glasgow, or some place, to be a nurse? You didn't go, then?"

"How could I go, with, with . . . och, how could I have gone anyway—isn't there only the one boat in the week? Monday, the next boat is. . . ."

"Don't go, then, Mary—don't you go," the man urged. "It's not worth it. Yon place is just a sink of iniquity, a trap for the unwary, whatever."

"Och, I'll manage fine," she asserted, cocking her small chin. "I'm maybe not so unwary as some folk. Besides, Glasgow might be different."

"So you're still for going, then? On Monday?"

"Why not? Would *you* stay here if . . . if you were my father's daughter?"

Ewan did not answer that—he did not have to. A shout reached them. They were down at the track that skirted the shore, now, amongst the scattered croft-houses, with Ailie MacCallum waiting for them to see which way to turn. From the gable-end of one, a man was calling, and waving. But a second glance established that he was not waving to them. He was looking behind him. And even as Ewan began to mutter the damnation of Archie Grumach, other figures appeared, to join him. And one of them, who stared, tugged at his beard, and then beckoned towards them imperiously, was Finlay Sim.

"There goes my dinner!" Ewan declared, almost snarled. "Damn it—I shouldn't have come down, at all!"

Mary stopped, looked from him to her father, and bit her lip. Then shaking her head, she slipped her arm through that of the other girl. "Come, you," she said, and turning, left him there. Over her shoulder she called back, "I will tell Mother."

Heavy-footed, Ewan moved down to meet the oncoming group of elders.

XVII

"IT'S a fine day keeping, and the oats coming on well,"
Ewan claimed, with strong determination, as they approached. "So long as the wind . . ."

He got no further. "In the name of God, Ewan Og—
where have you come from?" Finlay Sim demanded, with
the breathless sibilance he used when much moved.

"That is so, goodness me yes," Archie Grumach reinforced.

The young man decided that attack was probably the best
method of defence; besides, he felt like attack, there and then.
"From the mainland, just—where else!" he asserted. "Glad I
am to be back, too—it's a long long row."

"Row . . . ! Row, were you saying, man?"

"I was, yes. I've bought you that bit rowing-boat you
were wanting. A good price I got it for, too—twelve pounds,
and not a penny more!"

His uncle scratched a doubtful cheek. He had been
wanting a small boat for a while, yes, to be independent of
his deplorable brother Hector. "A boat . . . ?" he repeated
vaguely. "What's this, at all?"

"A boat for twelve pounds, only—oars and rowlocks and
all, for your own self, all the way from Moidart. It's a real
bargain—look what Hector the Boat paid for yon thing he
uses for the lobsters!"

"Och, maybe. But . . . but what about the other business,
man Ewan?"

"That's right," Murdo the Mill substantiated.

"Well may you ask," the younger man returned gravely.
"A bad business it is, too. Och, wicked, just wicked. You'll
need to watch out, all of you."

"Eh . . . ? What's this? Watch . . . ?" Finlay Sim looked around him, as though for moral support—an unusual procedure for him. "What are you talking about, whatever?"

"The salmon, just." Ewan nodded his head portentously. "That's the way I'm back so soon—to warn you. Those police are like bloodhounds, I tell you."

"Salmon . . . police . . . !" His uncle all but gobbled. "Save us all—are you out of your mind, man?"

"I am not. But I am hungry and tired—I have been on the water all night with your boatie, and no bite to eat. If you're not wanting to heed my warning, and just to make uncivil remarks—och, I'll just be leaving you!"

The elders stared at each other. Never had they heard such talk—and to Finlay Sim!

"The Lord forgive you your presumptuous words, Ewan Og!" that man said, his voice quivering. "Woe to the headstrong and rebellious man! What were you saying about salmon, at all?"

"Bloodhounds, he said," Duncan Macdougall put in. "What's bloodhounds to do with the salmon, my God?"

"It's the police," Ewan explained. "They're terrible excited about the salmon—there's a right campaign on about them. Anybody that has ever had a bit salmon without a licence and an Identity Card, is for the jail! Over yonder it's fair swarming with policemen in cars and bicycles, running folk into the cells. Och, likely they'll be out here any day now."

"Mother of God!" exclaimed Murdo the Mill, who had once had a Catholic grandfather. "Is that not just the limit!"

Finlay Sim wagged his beard. "But . . . but you don't mean you can't *eat* a bit salmon, Ewan? Och, you're not serious, are you . . . ?"

"Serious, is it! My goodness—I've spent most of these last four days and nights on the run, over land and sea, jumping out of windows, hiding in the heather, locked up in public lavatories and in the jail at Fort William—and all over a wee small bit salmon that Hector the Boat gave me for a woman at Dunstaffnage!" Ewan was quite enjoying this. "Serious, you say—and me without my own trousers to me! Damned—if they take *me* that seriously, what'll they be like with yourself that has salmon near every day of the week!"

"Och, gracious me—what a nonsense!" his uncle protested. "Here's me been enjoying a bite of salmon all my life, and the sea fair jumping with the creatures, out of the wisdom of the all-providing Creator! And isn't Hector the agent of the Lorne Salmon Fisheries Limited, my goodness! You wouldn't stop me having a bit fish to my tea, would you?"

"Not me, no. It's just the police, see you. Och, salmon's evidently not for the likes of you and me, these days."

"Then who's to get it, in the name of the Almighty?"

Ewan scratched his head. "I don't rightly know, at all. Nobody said who was to get them—except just not the ones that caught them. . . ."

Finlay Sim cleared his throat impressively. "And God said to man—have dominion over the fish of the sea and the fowl of the air and over every living thing that moveth upon the earth," he intoned, with entire authority.

"Aye. I'ph'mmm," his nephew acceded. "You tell that to the police Inspector-man when he comes. Well—I've warned you, anyway, in plenty time. Och, he'll not be here before Monday's boat, likely . . . unless they have a launch, maybe. I'll be away in now, and getting something to eat. My Chove, I'm tired. Uh-huh." And yawning elaborately, he raised one finger in easy salute, and turned to stroll off. "By the bye," he threw back, "the boatie is over at Camusnagal."

"But . . . now, look man," Finlay Sim cried. "What about the women, at all?" And he came stumping in pursuit, supported by his company.

"Hell's bells and damnation!" Ewan muttered, querulously disgusted.

At bay, as it were, he turned to face them again. "Devil roast the women!" he declared distinctly.

"Eh . . . ? What did you say? You don't mean . . . Ewan Og, you are not telling me . . . ?"

"I am so. You can keep your women—all of them. I'll manage fine without one—aye, I will."

"But . . . but what about the one you've fetched?" He gestured vaguely along to his own house. "Man, if you're after joking, let me tell you I don't like jokes, at all—not about such matters. I do not." That was severe. "What's her name, at all?"

"Och, Ailie MacCallum, just. But it's no joke, I tell you. She's a nice enough lassie. . . ."

"Glad I am to hear it," Finlay Sim said. "MacCallum has a nasty Campbell sound about it. You're not going to tell me that you're after bringing a Campbell back with you?"

"Och, goodness me—what does it matter? She's . . ."

"I knew a MacCallum, one time, in Barra, that was no kin to the Campbells, at all," Archie Grumach put in helpfully.

"Och, the bad blood could be getting right thinned down, by this," Murdo the Mill suggested.

"Aye," Finlay Sim sighed heavily. "She looks all right, does she? She doesn't squint, like so many of them, or anything? She'll be all right in the head . . . ?"

"My gracious—of course she's all right in the head!" Ewan cried. "My Chove—that's a terrible thing to say about a guest on Eorsa!"

"A guest! If it was just a guest it wouldn't be that important," his uncle reproved. "But this is serious. What was her mother's name?"

"How do I know her mother's name! Ask her your own self."

205

"I will," the older man asserted. "But I'd have thought that even the likes of you would have had the sense to ask an important thing like that. The blood is the very soul of the matter, whatever. My God—I'm hoping that you didn't forget *all* the other precautions, in your hurry, man? What about her teeth, and her feet? And och, the build of her. She didn't look so very broad-built, from here. . . ."

"My goodness—you've got it all wrong!" his nephew interrupted. "I didn't lift Ailie MacCallum out of Erismore to be marrying her. . . ."

"Erismore!" That was almost a scream. "Merciful Providence—Erismore, did you say! Och, by the Powers of Heaven —you've not landed a Campbell out of Erismore on us?"

"Tst-tst," Ewan said. "No, no. Will you not pay heed to what I'm telling you. Myself, I've not landed anything on you. She's just here for a wee whilie—till Monday morning. She'll be away by the first boat."

The elders looked at each other, lips moving but words at a premium. Murdo the Mill it was who found his tongue first. "My, my, Ewan," he said, head a-shake, "that's bad. Och, I wouldn't have thought it of your father's son. I would not."

"You shouldn't have done a thing like that, man," Archie Grumach reproached. "Not to be bringing her back with you. A bit fun in the hayshed's a thing we can all be understanding, but there's a limit!"

"Och, you lot of blethering old fools!" Ewan cried, quite beside himself. "Will you hold your tongues? I was giving the creature a lift just, in my boat. I never saw her before last night. She's nothing to do with me, at all. I've not got a woman, I haven't found a woman, and I don't *want* a woman! Is that clear?"

Out of the bewilderment, Finlay Sim made a quick recovery. "Are you going to tell me that you've come back with nothing arranged, at all? That you haven't found a one, out of all the women that's in it on the mainland! That you've been over there just on a sort of a holiday . . . ?"

"My Suffering Sam—a holiday!" Ewan almost choked. "Would you listen to that—after what I've been telling you! If yon's a holiday, then never again will I be taking another!"

"I . . . we sent you to find a woman for a wife, Ewan," his uncle went on severely, inexorably. "And you say you have not found a woman, not looked for one, maybe. Is it just a broken reed you are—failing us all, your children and the island, whatever?" He held up a commanding hand, as the young man's protests boiled up. "Did you or did you not approach any woman, Ewan Og? Answer me, now!"

"I did, yes. But mercy on us, the approaching is not the trouble, at all—it's the getting away again! You wouldn't believe what these mainland women are like—it's just not decent. . . ."

"Is that a fact, Ewan. Tell us what way, just, they are. . . ."

"Quiet you, Archie Grumach!" Finlay Sim said sternly. "I will have a word with my nephew about that, later, in private as is seemly. But, Ewan—if these women were so keen as that whatever, why have you not brought one at least of them back with you?"

"I told you. How could I be carrying a woman around, and half the police in Scotland on my tail? And, damn it— would you have me bringing bold brazen creatures the like of that back to Eorsa?"

"Och, a wee bit of spirit's not that ill a thing," Murdo the Mill suggested judiciously. "I mind, one time . . ."

"Eorsa needs new blood, strong vigorous blood," his uncle interrupted. "You need a woman, a wife. Your children need a mother. The position is serious—desperate, just. And yet you are frightened for a bit mettlesome girl—just the kind that we're after needing! It's just as I said—I should have come with you. I knew that you were weak, weak. If I had

207

been with you, man, there would have been none of this foolishness."

"If you had been with me, My Chove, Aunt Elspie would have been a widow . . . or a wronged woman, I'm thinking!" his disrespectful relation asserted.

"You . . . you ill-tongued scoffer, you mocker! You will answer for that to the Session, you will so! Get out of my sight now, before I forget that you are my own poor brother's son. . . ."

The young man frowned, sighed, shrugged, and turned about without another word. He had gone a dozen paces when his uncle's tremulous but decided voice followed him.

"After the corn is in, you will go back to the mainland, Ewan Og MacEwan—and I will go with you, as the Lord God's my witness!"

Ewan groaned, and walked on. But the route that he took was back whence he had so lately come. He would not eat in that man's house—he would not! Kirsty and Ewanie had been well enough for five days—they would do fine for a wee whilie longer. Scorning the track, he turned directly to face the slope to Corriemore.

XVIII

IT WAS early evening before Bally, having got wind that his employer was back, arrived up at Corriemore, to find Ewan sprawled asleep in the old armchair before a dead fire, the litter of his scratch meal around him, and the black porridge-pot lying on the floor at his feet. Actually, it was Luath the black-and-white sheep collie that joyously wakened her master—the collie was joyous, that is, not the master. Bally was joyous too, of course, and roared with innocent happy laughter, whilst beating Ewan about the back in an access of welcome.

It is to be feared that this heart-warming reception was but indifferently received and reciprocated. Ewan's back was sore, of course, from much rowing; he had a debit of at least another twenty hours' sleep to make up—and he was feeling less than kindly towards his fellow-Eorsans, one and all. What he said to Bally and the sheep-dog is more kindly left undisclosed—not that either of them minded in the least, however.

After a brief, fruitless, and soon-discontinued endeavour to discover what his minion had been doing while he was away, Ewan sourly dispatched him to round and shut up the poultry for the night, whilst he himself milked the cows. He had been sort of wondering if Mary might be up to the milking, again . . . but they were late already, and still out, lowing complainingly. Not that he could expect Mary to do any such thing. Och, no—not with himself back.

Curiously enough, though the milking might seem to be the longer job of the two, Ewan was fast asleep in his chair again by the time that his assistant eventually got back from

209

his poultry. Bally, after a paroxysm of discreetly silent mirth, drew up a second chair to the other side of the empty hearth, lowered himself into it blissfully, head back, and began to snore.

The twilight had faded into blue night when an especially violent soporiferous convulsion on Bally's part awoke his companion with a vigorous kick to the knee. Yawning mightily, and shivering a little, Ewan lurched to the doorway and stared gloweringly out into the terrible vacancy of the west. Only a pale star or two winked there, out of the stark void that the day had left in its dying, but infinitely nearer at hand, half-right, a scattering of yellow lights gleamed warmly from the houses down at the shore. Ought he to go away down— to have gone before this . . . ? Would they be expecting him—not that miserable uncle of his, but Mary and her mother? And the children . . . och, but they would be in their beds by this; Mary was the great one for them being in their beds in good time. There was no use in going down, now— not a bit. Better just to have a sort of decent sleep.

He threw out sundry cats that had found their way into the house, a pullet that Bally had missed, and then, with a considerable expenditure of precious and flagging energy, Bally himself. Luath he permitted to stay where she was. He shut the door on the night, and stumbled upstairs to bed.

He slept late in the morning—though not, apparently, so late as did his henchman—and went about the daily and necessary routine of the farm thereafter in a sort of gloomy lassitude. He was stiff, and ached in every single bone of his back, shoulders, and arms, and felt strongly and querulously in need of a wink of sleep. The man had not done much rowing for many a year, of course—and, when he came to think of it, he had walked quite a long way, recently; a hundred miles, at least, in less than that number of hours. And where the hell was that Bally?

He had a feeling that he ought maybe to be away down

collecting those youngsters of his—but, och, they'd just
be getting themselves into trouble if he fetched them up
while he still had all this work to do. If Bally had been in it,
he could have gone . . . no, damn it—he could not! That
wouldn't do, at all. But Mary might have fetched them up,
surely, and her with little else to do. He wasn't wanting to
meet that father of hers again, just now, my goodness. . . .

His mid-day meal over, such as it was, Ewan had another
think about going down that hill. He'd have just a bit scat
on the bench first, anyway, and a pull at his pipe. He reckoned that he deserved that. Then, he supposed, he'd better
go, right enough.

It was on the bench, then, that his Aunt Elspie and the
children found him, in mid-afternoon, his chin on his chest
and his pipe on his lap, not so much as lit.

It was a touching meeting. Kirsty and Ewan Beg made a race
of it, to see who could reach their father first. It looked like
a win for Kirsty, her legs being very slightly the longer, till,
a yard in front, she tripped over the wooden edging of the
garden-path and fell all her small length, whilst her slightly
more diminutive competitor scuttled on and past, crowing
triumphantly. That was too much for any young woman,
and getting to her feet, tears of everything but pain in her
eyes, she hurled herself not so much after as at her brother,
to teach him his manners. This she achieved by a good push
in the back—a favourite strategy with her sex—which sent
Ewanie sprawling into what had been once a rose-bed. The
son and heir of Corriemore had a lot to say about that—but
he did not confine his protest to words, or even screams. He
waded in with all that he had, to offer his sister a much-
needed corrective. The sum total of their uproar would have
wakened six other sleepers besides their father.

"My goodness me—what's this!" that man declared,
starting up, blinking. "Save us—whatna stramash! Och,

mercy—quiet, will you! Ewanie—don't you do that to your sister. It's . . . My Chove, Kirsty—that's a terrible way to carry on! Stop it, will you—the both of you!"

The parental lesson went unheeded, however, probably unheard, both contestants being intent on teaching a lesson of their own. To establish his authority, the man stepped forward, and took a hand—or, more accurately, an arm, a small arm in each hand. The vigour and unanimity with which both pugilists thereupon turned upon the father they had so lately been vying with each other to greet was astonishing, beating at him with tiny fists and feet, while in no way diminishing the intensity of their vocal assault upon each other. Much chagrined, Ewan held them away at arm's length, shook them, attempted to overcome the wordy cataract, failed dismally, and disgustedly thrust both disputatious offspring from him in opposite directions. They came together again, of course, with extraordinary rapidity, their mutual resentment only enhanced, and rejoined battle in a running fight that took them round the gable-end of the house and out of sight, if not of hearing, in only a little longer than it takes to tell.

"Well, by the Powers of Heaven—did you ever see the likes of that, My Chove!" the affronted parent complained to his aunt. "Is that not just deplorable!"

Elspie Cutach did not seem to be greatly upset—but then, Ewan never had seen her upset about anything, that he could remember. She smiled faintly, shook a gentle head, and said nothing. She was panting a little, of course, for it was a long climb up for a woman who had barely stepped outside her own garden gate for twenty years. Ewan had no recollection of her having been at Corriemore since his childhood. She gestured towards the bench which he had so lately left, and moved over to sit down.

The man eyed her small neat frail-seeming person with some doubt, forgot his parental indignation, and rubbed his chin. "You shouldn't have brought them up, Aunt Elspie," he said. "Och, no. No need, at all. I . . . I'd have been down my own self, in no time, just. I didn't . . ." His words died on him—as frequently happened in the presence of this unusual aunt of his; he tended either to lose his tongue or talk too much.

"You are back, then, Ewan," she said quietly.

"I am, yes," he admitted. "Yesterday, it was. Och, I was tired, see you, and . . . well, there it was."

His companion inclined her head understandingly.

Ewan cleared his throat. "My thanks for looking after the brollachs," he declared abruptly.

The merest lift of an eyebrow and a single shake of the head acknowledged his courtesy and dismissed it as unnecessary. She was looking out to sea, with the remote expression of one who sees far beyond normal horizons.

The calm of her, inscrutable yet nowise cold, the stillness, the sheer serenity of this small ageing woman, frightened, appalled, the man. He did not know her, at all, though she was his own aunt, though all his life she had lived within hail of his home, her house as familiar to him as his own. Did anyone know her, on the island? Did Finlay Sim, her husband, even . . . or Mary, herself? None spoke familiarly of her, no-one discussed her, nor even criticised—which was a strange thing in a small isolated community; though once, Ewan's own father, Ewan Mor, had in his son's hearing referred to her as Saint Elspie—but he had been a little less than sober at the time, and had never repeated the remark. She might well be of the stuff of saints—Ewan had always suspected that she had the second sight, at least, and knew all the foolish and shameful thoughts that were in his head.

"You are fine and well, Aunt Elspie, I hope?" he went on, since something had to be said. "The children were not too much for you?"

"No," she said.

213

Ewan did not sit down beside her, but with a foot on the end of the bench, and his arms folded on his knee, stared out to follow her own line of view—though his gaze did not take him much farther than Barra perhaps. So they did not look at each other. Racking his brains for suitable conversation, the man wondered what it was that had brought her up the long track to Corriemore.

"Mary . . . she was very good about the farm, and everything," he got out.

He heard just the tremor of a sigh from his aunt. "Mary, yes," she murmured. "Poor Mary."

"M'mmmm," he said doubtfully.

Another sigh. "She does not want to go."

"Go . . . ? You mean—to Glasgow? To be a nurse? Is she going, then?"

The woman nodded.

"Sorry I am, then," Ewan told her—and sounded it. "Och, I do not see the need, at all. It's not as if there wasn't plenty for her to do here in Eorsa."

"She will do what she must . . . if she has to," his aunt answered enigmatically.

"If she has to, yes—but why should she have to? What's driving her?"

"*You* are, Ewan—you, and Finlay Sim." That was a quiet statement of fact, and no mere suggestion.

"Me . . . ? Holy Smoke—why should I be driving her? Me it is that's wanting her to stay, whatever. Her father, it could be, right enough. . . ."

"Yes. But you only it is that could stop her—if you want to."

He turned to look at her now. "I want to, yes. But how can I stop her? Could I be doing what her own father—or her mother, indeed—cannot do?"

"You might—if you were wanting to, enough." His aunt's gentle unaccentuated voice was as calm, as tranquilly dispassionate as was her unaltered gaze. "How much would you do, Ewan, to keep her here?"

"I would do plenty—if it was any use, at all. You see I . . . I . . . och well, I like Mary—I like her fine, Aunt Elspie. I would do a lot to keep her here on Eorsa, whatever."

"Would you marry her, even, maybe?"

"In the name of God!" appealed Ewan MacEwan, and with difficulty.

Elspie Cutach turned her grey head to look at him. "Would you?"

"Me . . . ? But, I . . . och, my goodness—what's the use of saying that? Damnation—you know why I can't!" He spoke harshly now, fiercely even—no way to talk to an elderly lady. "You know the way it is—none better."

"That is so," she agreed, with no corresponding heightening to her soft lilting voice. "I know, yes." Almost she smiled. "You would marry her, Ewan, if you could?"

" 'D'Almighty—I would! Isn't that what . . . isn't that the way. . . . But, och—I couldn't do that. It is not possible. Finlay Sim would never have it. The Session . . . My own cousin . . ."

The other had resumed her scrutiny of the wide ocean. Now she shook her head. "No," she said. "She is not your cousin, at all."

The man stared at her, lips moving, wordless. "What . . . ?" he croaked, at length.

His companion pulled at the fringe of the tartan shawl that she wore around her shoulders, and then dropped it, her hand still again like the rest of her. "Mary is not your cousin, no," she repeated, so softly as to be almost inaudible. "She is not."

Ewan swallowed, noisily. "But . . . but, she is your daughter, and Finlay Sim's!"

"My daughter, yes—but not Finlay Sim's." The man had

215

no eyes to see it, but that pale flaccid cheek had taken on a delicate flush of pink.

Dumbfounded, the other shook his head. He took a couple of paces away, swung round, and came back. "But . . . she is your youngest! I do not understand," he said.

"I thought that you might, maybe. You have done sort of foolish things your own self, Ewan, perhaps!" Could it be—was there just a hint of an appeal in Elspie Cutach's gentle voice?

"Mercy on us—you mean . . . you . . . she's not . . . och, my goodness, I'll be damned!" He considered his little aunt with widely-opened eyes indeed. "Who *is* her father, then?" he wondered, with perhaps some lack of courtesy.

His companion lifted a shoulder in a peculiar but not ineloquent gesture. "Archie, his name was—Archie MacQuarrie, out of Erismore. But he has been dead these many years."

"Erismore! Well, d'you tell me that!"

"He was storm-bound. Fishing, they were—and their boat holed on the skerries, there. This Archie MacQuarrie broke his shoulder and was near drowned. A week or two he lived in our house, and me nursing him. A bonny laughing lad he was too, with the voice of a lark to him." There might have been the pale shadow of a sigh, there.

Ewan ran a hand through his hair. "Is that so," he said. "Well, now. And does she know—does Mary know?"

"No. Nobody knows, at all."

"Nobody . . . ? Not Finlay Sim?"

"Not Finlay Sim, no."

Her nephew's lips formed a soundless whistle, his mind chaotic. But his heart, cleverer than his mind, was singing. He sat down suddenly on the bench beside his aunt.

And now, strangely, Elspie Cutach was mildly chiding him. "It is not sitting you should be, now, Ewan—running would be more like it, surely."

216

"You mean . . . to Mary? Are you for telling her, then?"

"*You* are, I think."

"But . . . see you, if Mary is to know, and it is to make any, any difference to me—then others will have to know too. Finlay Sim . . . ?"

She nodded. "That is so."

"You have kept your secret all these years, Aunt Elspie. And now . . . ?"

"It was for Mary's sake that I kept it. It is for Mary's sake that I am telling it now. I am fond of Mary." That was simply said.

Ewan examined the toes of his boots, considering the many implications of that statement. He found it hard to consider calmly, reasonably, objectively. His impulse was to be up and away, that moment. But some part of his not always so reliable judgment restrained him. Mary's reaction to this astonishing revelation it was, that had to be considered. What effect would it have on the girl? He was not worrying all that much about Finlay Sim. . . . "I am fond of Mary, too," he declared heavily. "You think that . . . you think Mary will be happy to hear all this, whatever?" he wondered. "I wouldn't like to, to . . . och, to upset her, at all."

"Upset . . . ?" The other seemed to turn the word over in her mind. "There are worse things than an upset, I think. On the road of life, Ewan, is it not better to have an upset on the right road, than to be taking the wrong road, altogether?"

"It could be," the man assented, nodding. "But there is a risk, too."

"A risk, yes. There is always a risk in it. You have a risk to take with Mary—if you will. You it is that must decide whether to take it." Her hand rose and fell. "Myself, I have taken mine."

"Yes. Yes—I see that. If you think . . ." He stopped. "I will take that risk, yes."

"Then you will have to be taking it quickly. Now."

217

Surprised, he looked at her. "Tomorrow, the boat is. . . ."

"Mary is not waiting till tomorrow," his aunt informed. "She has had words with Finlay Sim. A quarrel. He says that she is not to go, now. She will not stay another night in his house. She is for off, now—today."

"But how? How can she go . . . ?"

"She is getting Hector the Boat to take her to Tobermory. She says that there is nothing for her on Eorsa, any more."

Ewan was on his feet again. "And Finlay Sim . . . ?"

"Finlay Sim does not know. Hector the Boat will do it, to spite his brother. You know how it is with them. . . ."

"Tonight, it is, then?"

"This afternoon. She is walking over to Camusnagal—to see your boatie, she says. But she has a bundle with her, in a basket. She will not come back, I think. Hector will be picking her up, round there."

"When . . . ?"

"When he goes to look at his lobster-pots, it will be. After his tea . . ."

"My Chove—that will be soon. An hour, maybe. Och, goodness me—could you not have told me this before!"

Elspie Cutach's smile glimmered. "Maybe your legs will prove faster than your head, whatever, Ewan," she said. "Go, you."

He went. At the corner of the house, he half-turned. "You will look after the children again?" he shouted. "Och, I don't know when I'll be back, just."

The small still woman on the bench inclined her head.

XIX

SO the man was back on the toilsome tramp to the sandy cove of Camusnagal, not much more than twenty-four hours after he had come therefrom—and much more strenuously, despite the aches and stiffness that still were with him. If Elspie Cutach was right, he reckoned that he had just over an hour to cover the four upheaved heather miles, and to say what had to be said at the end of it. Undoubtedly, he should have been rehearsing what he was going to say, but what with one thing and another, he was doing no such thing.

His shortest route lay up a long, long slope by a cattle and deer track, to the pass of Bealach na Bo, between Beinn Helival and its principal shoulder, and through to the high and boggy peat-lands of the watershed beyond, amongst which he must pick his cautious and exasperated way, before he could reach the stony but dry east-facing slopes, which slanted down in great sweeps to the fearsome cliffs of that barren seaboard. Along this spine of the island he was able to make good time, off-setting the delays of the peat-hags. He took it at a steady loping trot, dodging the outcrops and leaping the innumerable tiny burn-channels. At last, with the land falling away sharply before him, he looked down a series of steep aprons of scree and short heather to the miniature bay of Camusnagal, five hundred feet below, strikingly white amongst so much of black rock and brown and purple heather. The small boat lay high and dry where he had left it, but of Mary MacEwan or other human being there was no sign.

Disappointed and perplexed, Ewan stared down for a

little, panting. He could not have missed her, en route. If she started before his aunt left her house, she ought to have been here before this, even if she had followed the longer coastal route by west and north. Perhaps it was all a mistake? Perhaps . . . perhaps she had purposely misled her mother, and had her meeting-place with his Uncle Hector somewhere else altogether? Though, indeed, there were not so many spots on Eorsa's rock-bound coasts where a landing could be made, other than in the central and open main bay. She might be sitting amongst the shadows of some great rocks, down there, of course. . . .

Frowning, he began his zig-zag descent.

The man was something more than halfway to sea-level, when he saw her. She was not down at the shore at all, but up on the summit of a small headland that flanked the cove to the west, seemingly sitting on an outcrop at the edge of the cliff, and gazing back south and west, no doubt looking for the first signs of Hector and his boat. Ewan arrested his glissade, and started to slant left-handed to make as directly for her eyry as the terrain would permit.

So intent was the girl at her watching that he was no more than a dozen yards from her before his boot clinking against a stone jerked her head round. "Ewan!" she cried, gasped. Almost, she might have been at his berries again.

"Mary, *a ghraidh!*" he said. And though he had come all this way to say it, that was all.

They eyed each other questioningly, doubtfully.

"How . . . why are you here?" she asked, at last, and abruptly.

"I heard—och, I heard that you wanted to see my boatie, just." That was scarcely convincing.

"You followed me, then?"

"Well . . . sort of," he agreed.

Mary's voice was level, almost toneless. "You have been speaking to my mother," she stated.

"I have, yes," the man admitted. "I had to come, see you, Mary."

"Why?" That was bald.

He gestured with a hand towards the sea below them, and further still. "Because you were going away. I had to see you."

"Why?"

"Because . . . because, well, I could not let you go."

She raised her brows, and her voice a little. "Indeed? Has my father been speaking to you, as well as my mother, then?"

Ewan frowned at the bitterness there, that came so ill from Mary MacEwan of the smiles and the dimples. "No," he said. "I am here for my own sake, Mary—and yours, maybe."

"Is that so! And you cannot let me go, you say? Well, well. I wonder why you would be stopping me?" She had not risen from her outcrop, but looking up at him, her chin was held high.

The man groped urgently, desperately, to get his thoughts and his words into order. The order in which he put his points to her now was all-important, he recognised—to her, and therefore to himself. The wrong foot forward now, and there would be no stepping back. "I'll tell you why," he said, slowly, almost reluctantly. "It is because I cannot do without you, at all."

Her eyes widened to her sudden intake of breath. "*You* cannot . . . ?"

"No. I cannot. I have discovered that. Something else I have discovered, too—something I have known for a long time, I think, but . . . och, well—I'm fond of you, Mary. In fact, I love you, you see—I love you just something wicked!" He was away now, all his order and priorities forgotten. "I have loved you always, my goodness—even when I was away in yon Germany. I don't know what I was about, at all. . . . It was just, just . . ."

221

She was on her feet now, her eyes shining. "Dear God, Ewan—do you know what you're saying, man?"

"Aye, I do. Fine. Damn—I've been wishing I could say this for a long time. My Chove, I have! But I didn't know, see you. . . ."

"Blind you were, Ewan—and the thing staring you in the face!"

"Eh . . . ? How d'you mean? How, blind?" Astonished, the man floundered.

"Och, just that *I've* known that you loved me, for long enough—for years! Only, I didn't know whether you loved me enough, you see, to, to risk all, to throw over everything, not to care what anybody said or did, to go against my father, and the Session, the whole island . . . ! That was the way that you would have to love me, you see, if I, if you . . ."

Wonderingly he eyed her. "Yes . . . ?" he said hoarsely.

"If it was to be any good, at all," she cried, a trifle wildly. "Och, that was the way that I loved *you*, Ewan . . . !"

And then she was in his arms, her auburn head against his jacket, her slender body heaving between tears and laughter. "Oh, Ewan, Ewan!" she murmured into his chest, and actually shook him.

The man's lips on her hair, the edge of her brow, he murmured too, incoherencies, irrelevancies, foolishness. He sought for her mouth, and found it too.

When words again became of any consequence to either of them—and that was not by any means immediately—Ewan found himself still having to use his brain instead of leaving matters to his perfectly adequate impulses and instincts, as he would have much preferred. But the young woman, disentangling herself, became promptly bent on practicalities, as tends to be the way of such.

"So we'll get married, cousins or none, Ewan?" she said. "That's it, isn't it?"

The man cleared his throat. "Well . . . och, kind of, yes. You see, it's like this. . . ." He came however to a full stop. It is a tricky business to have to tell your newly-declared lover and future bride that her mother is not just entirely what she thought that she was—that she herself is, in fact, illegitimate.

Not that he was given much of a chance to frame things tactfully, judiciously. "Ewan MacEwan!" Mary cried. "Are you backing out, now! Is it a broken reed you are, after all? You're not going to fail me, now . . . ?"

"No, Gracious me, no. What d'you take me for, Mary . . . ?"

"You are going to marry me?"

"I am so. Isn't that what I'm here for, just, my goodness!"

"Good. That's fine, then. We'll get married just as soon as we can—and they can say what they like, and do what they like. Nothing else matters, at all—does it!"

He considered her fondly, but thoughtfully. "Is that how you feel, then, Mary?" he asked, slowly. "It suits you that way, does it? I mean, you don't mind about us being cousins? You are content to be my wife, cousin or none?"

"Of course I am. Isn't that what I'm saying? Mercy me— the way we love each other we've just got to marry. And there's no law against it, whatever . . . it is just my father and his stupid Session and his silly book! Don't tell me you are still worrying about being cousins, Ewan—after all!"

Her companion let out a long breath. "No," he said. "I am not. I am not worrying any more, about anything. My Chove, no!" He saw in his mind's eye a small grey quiet woman sitting on his bench and staring out into the infinity of the sea, and he knew a sudden and great content. Her secret could be safe, after all—her name clear. Mary need never know—nobody need ever know. Just Elspie Cutach and himself. Och, he had been the weak vessel, as Finlay Sim had said—damn him! But she, his Aunt Elspie, had strengthened him. He would fight Finlay Sim, now—he would fight them all. "I will so!" he declared aloud. "As cousins it is we'll be married."

"What else?" Mary agreed. "It's not . . ."

A whistle, thin but penetrating, reached them on their cliff-top. They turned to peer over and down. At the mouth of the little cove, their Uncle Hector's motor-boat lay, lifting gently to the echo of the long Atlantic swell. Its owner gestured to them, in question and perhaps just a little impatient.

"Och, now—what will we do with Uncle Hector, at all?" Mary wondered. "I had forgotten the poor man, altogether. We won't be needing him, now."

"He was to take you to Tobermory, was it?"

"Tobermory, yes. The nearest place, it is the best that I could do. Shall we send him away, just?"

"Tobermory . . . ?" Ewan repeated, tapping his teeth with a fingernail pensively. "Och, Tobermory's got more to it than just being the nearest place, Mary. It's got a church and a minister, see you—and we're in its parish. There's a thing you have got to be doing before you can get married, and that's having your banns cried. Three weeks crying, it takes. It's a wicked long time—but, och, we could be getting started, anyway. I'm thinking we might be keeping Hector the Boat to his bargain, after all."

"You mean . . . *you'll* come too? To Tobermory? Just you and me, together? My, oh my—my father is not going to be liking that!"

"Is anybody asking him, at all?" the man inquired. "You will be liking it, though, I'm thinking, Mary?"

She looked down, demurely. "Och, well—maybe," she said. "You think that we ought to go, Ewan?"

"We're going," her companion asserted, and with authority. "From now on, I do the deciding for this family, Mary MacEwan. Come, you."

"Yes, Ewan," that one agreed, and smiled her own smile.

They went down the hill towards the silver strand, arm in arm. And that was something of a feat, in itself.